JOE B

Chod

Best of luck with your new born child, and enjoy the read

Paul Heaven

JOE B

▼

Paul A. Newman

Writer's Showcase
San Jose New York Lincoln Shanghai

Joe B

Writer's Showcase
an imprint of iUniverse.com, Inc.

For information address:
iUniverse.com, Inc.
5220 S 16th, Ste. 200
Lincoln, NE 68512
www.iuniverse.com

For the reason that life is a mixture of experiences, depicting life in written form is a collage of those experiences. As such, the characters portrayed in this book are fictional having been drawn from tidbits of character I have observed throughout life. This is fiction, and if anyone feels akin to any one of the characters, then please bear in mind that we all have similar characteristcs. The places described are real, the story is an adaptation of a Biblical Chapter.

ISBN: 0-595-15008-X

Printed in the United States of America

To my wife
Merrilou
for the patience
for the fortitude
and for the support
she has shown me as I have scrivened this tome.

Contents

▼

PROLOGUE

▼

There was a man in the land of Uz, whose name was Job; and that man was perfect and upright, and one that feared God, and eschewed evil. And there were born unto him seven sons and three daughters. His substance also was seven thousand sheep, and three thousand camels, and five hundred yoke of oxen, and five hundred she asses, and a very great household; so that this man was the greatest of all men of the East. And his sons went and feasted in their houses, every one his day; and sent and called for their three sisters to eat and drink with them.

And it was so, when the days of their feasting were gone about, that Job sent and sanctified them, and rose up early in the morning, and offered burnt offerings according to the number of them all: for Job said, It may be that my sons have sinned, and cursed God in their hearts. Thus did Job continually.

Now there was a day when the sons of God came to present themselves before the Lord, and Satan came also among them.

And the Lord said unto Satan, Whence comest thou? Then Satan answered the Lord, and said, From going to and fro in the earth, and from walking up and down in it.

And the Lord said unto Satan, Hast thou considered my servant Job, that there is none like him in the earth, a perfect and an upright man, one that feareth God, and escheweth evil?

Then Satan answered the Lord, and said, Doth Job fear God for nought?

Hast not thou made an hedge about him, and about his house, and about all that he hath on every side? Thou hast blessed the work of his hands, and his substance is increased in the land.

But put forth thine hand now, and touch all that he hath, and he will curse thee to thy face.

And the Lord said unto Satan, Behold, all that he hath is in thy power; only upon himself put not forth thine hand. So Satan went forth from the presence of the Lord.

CHAPTER ONE

▼

A CHARITABLE BOARD OF TRUSTEES MEETS

Henry Jonathan Smith IV, called Hank by his friends, was on the Board of Trustees for the Interfaith Foundation. He had been elected chairman at the last annual meeting and was preparing to conduct his first formal meeting of the twenty-two member Board of Trustees. The Interfaith Foundation had amassed in excess of twenty million dollars which they dispensed in accordance with a set of principles of distribution drafted by the members of the Foundation. It was an organization devoted primarily to God, the Christian God, Jesus Christ. The Foundation was formed to enhance the performance of God's work on earth through the dispensation and disbursal of money. The Board of Trustees consisted of representatives of the Catholic, Methodist, Presbyterian, Jehovah's Witnesses, and Episcopal churches in the Cleveland area.

As the coffers of the Foundation grew, so too did the desire of each of the representatives to see that their particular faith was the beneficiary of the charity dispensed by the Foundation. Consequently, petty squabbles ensued over trivial matters. Politics. If one group thought another group was receiving too great an advantage, they would lobby to pare down that group's interest. In this manner, the Foundation was very selective in the projects it finally chose to fund.

On the agenda for the first meeting to be presided over by new chairman, Hank Smith IV, were three items, two of which would pass without much comment. But the third item, a request by a newly formed ad hoc Christian group operating out of a storefront in a black neighborhood for funds to help them proselytize their particular brand of evangelicism, but whose application was couched in language that brought it squarely within the principles of distribution, was going to be a bugaboo at the meeting. Hank knew it when he saw the item on the agenda; he had already received several calls from members of the Board expressing their disapproval.

Down deep Hank knew their disapproval stemmed from a bias against any form of religion but their own, especially an upstart religion that, although it extolled the virtues of Jesus Christ, was really only an alternative form which seemed to attract younger members away from an already established church.

None of the members of the Foundation would ever say anything about the new church being located in a black neighborhood and that it focused primarily on conversions of black people, or that the Reverend was black, but the bald fact stared them in the face and they were unable to deal with it.

The Interfaith Foundation, with its great sums of money, had parsimoniously purchased a small building, had two full time employees, and had refurbished the building in a manner befitting a twenty million dollar corporation. It was furnished lavishly; thick carpets, thick walls, and thin glassware, all in subdued earth tone colors to convey a quiet power and majesty. When the Trustees entered this building, they felt as if they had transformed themselves into instruments of angels. The ability to turn on the spigot of money vested them with a sublime feeling of charity and power, a feeling of magnanimity when they left a Trustees meeting. They had performed God's work on earth in a manner satisfying to themselves and to their ideal of doing good deeds.

The Trustees' meeting room was the showiest room of the entire building. Deep red carpet outlined with a thick border of black carpet. An original painting of The Last Supper that had cost over thirty thousand dollars covered most of the forty-foot long wall. Several statutes were appropriately placed in the corners on marble pedestals. Coffee, tea, or soft drinks were available for the Trustees on a highly polished cherry side table. The conference room table was a piece of art. It matched the cherry side tables, but it had oak, mahogany, and butternut wood inlays that blended together perfectly. The craftsmanship was superb; the forty-three thousand dollars price tag was something of which only the prior Chairman and Treasurer were aware. But everyone commented on the beauty of it. Trustees ran the palms of their hands over the joints of the inlays and marveled at the smoothness of the joining, so even, so deep, so...perfect.

Chairman Hank brought the gavel down on the wooden square placed on the table so the table itself would not be marred. The group quieted immediately.

"Ladies and gentlemen, welcome to the first meeting of 1997. We will take the roll."

The roll call was taken, minutes of the last meeting approved and accepted, and the treasurer's report showed an astounding $23,700,467.00 with its various investments and interest bearing accounts. The first item on the agenda was a request for an allocation for a group of nuns in El Salvador to fund certain medications dispensed from their missions. The sum was a mere fifteen thousand dollars; a motion was made, seconded, and passed.

The second item was to finance a nursery at an Episcopal Church to be utilized during church services. After a presentation showing a real need for the money, the motion passed without objection.

Hank looked at the third item on the agenda. He glanced down the table to the left and right. They were eager for the third item: the aggressive looks, sharp eyes, anticipatory, the facial smirks. They were ready for a fight.

"The third item on the agenda," said Hank, "is a request by the Prospect Avenue Church of Jesus Christ. Each of you has before you their prospectus requesting the sum of sixty thousand dollars. I have invited Reverend Herbert Stahl to present his request in person. He is the pastor of The Prospect Church of Jesus Christ."

Hank leaned towards the secretary on his right and whispered, "Joan, will you bring in the Reverend."

"While Joan is getting Reverend Stahl, I would like to set forth the procedure here. We will let Reverend Stahl make his entire presentation, and then we will open it up to questions. I know that several of you have some reservations about this project. That is why the Reverend is here, to respond to those reservations."

Joan preceded the Reverend through the door and showed him to the far end of the table. The Reverend slowly took in the impressive surroundings.

Hank introduced himself to Reverend Stahl, then introduced Reverend Stahl to the entire group.

"Reverend Stahl is here to present his request for funds and to answer any questions you might have. You have his application in front of you that has been filled out completely. Reverend?"

"Thank you Mr. Smith." Reverend Stahl bowed slightly to Hank. "Ladies and Gentlemen." He bowed slightly to the two ladies and then to the gentlemen in a sweeping bow that had a slightly circular theatrical motion to include the entire table. "I have applied for $60,000.00. That is a tremendous amount of money, but I want you to know that none of it goes into my pocket." He added with great volume. "None of it! I am not benefiting in any manner by this money. God benefits."

He paused for five seconds regarding the Trustees. In rapt attention, the Trustees all watched Reverend Stahl. He sounded like a high volume holy roller preacher, trying to sway them with emotion and histrionics.

"Yes, it is money that I am asking for to do God's work. I have detailed it out for you on the application. I need a copier and a computer. I need to get the written word out. Right now I have to pay to have my material printed. It is very expensive. Each time I have to go to the printer, I am losing time saving souls. Jesus, our Lord, suffers. He waits for me." Reverend Stahl's voice modulated with volume and softness. He smiled, he frowned, he looked pained, somehow all at once.

"I need to buy paper, lots of paper. My apostles are handing out reams of paper to the Philistines. We are winning them over. Our humble church has grown from five people to one thousand members in less than a year. But we need to get the word to them. We need to get the word to hundreds more, thousands more, millions more. The entire world needs to know about Jesus our savior. He is the light and the breath of this world."

Trustee Bob Johnson was squirming in his seat. He didn't like being preached to by some no account street preacher. He was a minister himself. He brought the word of God to his parishioners. He didn't have to walk in traffic at red lights to get the word of God out. He didn't have to demean the position of Reverend, not like this man was doing. As he squirmed, he geared himself ready to ask some questions of Reverend Stahl.

Finally, Reverend Johnson could stand it no longer. He interrupted Reverend Stahl.

"Excuse me, sir. You want this money primarily so that you can hand out literature at red lights when traffic is stopped?" The mere form of the question and the added intonation let everyone in the room know his position against Reverend Stahl.

Reverend Stahl stared at Reverend Johnson, five seconds, ten seconds, almost a full fifteen seconds before he answered.

"Yes sir, Mr. Johnson," he said loudly.

How did he know my name, thought Johnson.

"Yes sir," Stahl iterated loudly. "It is God's work we are doing. Do you think!," He paused for effect. "Do you think that the Lord Jesus worried about appearances when he washed the feet of his disciples. He took a bucket and washed their feet. Would you, sir, wash my feet? Would you? Yes, you look at me. You see an inner city preacher. Not educated. Not a fancy church, but we are doing God's work. We are converting souls. As I told you, in the last year we have converted one thousand souls. How many have you converted in the last year?" He paused.

"I am not here to embarrass you, ladies and gentlemen," he added quickly, "I am here to ask for your help in God's work."

"Reverend Stahl, if I may," asked Louise Mahler one of the layperson trustees. "Could you please tell us where the rest of the money will be spent? I know the paper and printing products, but the application seemed vague about where the rest of the money was going?"

"Certainly, my dear lady," bowed Reverend Stahl. "It will allow us to lease the space next door to our present facility. We now have fifteen hundred square feet of space. This rental would give us four thousand square feet. We need the space. On Sundays our church is filled to capacity with three services in a row. We must accommodate God's children. These are poor people, they don't have much money. They cannot even put a dollar in the collection basket, but they are much appreciative of God's word.

"We will also be able to lease the space on the second floor of the church for an additional four thousand square feet for a homeless shelter. I can put fifty bunks in there to house the homeless. These people are destitute. And they are not all winos. You may get the image of homeless people as drunken bums lying along the street in a state of drunken stupor. That is not the case. These are, in the main, good people. They need help. I am God's servant," he bellowed with a slow cadence, "it is my duty to help them. I will help them. Half of the money will be for the leases for eighteen months. The other half will outfit the place with bunks and allow us to set up a kitchen facility so that we can endeavor to feed these people."

Reverend Johnson, mentally reeling from the insult, said, "Sir," he wasn't ever going to call him Reverend, "do you mean to tell me that your converts are presently made up of these homeless people?" Score one for the established church, thought Johnson.

"I can feel it in my heart that you are against me, Reverend Johnson."

How did he know my name? thought Johnson again.

"The Lord underwent ridicule. They put a crown of thorns on him. They put a robe on him. Called him King of the Jews and laughed at him. Then they beat him." Stahl paused, inhaled deeply as if getting ready to shout.

Instead, in a whisper, he said, "And then they crucified him. Yes, they crucified him. And you sit here today. You make fun of me because I help the downtrodden, you..."

Hank Smith saw the antagonism on the face of Johnson. He saw also that Reverend Stahl was fair game to the battle. Hank acted.

"Gentlemen, please. We are not here to attack one another. We are all here to advance the cause of Jesus Christ. It is obvious to me that Reverend Stahl, although he does not advance the cause in the same manner as the established churches in the area, does indeed advance the cause. His willingness to undertake the chore, the obligation to help the homeless, is laudable. He deserves our support. There is a need. We in the suburbs do not know the day to day need. We are not there. Reverend Stahl is there. I note the exchange of ideas, of different approaches to the same goal. I do not want to see all these apostles of the Lord arguing over the best way to do God's work. It works all ways, many ways. But it must be done.

"Are there any more questions of a technical nature concerning the money?" Hank looked down the table. No one spoke, no one raised a finger. They were not going to get into an argument with this inner city preacher—because, it was obvious, they couldn't win.

"Fine then, Reverend Stahl, would you like to say a last word before we excuse you to discuss this matter?"

"Ladies and Gentlemen. We are here for God. He allows us to be on this earth. We must earn his reward. I am trying to do so. I beg your assistance. Thank you." He bowed again a full half circle and strode from the room.

When the door was closed, Hank said, "Well ladies and gentlemen, what is your pleasure. Do you wish to discuss the matter, or would you like to vote on it? Bob, you seemed interested, anything to say on it."

"I am against it."

"Why Bob?" asked Hank.

"The man's a charlatan. He's an Elmer Gantry. He's out to build a power base. He is clearly an egomaniac. God is on his side and no one else's. I don't buy his bunk."

"Anyone else?" asked Hank.

John Tomkins raised his hand. John was at the far end of the table, a small man with small glasses. He peered up at Hank.

"I tend to agree with Reverend Bob there. I didn't particularly like the way he had his holier than thou attitude. He compared himself with Jesus Christ. It doesn't go somehow. $60,000.00 is a lot of money, too. Doesn't seem right that we should fund his church to the exclusion of others. No," he hesitated, "I think Reverend Bob is right."

Hank could sense the mood shift, feel the emotion of envy and resentment flow against Reverend Stahl. It was time to halt this negative flow.

"Just a minute," said Hank. "Here we have a guy who is willing to go into a neighborhood and teach the word of God. Not just any neighborhood, but a neighborhood where the rest of us would be afraid to be in the daylight, let alone at night. I, myself, don't want to go down there. Should we just abandon the whole neighborhood? This guy, Reverend Stahl, you might not like his personality or his approach, but he is doing a job that none of us are doing in an area where none of us want to be. He has the guts to deal with these homeless people. I'm not comfortable dealing with them. Is his way of preaching the gospel the same as yours? No, I don't think so. But he is teaching it. If he has one thousand people coming to his church, more power to him. Is he making converts, changing people from agnostics to Christians? I hope so. I give the guy credit and I think this foundation should also. He asks for a measly $60,000.00 to renovate two floors of four thousand feet. That's a bargain. If it was new construction at seventy dollars a square foot, that would be two hundred and eighty thousand dollars. What do you think it will look like? It's going to be bare bones. The man is actually doing a tremendous job, and I say let's fund him. In fact, I say give him $100,000.00.

"Let's not attack him, let's analyze what he has done, what his vision is. These people he is converting, they will not be coming to your churches no matter what. So if they go to his and they listen to the word of God, then we are following the principles of this foundation that has twenty million dollars in its coffers. It's a drop in the bucket and it's why we are here."

Hank stopped, then drew a deep breath. He realized he had been spouting his own brand of religion, paused a second, then said. "Sorry for proselytizing myself." He grinned.

"Ok," said Hank, "We have the application of The Prospect Avenue Church of Jesus Christ for $60,000.00, do I have a motion to allow it?"

"I move to amend the application to $100,000.00 and to approve it," said Floyd Barris.

"I second," said Barbara Conger.

"Discussion?" asked Hank. No one said a word or moved. He stared at faces, some empty, some visibly troubled.

"All in favor, please raise your hands." Hank counted sixteen hands.

"All opposed, same sign please." Hank counted five hands.

"Motion carries," said Hank, "Any new business to come before the board?" No one moved.

"In that case, we are adjourned. Good job, fellows. I feel good about this, and, I am sure, Reverend Stahl will also. That's it." Hank stood up. The trustees started talking among themselves.

Two of the trustees remained seated talking softly as the remainder mingled, talked and left.

"Had me going he did," said Gary Prost, a tall lean insurance sales-man who sold commercial insurance. "I thought that Reverend Stahl was a pompous ass and I was going to vote against him. Hank changed my mind."

"Mine too," responded Edward Williams. "He really does have his heart in the right place. That's probably why we elected him president, huh?"

CHAPTER TWO

▼

A WIN.

Joe B walked out the Common Pleas Courthouse in Cleveland, briefcase in his right hand, coat buttoned against the incessant cold wind blowing down Lakeside Avenue. Bob from the office was coming up the steps.

"How'd it go?" asked Bob.

"We won!" Joe stuck his left thumb up in the air. "Twenty six-thousand dollars. They offered thirteen; we got twenty-six. I'm so delighted."

"So will the partners be. Good show," congratulated Bob, clapping Joe on the back and shaking his only free left hand vigorously. "What did the client think about it?"

"She was in seventh heaven. Just couldn't believe it."

Bob, sidling away said: "Don't have time to talk right now. Gotta run, I'm late for a hearing, tell me about it later." Bob bent his head to the wind and sprinted up the steps two at a time.

Joe reveled in the victory on his walk back to the office. A simple rear-ender with only two thousand three hundred dollars in medical damages.

The jury awarded ten times specials and the car damage. A great award. Juries frowned on claimants with soft tissue injuries. Plaintiffs complain their backs hurt, but no one seems to believe them. They never look like they are in pain. The jury just can't feel their pains. And with all the advertisements by the large insurance companies about the occasional large verdict and how deplorably the system has failed, they have turned the general populace into believing that every claimant is a faker or malingerer. Some are fakers, but this one wasn't. Her injury impaired her house cleaning business. She couldn't vacuum, wash toilets, or do anything that required her to bend over for any considerable period of time.

Joe was a junior member of a medium sized law firm, Smith, Post and Trivisonno. As an associate of nine years he hoped soon to be elevated to partnership; the committee considered him for some time and was progressing on the decision to accept him into full partnership. The law firm consisted of thirty lawyers in Cleveland, two more in Brussels, two in Washington, D.C., and two in San Diego. The hierarchy was staid and solid, with some flexibility on account of their modest size. They were a firm of only twenty-eight years. Notwithstanding, they represented large corporate clients. They wielded untold power. Memberships at the University Club, Grandview Golf Club, and The City Club only served to show the power base they had built financially, politically, and morally. The firm dealt fairly, billed according to the time devoted to the case, did not overreach, but was successful nonetheless. It was the most respected firm in Cleveland. It also represented the Cleveland Diocese. The Bishop visited the senior members of the firm regularly. They assisted generously in the Catholic Charities programs. They sponsored fundraisers for the Cathedral renovation. Within the legal circles they were highly respected.

The defendant's attorney, hired by the insurance company to represent the defendant, had only offered five thousand dollars to settle the case. On the day of the trial, the defense had upped the offer to thirteen thousand dollars, but it was too little too late. He made his mistake when he called her a "malingerer" in his opening argument. Her efforts to work and her past work history were too much for him. The jury believed her.

All the insurance company ads in the world in all the newspapers in the area had not totally convinced the people on the jury that every claimant was a liar and that the jurors will have to pay for it out of their own pocket. Insurance is supposed to spread the risk and provide just compensation. But insurance companies operate on a different level of sensibility than the rest of the population; that level concerns profit only. They cannot embrace the concept of conscience. They are a corporation for profit for their shareholders, not profit for their insureds or the claimants. The only way for them to make money is by not paying out money. Every dollar they can put into reserve on a claim that is not paid, is a dollar fifty in their pocket. They get to collect interest on the money while the claim is pending and the plaintiffs are so scared of what the juries will do, they are willing to settle for one or two times the medical bills. They got what they deserved on this case.

Joe had persisted for his client's case. He took the videotape deposition of the doctor, who would not appear live at the trial, at a cost of two thousand dollars. An outrageous amount, but it was necessary for evidence. The firm stood a chance of losing money on the case if the award was only five thousand dollars as the insurance company offered. But now they get one third of twenty-six thousand dollars and expenses, more than ten thousand dollars. Not bad, thought Joe.

Joe hoped the insurance company put his name on their list so the next time they came up against him they wouldn't want to try a case against him. They would merely acquiesce to a larger settlement.

CHAPTER THREE

▼

AN OLD FRIEND

Henry Jonathan Smith IV, the senior partner at Smith, Post and Trivisonno, stood looking out at the city of Cleveland from the full-length window of his office. He watched the traffic flowing continuously along the freeway, took in the expanse of Lake Erie, and tried to focus on the small boats fishing by the crib one mile out in Lake Erie where the city drew water for drinking. He viewed the stadium in its early stage of destruction. The avaricious owner of the Cleveland Browns, a team he followed closely, had moved the team to Baltimore, depriving Hank of his favorite entertainment, football. Hank's reverie was interrupted when his secretary paged him on the phone.

"Yes?" answered Hank to the beep.

"A Mr. Sam Hawkins here to see you, sir. He does not have an appointment. Shall I make one for him, sir?"

"Sam Hawkins, did you say?" asked Hank with surprise.

"Yes sir, Sam Hawkins," she repeated.

"Tell him I'll be right there."

It had been ten years since he had seen or heard from Sam Hawkins. He had not received a letter or even a card from him in all those years and he couldn't send one to Sam because Sam wandered all over the world—he never had an address. Occasionally Hank had heard that Sam was here or there in the world and he was surprised that he hadn't heard from him directly. They had been best friends in high school.

Their relationship had begun at Collinwood High School in the ninth grade. They hung around together, had their disagreements, and remained friends. While Hank continued to attend Christ the King Catholic Church regularly, Sam ceased his attendance. His parents thought he was attending, but he wasn't. They didn't attend, but required Sam to attend. There were more intriguing things to do, and Sam did them. He visited friends or tried to get Hank to miss church or Confraternity Classes. He was never successful in this regard, but it didn't stop him from trying.

It will be good to see Sam after all these years, Hank thought, ten years. What a life we had together. We had some good times, and boy oh boy, we had some bad times.

Sam's life at home had been extremely unpleasant. His father didn't care a thing about him; his only attention to Sam had been with screaming and the stick, a rung from an old playpen, harder than steel. Sam hated his father. Of all the wrestling matches Sam was in from the ninth to the twelfth grade, Sam's father and mother never attended one.

But Sam survived. He meshed with everyone in a crowd, was never without conversation. People liked him and they had fun with him. He was game for anything, actually he was too game for absolutely anything. He would try anything, and that got them into trouble too many times.

Sam had several sisters who were older than he by ten years. He never had a close relationship with them. Sam was the unwanted and less tolerated child, an accident of the rhythm method. His sisters' lives were intertwined with boys and marriage by the time Sam was old enough to give them recognition. As such, Sam was raised as a child is raised that is unwanted. His parents let him do as he pleased. They did not keep tabs on him like they had his sisters. They were tired of raising children, so they didn't do it anymore. Sam raised himself. His parents provided room, board, and immediate verbal or physical supervision, but not much else. When Sam was reported by the school or a neighbor for some transgression, the mode of discipline was progressive, first yelling, then hitting, then seclusion in his room for the bruises to heal. He had his own room; he was proud of that, but it was in the basement of their house. There was an entrance to the basement directly from the outside which afforded Sam countless opportunities to leave the house unknown to his parents. Not that they were concerned, just that they didn't know of his whereabouts.

When his sisters escaped the home to marry, Sam had asked for their bedroom, but was denied. The room was better used for a separate television room for his father. Father and mother watched different programs and therefore spent most of their married life separately since television was a principal part of their life experience.

As boys, Hank and Sam were inseparable. They did things together that made them close friends for life.

CHAPTER FOUR

▼

VICTORY APPLAUDED

At the seventeenth floor, the elevator door opened and Joe stepped into the opulent foyer.

"Congratulations Mr. B, we heard," said Lois, the receptionist.

"Thank you, Lois. My client is very happy."

Lois handed Joe his telephone messages, little pink slips of paper with the name, time of call, nature of call, and date of call. He had twelve messages. Perusing his messages, Joe turned to the reception area. He felt a presence, someone looking at him. His attention was drawn to a man with a khaki colored safari jacket casually staring at him. The man did not drop his gaze when Joe looked at him, but merely smiled slightly, a glint in his eye. His hands were at his sides, not in his pockets, not folded on his chest, just hanging at his sides. It looked odd. The man looked odd, but intense. Joe nodded, then turned away, he was in too good of a mood to think of anything else right now. Joe paged through the messages on the way back to his office. He received congratulations as he walked.

Joe walked down the hallway to his modest office two doors from the senior partner, Henry Smith, IV. Most of the work Joe did was generated from Hank's office. The case Joe had just won was handed to him by Hank. His client was a fellow parishioner of Hank's for whom Joe was doing a favor. "Come see me," said Hank, "I will put some young tiger on it that will get you just compensation." Joe had done just that.

Joe sat at his desk. The desk was made of mahogany, but the top could not be seen because of the cluttered paperwork. Piles of files were arranged in neat order. Joe arranged them in the order of preference to be worked on. Several photos of his family decorated the corner of the credenza. His girls in one photo, his boys in another. A third photo of Joe and his wife, Marsha, on a camping trip in Yellowstone National Park. On the vinyl wallpapered walls were his three education degrees, Barnard High School in Kansas, Kansas State University Bachelor of Arts in Political Science, and Case Western Reserve Law School. That was how Joe got to Cleveland, through law school. It was the most natural thing in the world to look for a job in the city where he went to school. And, he got a good job with a fast growing firm.

Joe married during his third year in law school. Marsha immediately became pregnant and delivered Joe Junior days after Joe was on his new job at Smith, Trivisonno and Post. Life had been good ever since. Four more children and nine years at the firm. He was primed for partnership and this victory for one of Hank's personal friends at his church was sure to secure him the partnership for which he had been working so long. Yes, Joe thought, as he put his feet up on the desk, hands intertwined behind his head, life is great. Great family, great job, great firm, great friends. God is good to me, he thought, and he offered a small prayer of thanks.

CHAPTER FIVE

▼

REUNION

As Sam waited in the reception area, the elevator constantly opened and closed, disgorging attorneys, clients, adjusters and a multitude of people. The receptionist answered twenty lines, put people on hold, passed them through, met and greeted everyone getting off the elevator, and kept glancing at Sam wandering around the reception area. He was tall, dressed in a safari suit. He walked around the glass coffee table ten times waiting for Mr. Smith. He watched out the windows for a while. She could see his tight little pony tail pulled together at the back of his head, more toward the base of the neck. He was neat and clean. He moved smoothly and stealthily, like a well oiled hinge.

But she kept glancing at him. Several times he was looking at her when she looked up. She blushed. He was good looking. A little old for her, though. He must be at least forty or fifty. His presence attracted her, but it disconcerted her. She messed up a phone call, put it through to the wrong office. She knew she made the mistake because she was thinking of the Mr. Hawkins in the waiting room. She looked up to see him smiling at her mistake. She turned red in an instant, looked away and thanked God the phone rang right away. She busied herself; she saw Mr. Smith from the corner of her eye going over to talk to Mr. Hawkins.

Hank entered the reception area; Sam was staring out the window at the expanse of Cleveland's skyline and bustling traffic. Hank took note of the short pony tail, the khaki safari jacket. Sam looked so natural. He immediately pictured Sam with fifty black porters following him through the jungle.

Sam turned when Hank was five feet from him—as if he knew Hank was there. Sam smiled the old smile, clean white, straight teeth, an engaging smile. They shook hands. They embraced without a word. Finally Sam said: "Don't you look good? Nice setup you have here."

"Sam, it's great to see you! What are you doing here? What have you been doing for the last ten years?"

"Ten years to the day, Hank," said Sam.

Hank looked puzzled.

"Yes, ten years to the day since we have seen one another. I would have come yesterday, but I wanted it to be exactly ten years."

Hank felt a twinge of unease, "Why, Sam?"

"No reason, I just thought it rounded out the time. So, let's see your digs here." Sam smiled and put his arm around Hank and they walked toward the hall. Sam gave a small wave to the receptionist. She blushed again.

"Are you married again?" asked Hank.

"Not for me, I learned my lesson. Four times is enough. I don't need to get married anymore. No siree," he drawled. "The last one was tough enough. How about you? Try something different yet?" The light in his eye showed he already knew the answer; Hank was monogamous.

Although the years had aged them both, it was as if they were teenagers again, they were their old selves. They slid slowly, but unconsciously and comfortably back into their lifelong relationship. Sam the leader, Hank the follower.

"So, it's quite the place you have here," said Sam, eyeing the artwork hanging on the walls as they walked to Hank's office. "Batemans, Seery Lester, are you turning into a nature freak?" asked Sam.

Hank ignored the taunt, but said, "They're originals, too. I met Seery Lester in San Francisco. Look at this one, it's one of my favorites, a mountain lion in the snow. So real. But then I have never seen a mountain lion in the snow, so I don't know, but the detail is so fine. What do you think?"

Sam surveyed the print matted in a light tan border to bring out the tone of the rocks and mountain lion in conjunction with an aluminum bronze color frame. "Looks too real. Leaves nothing to the imagination. Realism is not my type of painting. Give me something vague, something mysterious, religious, powerful. Not just a perfect rendition of what is already here, but something that is not here, something we want to be here, but isn't. If I want a photograph, I'll buy one. But a painting should not be a photograph. Know what I mean?"

"Hmm," answered Hank. "Like what, for instance?"

"Case in point, the Mona Lisa. Now that is mysterious. Or the Crucifixion by El Greco hanging in the Cleveland Museum of Art. Talk about powerful. Makes you feel the thunder. Makes you grow cold just looking at it, the sundering of the earth, you can feel it. Your spine starts to tingle. It is there, but it isn't there. The whole of mankind impacts on you when you look at it."

Sam glanced at Hank. Hank was looking at the Seery Lester print while Sam talked, but smiling, listening.

"Well?" asked Sam.

"I think I feel the same thing with this painting. I could be right there. I feel transported to the Sierras. Same feeling, different painting."

"No, no, no," said Sam. "Transporting one to the site is realism, drawing out the emotion, the force of one's feeling is mystery. To make you fearful of your existence, to question what is next. To ask what or why. That is a powerful painting. This,," he pointed to the Seery Lester with a wave of his hand with his middle finger extended, "is a pretty picture, technically perfect, of a mountain lion in the snow. Give me the Mona Lisa and I want to know why she is smiling that sly smile."

Sam laughed, "We don't change, do we?" He put his arm around Hank's shoulder. "Well, let's finish a tour of this place."

They turned the corner at Hank's office.

"Six partners. Two senior status, that is, next step to be partners. Three junior partners, that is usually between five and ten years at the firm. And eleven associates, beginning attorneys. They get to do all the grunt work," Hank chuckled.

"Grunts, huh?" said Sam.

"Yes and no. They do put out the work. Lets the partners have some time off."

"What kind of work do you do?"

"Pretty much everything. We have a several Fortune 500 corporations that we do the trial work for. Then the Catholic Diocese. They have lots of work, surprisingly."

"Still connected to the church, I see."

"Oh yes, connected until after death. I take it you are still not involved in church?"

"In church, no. In religion, yes."

"Meaning what?"

"Means I am into religions. I know religion. I have seen religions. But church. No thank you. Not for me. Some priest telling me what to do. Hah!" After a slight pause, he asked, "How's the wife by the way?"

"Marian? She's ok. We've been married a long time. After you have been married a long time, something you, of course, will never know," Hank and Sam both chuckled. "Well, you kind of grow apart. Do your own things. Your interests in your younger years are not the same as when you grow older, neither are hers. So we live together, but that's about it. Sometimes we go to functions together, when necessary for business, and sometimes, but few and far between, for pleasure."

"Oh well, she never liked me anyways."

"You got that right. From day one. Maybe she was jealous. Who knows? And at this point in our marriage, who really cares? The amore has disappeared. We are partners in different lives or different paths. We tolerate each other. I guess we are happy. How does that sound?"

"Sounds like you're married." Both laughed softly again.

"How about the kids," asked Sam.

"All finished college. Gone from the house. The house is quiet. Even the dog died." They laughed again, commisserating.

"The kids are doing fine. I even have two grandchildren from Beth. Great kids. One is three, the other is two. What a couple of munchkins. They live in Atlanta, so I only see them about once a year, but they're fun. Kids, I love em."

"Yeah," said Sam ruefully.

Hank glanced quickly at Sam. The subject of kids was not pleasant to Sam. He had had one in the hopper, but he let it go, never had another. Hank beleived Sam wanted kids, but would never show it.

The friends talked. Old times, experiences, friends. Hank, who had built a powerful influential law firm, and who had an outward, efficacious, engaging personality, simply slipped back in time and emotion to his previous relationship with Sam. He didn't know it, it just seemed to always happen that way.

CHAPTER SIX

▼

AN INTRODUCTION

Joe sat at his desk, raised his feet to the corner edge, folded his hands behind his neck, and dreamily looked out the window soaking up the feeling of warmth and success of the day's victory. Basking in the temporary glory that goes with a legal win.

Steve Bond entered with a thick file under his right arm, plopped it down on Joe's desk jolting Joe out of his reverie.

"Well," said Steve, grinning, "I guess you pulled this one out of your hat. Good show. It will make the old boys look just a little bit more closely at you."

"More closely?" Joe cocked his head and arched his eyes. "It was just great, Steve. Just great. You wouldn't believe the lies I caught him in. He just lied on the stand. And when I confronted him with the contradictions, he just bulled his way through sticking to what he had just said and not what he had previously sworn to. The jury hated him. It was great. It is the reason we do this. It was just great." Joe had kept his feet on the desk, his hands behind his head, chair tilted.

"Are you ready for the next one?" asked Steve, pointing to the file he placed on the desk. "These victories are short lived—transient. Wait until you see this one. Impossible situation. A zoning problem. Our client is an asshole, but he is probably right. Give yourself a day off and take it easy for a change. Go home early today, but start early tomorrow." He laughed.

"I think I will go home early. I won't get anything done today. Bobby has baseball practice tonight. Doesn't Jim?"

Jim was Steve's son, age six, who played in a T-Ball league with Joe's son, Bobby; there is no pitcher, just a ball placed on a T and the child hits it. It introduces the child to the game without the danger of being injured by wild pitches.

"Yes, why don't you pick him up also. That way I can stay here and get some work done. There's a ton of it."

"Sure, no problem. I like watching those kids scramble around. That Jim is going to be a hitter."

"That Jim," said Steve, "is going to be the death of me. The kid leaves stuff all over the steps at home. I almost killed myself coming down the steps this morning. I yelled at him and he broke into tears. You got to love them as you yell at them."

"Steve, you got to love them always. They make the world go around. They're better than winning twenty-six thousand dollars on a ten thousand dollar case."

Senior partner, Henry Smith IV, came into the office. He was dressed in a dark blue pinstriped suit with a red paisley tie, monogrammed shirt and shiny shoes. Perfectly coiffed. Behind him was Sam, The man Joe saw in the reception room. The man glided behind Hank, smoothly. He wore a small pony tail at the base of his neck. Unlike Hank's hair, Sam's was a deep brown with no gray whatsoever. He looked younger than Hank by years. Joe dropped his feet off the desk and stood with the same movement.

"I heard," said Hank pumping Joe's hand. "Nice job. How did Nadine take it?"

"She was in heaven. She kissed me and hugged me. Kind of embarrassing, but she was delighted."

"Good. I'm proud of you, you make us look good."

Meanwhile, Sam was examining the certificates hanging on Joe's wall, College, Law School, Supreme Court license, Federal Court license, Sixth Appellate Circuit, St. Mary's Certificate of Appreciation, etc.

Hank said, "Joe, Steve, this is Sam Hawkins, a very old friend of mine."

"Not as old as you, you old goat," said Sam winking to Joe as he shook hands with Joe and Steve.

Joe surprised, quickly looked at Hank for a reaction, but saw none. Hank paid no notice to Sam's jibe. "Sam wanted to meet the stalwart, good, young attorneys in the office. I'm glad he got to meet both of you at the same time." After a moment, he said to Sam, "Joe just won a jury trial today for a very good friend of mine. He made a lot more out of the case than it was worth. Did us proud today, he did."

"Yes," said Sam, "I heard the receptionist congratulate him."

At that moment, whether it was the way it was said, or the tone of voice, Joe felt an unaccountable queasiness—a cold breeze wafted.

Hank turned to leave, "Once again, Joe, great job for Nadine. Now I can hold my head up when I see her again."

Steve made sure they were out of earshot before he spoke.

"You don't see old dudes wearing pony tails like that very often. Think old Hank was a hippie in the 60's?"

"Looked a lot younger than Hank, didn't he?" said Joe.

"Yeah. Shows what hard work will do to you, gray hair and and advancing wrinkles." He hesitated a moment. "Didn't know there were still hippie types around. Old friends. Strange looking guy. He actually was reading your certificates. No one ever does that. I don't know, he kinda gave me the creeps," he laughed.

"Not your impression of a forthright guy, is he?" continued Steve. "That's not the word, what is the word?"

"I know what you mean. Up front. Upstanding. Clean. Sincere," muttered Joe. "I don't know the exact word you are looking for, but I know exactly what you mean. Oh well, he's Hank's problem, not ours. So, I'll take a look at this file, maybe tomorrow. Right now I am going to get out of here and go see my family. I'll pick up Jim for you."

"I'm off," said Steve. "See you later when you drop off Jim. And thanks, and also, good job." Steve gave a halfhearted wave and was gone.

Joe breifly thought about Sam. There was something musty about him. Something hidden in that face. A superior knowledge, some presence, a force. He felt it, but could not identify it. Strange reaction to meeting someone for the first time.

CHAPTER SEVEN

▼

A COMPACT IN A CHINESE RESTAURANT

Hank and Sam turned into the parking lot of Peking East twenty blocks from Hank's office with a view of seedy buildings.

"Ten years doesn't change a thing, does it?" Hank said, smiling. Sam was always one to move right in and be comfortable. Sam had the ability to make himself comfortable without anyone else in the room becoming uncomfortable with him. He used to drape himself all over the furniture at Hanks' home and Hanks' mother wouldn't say a word about it. But if another friend had done the same, a sharp word from his mother curbed their behavior quickly.

"You know what I have been doing for the last ten years. Working." Said Hank. "What about you, what have you been doing? Where have you been traveling?"

"From going to and fro in the earth, and from walking up and down in it."

"What kind of answer is that?"

"More like, what kind of question is that? The answer fits the question perfectly. I've been everywhere in the earth, under it, over it, on it. You name it. I've been there. I even learned a thing or two while doing it."

"But what have you been doing?

"Let's see, I was a steelworker in Brazil, clerk in Argentina, maintenance man in Japan, yak herder in Manchuria, mercenary in Angola, marble cutter in India, anything you want, I was it at one time or another. It is quite the world. As I said, to and fro in the earth and from walking up and down in it. It is true."

"Amazing." said Hank in an astonished tone. "So what are you doing back here?"

"I felt it was time to come back. I can do whatever I want now just because I feel like it. It's a great feeling. I wanted to see you. Real friends are hard to come by. Keeping friends is even harder. I wanted to see old friends."

"How long have you been back?"

"I came in yesterday morning."

"Where are you staying? I have room at my house. You're welcome there."

"No, no, no." Sam waved him away. "I'm staying with my bastard father. I thought it was time to see him also. He's going to kick the bucket soon, so I thought I'd spend some time with him," he paused, Abesides… Marian? She's not too keen on me, you know."

"Yes, I suppose so," said Hank, quickly dismissing the idea.

The look in Sam's eyes and the tone in his voice left Hank wondering if Sam wanted to be with his father or not. Sam had never gotten along with his father in his younger years. His father had been abusive, hit Sam whenever the moment urged him, penalized him for nothing, paid no attention to him throughout his high school years, and never attended a single wrestling match of Sam's even though he had been varsity for three years. His Dad always seemed not to like Sam at all. He seemed to like Hank more than Sam.

Sam continued in the same facetious tone. "I intend to make his last months on this earth as painful and full of suffering as he made my first eighteen years." Sam laughed as if he had made a joke, but there was malevolence in the sound and Hank felt a certain truth in the statement. He changed the subject.

Sam began describing his travels and the different religions he had seen and experienced.

"I'm telling you, the only religion I've seen that makes any sense is the Hindu religion," Sam said superiorly and with a hint of facetiousness. "You can pick the god you want to worship that fits you, fits your own lifestyle, worship him or her or it in the manner you want, and get the same or better satisfaction or peace of mind than from any religion in the world. There are a million gods in the Hindu religion, Shiva, Krishna, Vishnu, Saraswati, Ganesha, and on and on. My favorite is Saraswati, the goddess of learning and knowledge. She is the divine energy and is the source of spiritual light, remover of ignorance and promoter of knowledge." Sam was beaming in her praise.

"She has four arms, one holding a book, the other a rosary, yes, a rosary, you probably thought only Catholics used them, but they use them in all faiths. Two of her hands hold a musical instrument. She sits on a lotus and the peacock is the vehicle she uses to represent equanimity in prosperity. However, some areas give her a swan for this vehicle, but the peacock is so much prettier."

They got out of the car, shut the doors. Hank pressed his remote lock and alarm.

Hank countered, "I'll stick to Catholicism, it's what I know."

"That's it," said Sam. "It's what you know, not necessarily what is right or truth, but the way you were brought up. Is that any way to pick a religion? Faith by forced inculcation."

As they crossed the street, a homeless bum dressed in a dirty white shirt with an overcoat and peeling shoes approached them with his hand out. Hank began to fish into his pocket for a coin. Sam looked at the man and growled a low growl. The bum looked into Sam's face, froze for an instant, quickly turned and left.

"What the hell was that?"

"I let him know that he wasn't getting a free handout from me. I growled at him. He thought I was going to bite him." Sam laughed. Hank frowned.

They walked through the restaurant's foyer, two sets of doors—a small attempt to keep out the winter's blast on cold days—to the counter where a Chinese woman stood in a long dark green short sleeved dress with slits up the sides to her mid-thigh and buttoned at the neck. Short dark hair with a bored smile.

Two waitresses, clearing a table ten feet away, looked at the two entering the restaurant and spoke to each other in Mandarin Chinese. Sam listened; Hank spoke to the hostess for seats for two. She led them to a table on the far wall that seated four. Sam sat with his back to the wall. The two waitresses were giggling and throwing glances at the two men. The restaurant had only a few patrons this early. The walls were decorated in relief paintings of Chinese pagodas on a black lacquer background. Bright red Chinese lanterns hung over each table with tassels dangling and gently moving with the breeze. The hostess handed them menus, asked if they wanted water or tea. They ordered hot green tea.

One of the waitresses who had been looking at the two men came over with a pot of hot tea and poured it into the little tea cups. Sam addressed her in Mandarin. She blushed, hesitated a few seconds and answered in Mandarin. Sam smiled at her, responding in a long-winded sentence, moving his hands above his head as if he was making the outline of someone's profile, and laughed again. The waitress gave a curt bow, said thank you in English, and left quickly.

"You speaka Chinese, Sam?"

"Oh yes," Sam answered. "I speak that dialect of Mandarin very well."

"How did you learn it?"

"I was in a prison for six months in Northern China. My guard was from Peking and he taught me Mandarin, but he didn't know it. I learned it from listening to him talk to another guard and several inmates. I was the only gringo there. So I learned it and it has stood me well since."

"In prison! What for?"

"Some trumped up charge against a foreigner. They made it up. And made it stick. But the girls," Sam nodded toward the two girls who were whispering on the far side of the room, "were talking about us as we came in. They like you quite a bit. They were talking about the prospective size of your penis."

"No way, those cute little things over there?" Hank gave a mock look of shock.

"Yes they were. I asked her if she would like you to demonstrate for her at the table. I told her you were a paid stud and that you could make it stand up on command. That her wish was your command. That was when she blushed. Cute, wasn't she?"

"No, that's strange," Hank puzzled, "who would've ever thought two young girls would be talking about something like that about two old guys?"

"When people think you cannot understand them, they will say anything in front of you. I've heard husbands talking to their wives about bedroom behavior, priests about their parishioners, doctors about their patients, and young girls about a middle-aged man's penis." Sam laughed and drank his tea in one swallow, refilled his tea cup and drank again.

"In prison," Hank mused looking at Sam wonderingly. "Isn't that the cat's meow?" Hank was thinking. What was the trumped up charge against a foreigner? Six months in prison in Ohio was a first degree misdemeanor, assault, negligent vehicular homicide, a lesser sex crime?

Sam and Hank broke open fortune cookies at the end of their meal. Sam read his aloud: "You will meet a good friend soon."

Hank read his: "Beware of wolves in sheep's clothing. Many are there who are not what they seem."

"Sounds ominous. Must be business related?" said Sam.

"Probably talking about you, huh?" responded Hank.

"No doubt about it," Sam pointed to himself pursing his lips together in a forced smirk.

Hank briefly reflected, Sam was not the same person he had known in his youth. Sam's outlook was so different. Maybe too many marriages, no kids—that would jaundice anyone in this world—too many bad times? Maybe, just maybe, Hank thought, maybe he himself had changed. Or maybe the ten year absence clarified the differences between them. Sam appeared to have no compassion, no mercy, no nothing. Hank couldn't pinpoint the difference, but their relationship had shifted ever so slightly.

"And so," Sam drawled, putting his hand through his long hair as if putting back any loose hairs from his pony tail, "The man who tells you he has faith is talking pure bullshit. It doesn't mean anything and the person who thinks he has it, doesn't. Faith is nothing more than blind obedience to a concept that has no significance."

"What you're saying is that life is nothing," Hank said. "I don't buy it, Sam. If one believes in one's religion, and he has faith in that religion, then that belief attains for him the kingdom of heaven."

"Really, Hank. You are 56 years old. Who do you know who has faith anymore? Who would give up everything for their god? Either the pagan god with a small G, or even the Christian God with a big G? Do you think there are people in your church who would give it all up? If God said to you, Hank, put your son on the altar and sacrifice him to me,' would you do it? I don't think so."

"Those were different times, Sam. Our God is the God of love and peace, not vengeance. Ours is the New Testament, not the Old."

"You mean your God doesn't tax you? Your God doesn't require you to do things to obtain heaven or the state of grace for permission to get into heaven?"

"Of course he does, but it's not the same as in Israel of old. The Catholic Church requires faith in God. Along with that are the sacraments, good deeds, a Christian faith."

"You are repeating yourself." Sam's green eyes glittered. "Faith! Ha! I laugh at it, Hank. I have seen too much, everywhere, to have any faith in faith." He laughed derisively. "You give me someone from your church and we will test his faith. You think there are any "brahams out there? No siree. Anyone you choose. I can devise something to test his faith. I just don't believe there is faith anymore, if…there ever was. It can't exist unless it is in a mindless vegetable with a cross in his hand in a nursing home laying in his bed with drool wetting his pillow."

"Oh ye man of little faith," snickered Hank. "The phrase has never been more apropos. You've got to be joking." Hank thought, he should be joking, but I don't think he is, something in his face seemed hard and searching. "I don't know that testing someone is the right thing to do. We are not God. But let's assume I even entertained the idea. How would you test someone's faith?"

Sam said eagerly, "How did your Lord test Abraham, Noah, Job, St. Paul, Simon the Cyrenian. We can test anyone. What's a little faith? For Abraham it almost cost him his only son. For Job, it cost him his children, his wealth. St. Paul, struck blind, Simon the Cyrenian, how would you like to help some poor schmuck carry a heavy wooden cross down the streets of Jerusalem? Picked out of a crowd to help someone everyone despises. Faith, I laugh at it. I detest it. I don't believe it for a second."

"You are dead wrong Sam." Hank said, suddenly very intent. He looked at Sam as if he was looking through him. "Faith is the foundation of the church, it is the personal adherence of man to God, and it is man's free assent to the whole truth that God has revealed."

Sam leaned back in his chair, furrowed brow, narrowed eyes, he watched Hank.

"Faith is a gift from God," Hank continued, "a supernatural virtue infused by him. Man must have the grace of God before this faith can be exercised. It's our entrance to salvation. Without faith, man cannot please God. There are people within the church, within my church whose faith is strong, so strong they can be considered the embodiment of Abraham."

"Hank, let's cut to the chase." Sam cut in abruptly, waiving his hand in dismissal. "Suppose one of your fellow parishioners, who you valiantly infuse with this concept of faith, loses all his money, has to sell his house, is spurned by his friends? Suppose one of your fellow parishioners is a Job? Do you think in today's world, the very early twenty-first century, that someone can and will adhere to his faith?" Sam looked questioning at Hank, then added. "I don't think so, Hank."

Sam waved his hand in dismissal again, then put his elbow on the table, propped his chin on his hand and looked at Hank. Hank did not answer for almost a minute.

The die was set. The relationship of youth had reasserted itself in middle age. The force of Sam's personality gave credence to his arguments. Hank, even with the ten year absence, was locked, once again, into the same gears of life he had formed with Sam thirty years prior.

Hank persisted: "I say again, Sam, you are dead wrong. I believe that any person in my parish will have the conviction of their beliefs. For instance, you met Joe B. at the office today. He is a prime example. He is a member of my church, participates on various committees, and *he*," Hank leaned forward and spoke slowly, *"he* has faith."

"You really think if he got the Job treatment, like in the Old Testament, that he would continue in his faith?" Sam shook his head slowly. "We obviously disagree," said Sam.

"Sam, I don't believe there's anything you could do to shake his faith. I'm certain of it."

"Two dollars says you are wrong, Hank. Two dollars." Sam smiled, brushed his hair back with his right hand, flicked his head at the same time in a gesture of superiority and looked at Hank to take him up on the bet.

"Two dollars," said Hank. Two dollars, that was the bet. It brought back all the bets they ever had. Hank owed thousands of dollars to Sam in two dollar bets. Hank remembered the first two dollar bet.

Nine-mile Creek along Belvoir Blvd, hardly nine miles long, but for some unknown reason the name had stuck, was a half mile creek that poured into large underground cement sewers. When the boys were younger, they got flashlights and boots and investigated the sewers. One time they had walked for three quarters of a mile through the sewers and came up in the middle of Euclid Avenue. Traffic stopped for them while they climbed out of the manhole in the middle of the road where people stared at them. But walking in the sewers as kids with the smell of sewage for excitement was in days bygone; however, at age sixteen, they used Nine-mile Creek as a stash for liquor. They had been sneaking small amounts of liquor from their parents liquor bottles and hiding it in the woods by Nine-mile Creek. Just the two of them. They had an odd collection of bottles and canisters. They had three beers, a bottle of Ripple, Thunderbird, and Mogen David 20/20 which they got through Slim, the local homeless person. Slim was raggy, with a rough beard, skinny, dirty, and slept in anyone's unlocked car, but Slim had given them a difficult time to purchase the wine. They had to give Slim an extra three dollars to perform the chore, but he accomplished the task and got some wine for himself in the bargain.

Also included in the stash was a small bottle with four shots of Kentucky whiskey, a jar with two shots of Scotch, another with three shots of vodka, and the last with four shots of Galiano. None of the two had ever been drunk before. Their parents had let them have a taste or so of various drinks, but they had never been drunk. It was time for them to get drunk. A rite of passage to adulthood.

The appointed day was a cool, clear fall day, colored by orange maples, yellow beeches, and brown catalpas. They put on warm clothes for the sixty-degree weather; when you sit in the shade, it gets cool if you don't move around. At nine A.M., they started early; it was to be an all day experiment and they wanted to be sober before they got home in the evening. Sam went to Hank's house, one of the nicer homes overlooking Hillsboro Road with a great view of the Nine Mile Creek valley. Where they were going was the only wooded area nearby unless they went to the Metro Park two miles away. The terrain was hilly and had not yet been invaded by developers.

Sam knocked on the back door of Hank's house. Delores Smith, a women in her late forties, answered. Hank was the last of three children. Delores had been fighting the midriff bulge problem for several years and was losing. She wore a robe which showed plunging cleavage. Sam looked without looking. Nice tits, he thought, too bad she's getting fat. Delores invited Sam into the house and offered him breakfast. Sam ate toast with orange marmalade. He hated the bitter orange marmalade with the orange peels still in it, but he was courteous. He would have eaten the toast without anything, but Mrs. Smith put the marmalade on it.

"Mrs. S, that was the best toast, thank you," said Sam, smiling.

"Enough, Sam. I know when you are fibbing," she said, waving him off, thinking, what a con man! And what a beautiful boy he is. A very attractive boy who will break hearts some day, if he hasn't already. He could be an actor for all the sincerity he could put into a sentence he didn't mean. He will say anything to anyone, she thought, but he is a nice boy. And they do get along, those two.

"Where are you boys going today?"

"Bowling at 20th Century Lanes. There's a bunch of guys from the wrestling team that are going to be there."

"Sounds like fun."

"It should be." Small talk with mothers was easy for Sam. He bit the toast. Ugh, marmalade. He smiled at her.

"Sam," she said as she got up from the chair. "I've got to get some work done around here, so you boys have fun. Hank should be down in a minute. Help yourself to whatever you need here in the kitchen. "She wiggled her heavy ass out of the kitchen. Sam watched appreciatively, but her tits really drew him in, mentally.

He heard Hank thunder down the stairs, then they were out the door walking down Hillsboro Road to Belvoir Road to Nine Mile Creek.

They were off, walking, talking of Marilyn Shade's body, the curves, her tits, Bob Aker's acne, and who liked whom. Of nothing, of everything. They were buddies.

They ambled down Hillsboro Road to Sandy Hills, a bare, muddy, shale area where in the winter, with some snow, they'd go sliding down the hill on a piece of cardboard. The steep hill was about 150 feet long and very steep. If they didn't pay close attention to the sled path, they collided with a tree. Down this hill, they slid sideways. Their objective was the west side of Belvoir Blvd.

Sam slipped, caught himself, slipped again and slid on his butt three feet before his feet dug in. As he got up, he spotted a black metal object. He scrambled over to it; it was a gun. He picked it up, it looked real, it felt heavy. Sam's heart double timed, he yelled to Hank, already down the hill.

"Hey look, a gun. I found a gun. Holy shit, a fucking gun. I think it's real."

Hank started back up the hill. Sam came down slowly, looking at the gun and his footing at the same time. Sam's feet slipped downwards, he fell on his already dirt smeared rear, the gun flew. Sam got up with a bounce, quickly wiped off the dirt. Hank went for the gun, picked it up, turned it over in his hands examining it.

"Yeah, I think it is real. Who would throw this away?"

"Let's see it. Are there any bullets in it?"

The gun was a Smith and Wesson 38 caliber revolver. Sam looked down the barrel.

"Don't point that thing at your head. It could go off," exploded Hank.

"No, it can't. Not unless you pull the trigger. Besides, I was just trying to see if there were any bullets in it. Look, there are some bullets, you can see them."

"Don't point that thing at me. Shit, you don't know, it might have a hair trigger." Hank sidestepped to avoid the gun being pointed at him and waved his arms at Sam.

"Wait a minute," said Sam. "Look. You can take it apart with this lever."

Sam pulled the pin that allowed the cylinder to tilt out for loading and exposed six bullets.

"Here's the bullets," said Sam.

Sam tilted the gun, four of the bullets slid out, two fell on the ground. Hank picked them out of the leaves. Sam used his fingernail to pry the other two bullets out. One had been fired.

"Holy shit, one of these has been shot! There's no bullet, only a shell. Look at this dent in the back. That must be where the firing pin hits it."

They both stared at the bullets in Sam's and Hank's hands. At least twenty seconds of silence passed as they looked.

Hank spoke first: "Who would throw away a gun after shooting one bullet? Maybe somebody was murdered with it. Now your fingerprints are on it."

"I don't know. What should we do with it?"

"I guess we have to call the police."

"Aw, shit," Sam grimaced, "that will screw up our whole day. We'd have to go back to the house to call the police. They'll ask us a bunch of questions about it; and your mom would wonder why we were here at Sandy Hills, instead of walking down Algonac to 20th Century Lanes. She'd know we lied to her. "

Sam thought for a second, then said. "I know, let's take it with us, and we can say that after bowling we were playing around on this hill and found it. That would sound better, and it wouldn't be a lie."

Hank screwed up his face as he thought. "Yeah, I guess so, I don't know. A gun with one bullet gone. Geesh. I feel kinda creepy about this gun. It did something bad. It might bring us bad luck."

"Aw, bullshit. It's just a gun. We'll keep it with us, so no one else finds it. Look, it fits in my pocket." Sam put the gun, barrel first into his jacket pocket. The gun was so heavy, he had to hold the outside of his pocket with his hand. Hank handed the bullets into Sam's outstretched hand, which he put into his other pocket.

They hiked down the hill into the woods, crossed the grassy area to the road, over the ditch, crossed Belvoir Blvd., went into the woods, climbed under the fence along the woods fifty feet in, and made their way to their alcohol stash. The booty uncovered, they took stock and lined up the bottles: Mogen David 20/20, Ripple, Thunderbird, a jelly jar with four shots of Kentucky whiskey, a baby food jar with two shots of Scotch, another baby food jar, creamed peaches label still on it, with three shots of vodka, a flask borrowed from Hank's Dad with four shots of Galiano, and three beers. Sam glanced at Hank.

"Are you ready?" he asked. Sam's eyes glittered and narrowed.

"I guess it's time." Hank looked at his watch. "It is 10:30 a.m., 1955 the year of our lord, and we pray that this elixir will awaken us to the sensitivities of the world, we pray that…"

"Oh, sit down and quit that crap," interrupted Sam, who laughed. "What do you want to start with?" asked Sam.

"Hmmmm. How about the Galiano? If it looks like piss, it probably tastes like it." Hank sat on some leaves. He opened the flask. The top had a little chain holding the lid to the body of the flask. It was understandable that someone drinking from a flask might misplace the lid, so having it secured was a safety factor the boys could appreciate. Hank had to be sure to return the flask to the cabinet, cleaned, of course. His dad would surely notice an absent lid.

"Well, here goes." He tilted the flask, sipped half a shot, swirled it around in his mouth, swallowed it, gave a slight frown, then grinned.

"Tastes like licorice, not bad. Can't taste the alcohol at all." He handed the flask to Sam. He swirled the golden liquid in his mouth and forced a swallow.

"Ok, here we go." He took another drink.

They drank all the Galiano, they didn't like the scotch, they forced the whiskey down because they were macho men, sipping beer to wash away the taste. The beer tasted only a little bettter than the whiskey. They got halfway through the bottle of Ripple, gulped the vodka, and tried to drink the Mogen David, but couldn't. Energized, they started to throw things into the pond—rocks, tree limbs, anything, the empty baby jars. Sam pulled his pants down and shot a moon to Hank, Hank laughed. Sam fell over on a rock. He fell on the gun in his pocket, it jabbed into his ribs, he felt it, but was too drunk to notice the bruise he would feel tomorrow. He had forgotten about it. He hadn't felt the weight of the gun while he was sitting on the ground. He took out the gun. He was dizzily drunk.

"Hey, Hank, look, the gun. Let's shoot it. What the hell, let's shoot it."

"Well shit, what the hell, let's shoot it. That's what it's for, isn't it?" Hank was laid out on the ground spreadeagled, looking at the sky. The sky reeled, the trees did not stay still against the sky. He felt lazy, but full of energy.

"We need a skunk to shoot at. There's lots of skunks around here. What do you want to aim at? Let's have a contest. You ever shoot a gun before?"

"Not me. I never had a gun in my hand in my life."

"Me neither. Let me figure out how to load this thing." Sam got the bullets out of his pocket, opened the gun and placed five bullets into five of the six slots.

"Let's do it. That tree over there." He pointed the gun, wavering, at a tall beech twenty inches in diameter.

"Which tree?" Hank was on his feet, swaying, trying to locate the tree that Sam was pointing out. The tree was thirty feet away across the corner of the pond, toward the fence, beyond which was the grassy area, the ditch and the road.

"That one with the smooth bark, the small yellow leaves. I don't know what kind it is. It's big enough. We should be able to hit it."

"It's a beech. Got that, shoot the beech!" They laughed. Then together they said in unison: "Shoot the *beech*, shoot the *beech*."

"Ok, let her rip." Hank had located the tree by standing behind Sam when he pointed.

"Isn't there a safety or something on this thing? . Yeah, here it is, I think." Sam turned a small lever from horizontal to vertical.

"Do you cock it or just pull it? In the westerns they cock'em. Fan'em." Hank pantomimed drawing and fanning a revolver; acting, in his alcohol induced dizziness, like Gene Autry fighting the bad guys.

"I don't know. Let me try to cock it." Sam pulled the hammer back until it clicked and locked. "I guess it cocks, it's stuck back here. Let me see what happens if I pull the trigger."

Sam turned to aim at the tree, he also aimed at Hank, but Hank was so drunk he didn't notice and it didn't make a difference.

Sam aimed at the tree, his hand swayed left, then right. He lowered the gun, raised it again.

"I can't get a goddamn aim on that tree. It keeps moving."

"What's that, the tree, or your hand? You're too drunk."

"You can bet your sweet ass I am. I'm completely drunk. I don't know what the fuck I am doing. But here goes."

Sam took aim, unsteadily, pulled the trigger, the hammer fell and the loudest bang in the world deafened their ears. There was silence.

"Holy shit." said Sam. "I can't hear a thing. That was so loud."

"My ears are ringing. Whoa, baby! That was a shot heard round the world. Loud, loud, loud. Did you even hit the tree?"

"I don't think so, there's no mark on it. Let's go look at it."

"Put the gun down. I don't want you walking around with it. You're liable to shoot me."

"Ahh, bullshit." said Sam, but he put the gun down and walked around the swampy corner of the pond to the tree with Hank.

"Nothing. Great shot, Wyatt Earp. My turn."

"Yeah, let's see you do any better." They went back to the gun. Hank picked it up.

"I gotta cock it, right?"

"Yeah, just pull it back."

Hank pulled the hammer back until it locked, the cylinder moved one notch. He took aim.

"They say you're supposed to squeeze the trigger slowly."

"Then squeeze it slowly, just get on with it." Sam stuck his fingers in his ears. He stood slightly behind to the left of Hank so he could see the aim.

Hank fired. Again the sound was the loudest sound they'd ever heard.

"I hit it! Look, I hit it!" Hank looked at the spot on the tree about three feet above the ground on the edge of the tree where the bullet had splattered the bark.

"I see. Give me that gun. I can hit that sucker." Sam stepped up, took the gun quickly, cocked it, took his stance, left hand on his hip, right arm straight out from the side of his body, head turned, and he shot. Missed again.

"Missed, dammit. Once more." He aimed again, shot quickly and hit the tree two feet above where Hank had hit.

"Bout time." said Hank. "OK, I get one more. Last bullet, right, there are only five, aren't there?"

"Yeah, I think so. Have at it."

"Watch this." Hank took the gun, got into position. "I'm going to hit that second branch where it comes out of the tree. See it."

"Yeah, I see it. Bull. You can't hit it."

Hank shot.

Sam laughed, "You missed." They heard a car screech. They looked beyond the woods, saw a yellow 1954 Mercury fishtail and come to a stop.

"Shit, I think you hit that car! Look. The window is broken."

They were quiet, they could hear a woman screaming.

"Get down, get down," hissed Sam, crouching.

They heard a man shouting, but could not understand the words. The car jerked in a half turn, backed up, and accelerated north on Belvoir Blvd.

"I think you hit the car."

"I think so." Hank spoke so slowly it sounded like a drawl. "I wonder if anyone inside got hit."

"I don't know, but I think we better get the hell outa here, and not across that road, they might be waiting."

Hank watched the car speed away. He began to pee his pants, but stopped it almost immediately. Not bad enough to show. That would be embarrassing.

"Let's get out of here." Sam warned. "First, let's get rid of this stuff." Hank, eyes out of focus, stood there. He couldn't believe it.

"Com'on, move it!" expostulated Sam.

Hank, focused again, took the baby jar that held the Scotch and threw it into the pond.

"Open the tops, pour that shit out. That son of a bitch is going to float." said Sam.

Sam threw the bottle of Mogen David at the baby jar of scotch floating at surface level and hit it with the first throw. The baby jar broke.

"Great shot, huh? Better than your damn shot." Sam said sarcastically.

Hank said nothing.

They tossed all the bottles except the flask which Hank put into his hip pocket. They were still very drunk.

Sam took the gun and threw it into the pond.

The bullet had traveled through the leaves, over the fence, and through the closed window of the Mercury, blowing a hole the size of a baseball in the window, permitting the bullet to crash into the skull of a child laying against the breast of his mother. The child died instantly although she convulsed spasmodically for about thirty seconds. The mother screamed, hysterical. The father slammed on the brakes, the Mercury skidded to a stop. The father assessed the situation, yelled at the mother to shut up, turned the car around and rushed to Euclid Avenue, then to Huron Road Hospital. The child was dead, the mother uncontrollable, hysterical. The police were called, they did not find any evidence of anyone. They did not climb the fence, they didn't know exactly where the car was on Belvoir Road when the child was shot and they did not take the time to walk the woods on the other side of the fence. The father walked the wooded area for weeks, climbed the fence, searched the area, but found nothing. He went to the area at least once a month for the next three years wandering aimlessly through the woods. He never saw Hank or Sam.

They never returned to the scene again.

Hank awakened the next morning at 5:15am after a fitful disturbed sleep to deliver the Cleveland Plain Dealer. He dressed, got his canvas newspaper bag, a bag he had to purchase for three dollars, but which lasted for years. Hank delivered the Plain Dealer for the past three years, it gave him spending money, which every fifteen year old needed. The real difficulty was collecting money. Some people avoided paying the paper boy whenever they could. It was a frustrating process although he got quite clever at figuring out when to knock on certain doors to make sure they were home. Once confronted with the paper boy, face to face, it was harder to make excuses, but, of course, they still tried.

He walked to the corner of Hillsboro Road. where the Plain Dealer delivery truck dropped off his forty-two papers every morning, but Sunday. On Sundays the papers were dropped off at his home; then he had to insert the funnies section with the metro section and then put them both into the front page section. He used a wagon he'd won in a contest by getting ten new subscribers in one month. The Sunday papers were too heavy to carry.

Hank undid the twine around the papers, folded the single sheet of brown paper at the top and bottom of the bundle, used to protect the newspapers, and placed it in the bottom of his canvas sack. As he folded up the cover paper, he always casually read the front page. This morning he was keenly interested to see if there was anything about yesterday's scare.

Hank discovered the extent of his crime on page two, column one, which read as follows:

STRAY BULLET KILLS CHILD

A stray bullet shot through the window of the car of Robert Elliott yesterday killed his three-month old child, Robert Elliot, Jr., sitting on his mother's lap. Mr. Elliott had been taking his family on a car trip to visit his mother in Pennsylvania. He was on Belvoir Blvd. in East Cleveland when a bullet of unknown origin pierced the car window striking the child in the head. Mrs. Elliott was unavailable for comment. The Police scoured the area but were unable to find any clues.

Hank, with shaking hands, carefully tore the article out of the paper, folded it, and put it into his pocket. He delivered his papers, throwing the papers onto porches in such a frenzy that the papers skidded across the porches and slid into the walls or across the porches and into the bushes. He even delivered the paper from which he ripped the article. He didn't care. Going through his mind over and over was the picture of the child he had not seen, but who he imagined, bleeding its life out all over the car and all over its mother. He had killed a child. He didn't know what to do. He did nothing but deliver his papers in a frenetic panic.

He called Sam, he had to see him. When they met later in the day, Hank showed Sam the news clipping.

"Mum's the word," said Sam. "You understand me? Mum's the word. Not a damn thing to anyone."

"We can't not do anything." said Hank. "I killed a child. Do you understand me? I'm going to hell. I killed a goddamn child and I am a god-
damned murderer. Oh, shit."

Hank collapsed on the stone wall by the apartments where he delivered
papers, covering his face with his hands, his elbows on his knees with his
legs tucked up. His glazed eyes stared vacantly at traffic on Euclid Avenue.

"Look," said Sam, "You can't do anything for that kid now. He or she,
whatever it was, is dead. There is nothing you can do for it. And," he said
sternly, "there is nothing you can do for yourself by telling anyone. What's
going to happen if you tell anyone? They'll put you in the detention home.
Then what will happen to you? No, you can't say or do anything about it.
It's over."

Hank was almost crying, but he wasn't going to cry in front of Sam.
"Shit, shit, shit," he moaned.

"And what about your parents? What'll this do to them? They'd shit a
brick, then kick your ass, let juvenile court kick your ass, and then let
them take you away.

"No one knows that we are involved in it, so let it stay that way. Forget
it. I'm as involved in it as you are, and I sure as shit don't want to go to the
detention home. My dad would be in ectasy if he could get rid of me that
easy. So fuck him. Mum's the word."

Hank looked at him through thick teary eyes. Sam's narrowed eyes
looked straight at Hank. They stared at each other for a full minute before
Hank looked away.

"You're right, but it feels so wrong. I can't believe this."

"Hey, it was an accident, an accident," said Sam.

"Shit, shit, shit," repeated Hank.

"Yeah, yeah. Look, Hank. We are the best of friends. If friendship
means anything, then we must not, I repeat, we must not say a word about
this to anyone. Not in a joke. Not seriously, not ever. Not even between
you and me. Someone might overhear us. Not ever. You got it?"

Sam looked at Hank, grabbed Hank by both forearms and made him look into his eyes.

"We are friends." said Sam. "We say nothing, ever. We stay friends forever. If we don't, we're dead meat. You got it?"

Hank looked at him and said: "We are friends, mum forever."

"Shake on it."

Friends they remained, and the incident dictated their relationship. Sam was the leader, the decider, the controller. Hank was the companion, the foil reflecting the actions of Sam. Sam acted, Hank supported.

They were inseparable. The mention of one of them, brought the other to mind.

However, the incident haunted Hank. He thought of it often. He knew he couldn't tell anyone. But the thought was with him, he couldn't shake it, he had killed a child. He had caused untold and unimaginable suffering to a mother. He had killed a child in the arms of its mother. His punishment was in the secrecy of his remorse. What he had done was wrong, but there was no way to right it. As a consequence, he became closer to the Church. He continued to be an altar boy even though he attended a public school. He joined the Catholic Church youth group. Sam refused and this was the one activity that they did not do together. Hank leaned on the Church. Sam leaned away from any church.

Occasionally Sam would mock Hank for his attentiveness to church, but Hank let it roll past him. There was one thing different between them and Hank knew it; he had a conscience, he felt for people. Sam didn't care about anyone. Even on small items, Sam was in it for Sam. To hell with everyone, they are out to get you, so you better look out for yourself.

They were bound together by silence, by trust, by mistrust, by fear, by guilt and by friendship.

Infrequently they spoke of the incident. They checked to see if they were alone, they spoke softly. There was nothing to do about the incident, but it kept coming back to Hank. He repressed it as well as he could, but it resurfaced and a pang of guilt enveloped him.

Less than a month after the terrible event, Sam and Hank were going on a picnic with the Jonke twins. They walked to the Jonke home. Hank's mom had made sandwiches, stuffed pop cans and a treat for dessert into a paper grocery bag for all four of them. They were going to the Ferguson playground by Green Road Shopping Center. It was only a twenty minute walk. That was the best time with the girls anyway, walking and talking.

Sam knocked on the Jonke door. Mrs. Jonke invited them in to wait for several minutes while the girls finished what they were doing. Maryanne was bottle feeding a nine-month old child when they entered.

"Hi Sam," said Maryanne as she looked up and smiled. She had eyes only for Sam although the double date was supposed to be non-specific as to who was with whom. Maryanne knew with whom she wanted to be.

"Hi," smiled Sam.

"I'll tell Ann Marie," said Mrs. Jonke exiting.

"What's the kid's name?" asked Hank.

"Joey. Cute isn't he? Likes these bottles. He'll be asleep in a minute after he finishes this bottle." Joey made slurpy sucking sounds of satisfying pleasure.

Hank went over, took Joey's hand, the fingers clasped Hank's index finger.

"Quite a grip, little fella." Hank crouched to eye level with Joey whose eyes were slowly narrowing into sleepiness.

"Won't be long now," said Hank. "He's tottering into netherland."

"He's a good baby. We love him so much. Ann Marie and I have to flip a coin to see who gets to feed him."

Sam sat on the single chair with an ottoman, put his feet up, relaxed.

"I might just go to sleep myself. Maryanne, will you feed me, please?"

Maryanne looked up at Sam. Smiled. "Hmm, I just might. But you better not go to sleep if I do."

"Wouldn't it be terrible if Joey got shot like that baby on Belvoir Blvd.?" said Maryanne.

Hank stood bolt upright. "What?"

"Didn't you read about that baby? A little baby got shot by a bullet on Belvoir. I'd sure hate it if we lost Joey like that. Actually, I'd hate it if we lost him any way. He is such a good little baby." Maryanne was oblivious to the looks exchanged between Hank and Sam.

"I'll wait on the porch," said Hank hurrying out the door breathing deeply.

Before Hank could get to the door, Sam asked, "So how's your mum?"

"My mum? You mean my mom? You just saw her. She is fine. What's the matter with him?" asked Maryanne.

"Need's fresh air, I guess," answered Sam.

Sam's comment was not lost on Hank. He knew exactly what Sam meant. Mum's the word.

Hank sat on the top step of the porch. It all came back in a rush. He had killed a child. He could say nothing. What were the odds that Maryanne would have read that story, and then to have repeated it to Hank? He stood, quickly descended the steps and strode around the house with his hands in his pockets, sweat beaded on his brow.

It wouldn't leave him, he knew it. The guilt enveloped him. It happened everytime he watched parents with young children. He saw the bond of love, the animalistic and human attraction; he knew he had severed that bond in one family and he felt unquenchable guilt.

He also felt inextricably bound to Sam. Sam knew his deed. Sam was his friend, but Hank felt certain that if Sam wished, he would use the incident as leverage. "How's your mum?" Sam drove it home. Stuck it in and twisted it ever so slightly. Sam hadn't used the incident as leverage yet, but Hank was ever so watchful that it could happen. Hank might be best friends with Sam, but he didn't fully trust him. Hank purposely did not allow any of their disagreements to deteriorate to that point. Hank developed an attitude of acceding to Sam's wishes.

"Did you hear me, Hank? Yoohoo, wake up. What are you? Dreaming?" asked Sam.

"Yes, for a second there I was," said Hank, snapping back to reality. "The old two dollar bet, huh? Two dollars for what? To make Joe lose all his money? First, you couldn't do it. Secondly, it's not right that you should. I'm not going to bet a man's livelihood away. I couldn't do that."

"Right, right," expostulated Sam frowning derisively. "I don't know what is right. There is no right in the world. You tell me the man has faith. Let me see if he really does. You want a test of his faith. Let me worry about how the test is conducted. If I make someone lose money, then I can make sure any loss of money is only temporary. If I did it, I'd damn sure make sure he'd get it all back, with interest. But it's the thought of the loss." Sam drew it out. "Ahh, he will curse your God. His faith will plummet."

"It doesn't sound right, Sam. You just can't play with someone's life."

"That's exactly my point. You profess that a man has faith, but there is no way for you to demonstrate his faith. It is like your law practice, an argument without proof, is nothing. As I say, there is no faith in this world. It doesn't exist. I am not attempting to ruin this young man's life, but only to test his faith in this God of the Catholic Religion—a simple trick." Sam looked expectantly at Hank.

Hank was red-faced. He didn't want to bet two dollars to test Joe B's faith. Especially not Joe B, a man he knew and liked. Hank felt boxed in. He couldn't carry the argument without proof. His statements about the goodness of God just seemed to fall flat.

The relationship of the friendship of Sam and Hank, exerted for more than fifty years, with Sam clearly in control, made itself paramount. It had to be wrong to let Sam try to test someone's faith, but really, what could

Sam do? Hank recognized the wrongness of it, but was powerless. What could he do? Nothing, really.

Sam always turned the littlest project into a bet. Who can reach the corner first, who can jump the highest, who can piss off the teacher. Always a bet, always two dollars. It was never paid. The bets meant nothing, just the idea that Sam had competition, something to work for or against. What could he really do to test Joe B's faith? I mean, after all, you can't play with a man's life. Have him suffer a financial loss? He says he would make him whole. Sam is a liar, but not that big of a liar. Sam lied all his life, but not on a bet. The bet was sacred. Sure, right word for this discussion, Asacred".

Hank knew it was going to happen, no matter what he did. He felt trapped. He couldn't just say no, go to hell. It wouldn't end there. Sam would do it anyways. It wouldn't end until Sam lost the bet. Sam was like a pit bull terrier, he got his teeth into something and held on til he got bludgeoned off. Sam kept coming back to it over and over again. It was going to happen, so Hank might as well make the best of it.

"You tell me, Sam," Hank said resignedly, "What exactly are you planning to do? How are you going to test his faith?"

"I don't know—lose some money somehow?" Sam's grin evidenced that he knew he had bested Hank—the bet was on. The old relationship continued. Sam was in control. He baited Hank, and Hank went along with it. Not because he thought it was the right thing to do, but because it was the easiest way out of the argument. Sam was so full of himself on this one. Was Hank making a conscious decision? He didn't know, but he felt uncomfortable. And the loss of a little money would not affect Joe B's faith at all. The man was solid.

Sam continued, "I'll have to think about it for a while, but two dollars, that's the bet. What's his name again? Joe? Joe B, that's it. Well, Joe B, do you have faith in your God? Are you an Abraham, a Jacob, a Job? Faith. Ahh, yes, I scoff at it."

"A little money, Sam," Hank said cautiously. "But you can't do anything to Joe B. The kid will bear up like a trooper."

Sam with a knowing smile extended his hand across the table. Hank, resignedly, took it. They shook and looked at each other for a long time.

"You have my word," said Sam with a wry grin, "I'm not going to harm him. I'll figure out a way to test his faith and I'll make sure he gets whatever money we delete from whatever accounts he has is fully returned; and, we'll meet again."

CHAPTER EIGHT

▼

AN AMERICAN FAMILY

Joe's win exhilarated his drive home. He drove east on Route 90 from Cleveland in his two-year-old Chrysler LeBaron to suburban Willoughby, out of the tall buildings to the cul de sacs, to the houses with an hour's worth of lawn cutting every week in the summer with a riding mower. Joe's home, a ranch style on two acres of land, had woods on one-third of an acre in the rear; or, as Joe liked to say, weeds. The house was built in the early sixties and well maintained. He would have to move in several years; Joe Jr. and Edward weren't happy sharing a room any longer. Jenny and Samantha didn't know yet what privacy was, but they would clamor for it in another couple of years.

Life was good when you were winning, thought Joe. To be thrown into the fray and come out scratched, but successful. And to still get along with the opposing attorney after beating him so badly was a feat that Joe was able to handle by the force of his engaging personality. He didn't personalize the legal battle so as to alienate his opponent, nor did he allow his opponent to personalize the battle so he resented Joe. Treat others as you would be treated was his motto. He lived by it: it worked for him.

Hank was pleased with his victory. Partnership track. He had impressed them today. And that guy with Hank—looked worldly. Not the sort of person I'd imagine a friend of Hank's. He exuded something earthy, fecund, fetid. Can't exactly put a finger on it, but the tight little pony tail was a different look for a friend of Hank's. The safari jacket automatically made him a traveler. Hank's friend—Sam was his name— had a presence. You knew he was in the room, even when your back was to him, you knew he entered. Why did he stare at me in the reception room. Maybe it was smell. Man's sense of smell is keen, he just doesn't know how to rely on it. What smell would Sam give to announce his presence? Sulfur. Wet earth. A damp basement? Why do those things come to mind so quickly? Fecund wet dirt, swamp water. He can smell them now; yes, the man had a presence. Something apart, different. A slight involuntary shiver tingled down Joe's spine. He shut off the air conditioning. It was too cold in the car.

As Joe pulled into the paved driveway of his home, Jenny, four years old with short blonde hair, came running out the front door yelling: "Daddy, Daddy Daddy. Daddy's home, Daddy's home, Daddy's home." She raised her arms, dropped them, raised them again and ran behind the car to the driver's door. She hugged Joe's leg when he got out of the car.

"Daddy's home. Daddy, Daddy, Daddy."

"Hello, Jenny." He picked her up and gave her a kiss on her cheek.

"Give me a real hug now." She squeezed him tight. He heard noises of the kids in the backyard, and carried her around the house.

"Eddie did something bad today, Daddy." She kissed him on the cheek.

"Oh, oh, what did Eddie do? Is he going to be in trouble?"

"He's in his room. He was a bad boy."

"What did he do, pumpkin?" Joe reached the back yard and watched Bobby and Joe Jr. hitting the tether ball, jumping and screaming with each punch.

"He hit a girl at school. He is a bad boy."

"If he hit a girl, he is a bad boy. Why did he hit a girl?"

"He hit her and the teacher called mommy. He is a bad boy, Daddy. Don't let him hit me."

"I won't let him hit you, pumpkin. If he ever hits you, you let me know. Why did he hit the girl at school, do you know?"

"She spit on him, so he hit her. I won't spit on Eddie, Daddy. He will hit me then. He is a bad boy, Daddy."

"Yes, he is a bad boy, isn't he?" The boys were so busy hitting the tether ball, they didn't see their father watching them. He stood there watching, appreciating his children. His wonderful children. They were such good children, even when they were bad boys like Eddie, they were good. Life couldn't get any better than it was today, thought Joe. Great kids, great family, great job, great friends. And none of the machinery or electrical appliances have broken down so as to need fixing. Great, great, great. God is good and life is great.

Marsha called Eddie out of his room for dinner. Marsha was short with light brown hair, industrious, and had a smile that brought a return smile from anyone. Her movements were quick and smooth. Her coordination had passed on to the children. They had held off having children until Joe was assured of employment, but then they created one after the other.

Their life was their children. Everything they did revolved around their children; Joe Jr.'s guitar lessons, Eddie's computer interest, Bobby's baseball, Jenny's singing and dancing, and Samantha's being smothered by love. Marsha was dedicated to raising children. She spent much time volunteering at the church. Father Bill was so understanding and helpful. She was in the St. Vincent DePaul Society, collecting and organizing donations for the poor, delivering them to the outlet store in downtown Cleveland. She took Samantha with her on these forays; she wanted Samantha to learn from her earliest memories to help others less fortunate than her.

Dinner of macaroni and cheese was one of the kids' favorites, with peas and a small salad on the side. Ice tea for the adults and 1% milk for the kids, to keep the fat out of their diets. All of the children except Eddie were sitting at the table when Marsha yelled for him.

"Eddie, time to eat." No response came from Eddie's room. "I'll get him. Give me a minute. Go ahead and start without me, right after our blessing," said Joe.

"Ok kids, give me your hands. Bobby, you say the prayer today," Joe said. He stretched his arms to hold Bobby's and Jenny's hands.

"Jesus," Bobby said, "Bless this food we eat this evening, we thank the Lord our God for this food, for our family, for our house, and especially for Eddie who is in trouble today. Amen."

Joe smiling said: "Nice job, Bobby. You might even grow up to be a priest." Joe headed to Eddie's room. The family began to eat and talk at the same time.

"My favorite." Said Jenny scooping up some macaroni. Joe Jr. had a line of milk on his upper lip from drinking deeply.

Joe knocked and entered Eddie's room. A small room with bunk beds on one side, Eddie got the top bunk, Bobby was on the bottom, Joe Jr. got the single bed on the far side of the room because he was the oldest; a mirror and dresser, each had two drawers in the dresser, on the end of the room; posters of Spider Man and comic hero Thor hanging on the walls,

clothes on the floor which Joe looked at and frowned. The kids knew better than to throw their clothes on the floor.

Eddie, a third grader at St. Mary's School, lay on his back, staring at the
ceiling. Joe came to the side of the bed and looked.

"What's up, sport? Hear you got yourself in some trouble. Want to tell
me about it?"

"No, mom already told you."

"Well, she told me you hit a girl and that the girl spit on you. Do you
want to tell me about it?"

"No, there's nothing to tell. Mary Addison spit on me so I hit her. She
deserved it."

A pause ensued. No one spoke for ten seconds.

"Why did she deserve it, Eddie?"

"Richie Harrington called her a fatty, fatty two-by-four and she
thought it was me, so she spit on me. I didn't do anything to her. She just
spit on me."

"Did you try to explain to her that it wasn't you who called her names?"

"No, I'm not going to squeal on Richie, but she shouldn't have spit on
me. It was gross."

"Do you think Mary was happy about it? About someone making fun
of her?" Eddie did not answer.

"Eddie? Do you think Mary liked being made fun of? Were there other
people around to see her being called names?"

"No, she didn't like it, but she shouldn't have spit on me."

"Should she have spit on someone else?"

"Richie."

"So it was okay for her to spit on the person who called her names?"

"No, yes…Probably not, but he should have got it, not me."

"But Mary thought you did it, didn't she?"

"Yes," Eddie sulked.

"So if it was okay for Mary to spit on someone who called her a name, then
you hit her for making a mistake. She just got the wrong person, didn't she?"

"Yes," Eddie continued sulking.

"Should she be hit for making a mistake?"

"She shouldn't have spit on me."

"Would you want someone to hit you whenever you make a mistake? How about when you dropped the glass last week and it broke. Would you want someone to hit you for making that mistake?"

"No."

"So do you think you should hit Mary for making a mistake?"

"No."

"So what happens now?"

Eddie hesitated, he looked as guilty as a third grader could look.

"I write an apology?"

"Yes, of course you do. But what about hitting people? First, you know you shouldn't hit someone for making a mistake, but what about hitting people at all? What if everyone went around hitting everyone else for things they didn't like. The whole world would be beating each other up. You wouldn't like to get hit all the time, would you?"

"No."

"Well, then, Eddie, I don't want to hear of you hitting anyone, especially a girl, again. If you can't talk your way out of it, then you leave. Do you understand?"

"Yes."

"We can do the apology after dinner—no, I mean after Bobby's T-ball practice. But let's eat now. Do I have your promise that you won't hit people for making mistakes? Eddie?"

"Yes, I won't hit people."

"Ok, let's eat, I'm starved, Sport." Joe extended his hand to help Eddie up.

The family was seated around the table, passing food back and forth, making small talk. Even Eddie bounced back into the gaily bantering conversations once he realized he was no longer the focus of everyone's attention. Bobby asked his father if they were going to pickup Jim for T-ball practice when Joe Jr. announced: "Melissa Perkins' sister died yesterday."

Everyone was silent and stared at Joe Jr.

"What did you say?" asked Joe.

"Melissa Perkins' sister died yesterday. She was only three years old. Leuky something, I don't remember. Melissa missed school today and won't be there tomorrow either."

"Oh, that is so sad," said Marsha. "That poor woman. Oh Joe, we have to send them something. Oh, her grief must be horrible. I knew the child had leukemia, but I thought they had it under control."

"Flowers? I'll take care of it tomorrow," said Joe.

"I'll make a casserole and deliver it tomorrow,"

Marsha added. "Why does that happen, Daddy?" asked Bobby. He was a first grader at St. Mary's School; Sister Bridgette was his teacher, one of the few nuns still teaching school. Bobby's crew haircut made him look like his favorite baseball player, Cal Ripken.

"What do you mean?" asked Joe.

"Why do kids die? Why does Jesus let that happen? What did that baby do to have to die for?"

Joe sat thinking for a moment. The children and Marsha looked at him. He didn't have an answer, but the child needed an answer. Joe needed an answer. Why do children have to die? What a question. Only God could answer it, but Bobby and the rest of his children needed an answer. It was taking him much too long to answer. He sat poised to answer but nothing was coming out of his mouth, nothing came into his mind to answer. With his right elbow on the table holding the fork suspended in air, he appeared to be sticking himself in the eye while he was thinking.

"Joe, aren't you going to answer?" asked Marsha, finally.

"Yes," said Joe, anguished.

"Well, Bobby, there is no real answer to your question. God does things for a purpose. He must have a greater reason for taking the little child. He may have wanted someone pure in spirit and full of grace at his side in Heaven." Joe thought hard for more answers for Bobby. After all, these were children he was talking to, not a jury he was trying to convince to award money for an injured client.

"We don't know the full perspective seen by God. He sees everything. He might be testing the other people he left on earth; to test their faith in the Lord. He might be actually saving the child from a worse fate down the road of life. He might be doing a good thing. We don't know. We do know that what the Lord does, he does for a reason; and, we must believe in Him for whatever reason he does it even though we don't know the reason. We must have faith in the Lord Jesus. Can you understand that, Bobby?"

"Sure, Dad," answered Bobby, squinching his face in a puzzled look.

Jenny piped up, anxious to get into the conversation.

"The other Jenny in my class fell off the slide today and broke her arm. The amblance came and got her."

"That's am-bu-lance, Jenny. Can you say it? Am-bu-lance. Say it," said Marsha.

"Am-blance."

"Am-bu"

"Am-bu."

"Am-bu-lance."

"Am-blance."

"Ok, kids, that's enough about bad things happening to people for today. Let's talk about good things," said Marsha.

"Did you know Daddy won a big case today? A big case that will help him get a promotion in the firm. A promotion that will get us a bigger house in a year or two."

Marsha smiled at Joe.

Joe gave a thumbs up with a fork in his hand, smiled back. Everyone started to chatter for food and life went on as normal.

Life was good.

CHAPTER NINE

▼

BREAKFAST WITH MARIAN

The routine of married life was set with Hank and Marian Smith after thirty-two years of marriage. By the time Hank awoke, Marian had already retrieved the two newspapers, the Cleveland Plain Dealer and The News Herald. She sat at the kitchen counter with the papers piled on top of each other, paging through one, then the other, sipping a double mug of coffee from an insulated plastic container. For as long as it took her to drink the coffee, it remained warm to the last drop. The butcher block counter had papers piled on one end—at least four days worth. Glasses, cups and plates in the left side of the double sink were unwashed. When the sink filled she would put the items in the dishwasher, unless Hank got so frustrated by the mess that he would jump the gun and put them in the dishwasher himself. This occurred more often than not.

Their main contact was in the mornings. Both Hank and Marian had evening meetings which seemed never to coincide. Dinner in the evening was on your own and had been for years. Hank liked it like that. Hank learned to cook for himself with an efficiency that involved few dishes; a sandwich, grilled steak, or a bowl of soup. Simple.

Hank didn't see Marian last night, she got home after he was asleep. She heard him come down the steps, the squeak on the fourth to last step announced his closeness. Why he always stepped on the squeaky part annoyed Marian, but she said nothing.

Hank went to the coffee pot, lifted it and poured coffee into the waiting cup with sugar and non-fat dairy creamer already in it. One of the nice things Marian did for him. Really, about the only nice thing anymore.

"Morning," said Hank.

"Morning."

"Saw one of your favorite people yesterday, guess who?" said Hank.

Marian didn't answer, but continued to read the newspaper. She hated guessing games; he knew it, but insisted on trying to goad her into them.

After an appreciable pause, Hank said, "Sam Hawkins stopped at the office yesterday."

"That SOB!" Marian lifted her head from the paper just enough for Hank to see her scowl.

"He asked about you too."

"Who's he come to do dirty this time? Is he going to shaft another poor girl that he married?" Marian sipped her coffee peering at Hank over the rim of the mug.

Hank remembered, right after Hank married, Sam married. Sam remarried three more times. Hank liked each of Sam's wives; he was best man at each wedding except for the last which occurred overseas and was on the spur of the moment. Hank watched the deterioration of each of Sam's marriages. Sam was selfish, inconsiderate, too often mean—a lot like his father. Hank saw the earmarks of each pending divorce. The look of concern on the face of Sam's wife, her inquiries to Hank, to Hank's wife, the crying, the hurt, the acceptance, the anger, and the divorce. Sam always forced the woman to seek the divorce. He just treated them badly until they desperately wanted to get away.

"He really is a bastard," added Marian, seeing no response from Hank. "I don't know why you tolerate him?" Then she shrugged and refocused on the paper.

"I guess his Dad is sick, so he came into town to be with him awhile."

"As if he ever liked his Dad. Probably came to bury him. I know his Dad never liked him." Marian paused, "What's he really doing here?"

Hank thought of Sam's father. A man Sam never got along with. Sam was independently wealthy. He inherited a large sum of money from his grandfather. His grandfather had invested in Standard Oil, made much money, put it into trust, and promptly died. Sam was the inheritor of all of his grandfather's money. His grandfather had refused to leave any money to his own son, Sam's father. There was a feeling of ill will. Sam never knew his grandfather well, but he inherited well. The banks that acted as trustees excelled at multiplying the money hundredfold. Sam never had to work a day in his life after he reached the age of thirty when the proceeds of the trust were available to him, but he did work. He worked very hard, but not at anything for a long time. His work consisted of con games. He made money at the expense of someone else. If he could pilfer, he would. If he needed to steal, he would. If he could cause some poor sap to spend his last cent on Sam, he would.

Sam didn't act this way out of malice, or if he did, he wasn't conscious of it. He merely acted this way because it was his nature. It was a game, his challenge. No one bred it into him. The growth of it emanated from Sam. He took great glee in a trick or the unexpected result of a slight oversight. He didn't believe in anything. He didn't believe in the afterlife, the trinity, Jesus Christ, or anything. He did believe in a good time, a good contest, a good test. He thought faith was a hollow puzzle created by the Catholic Church to ensnare the sheep so they would not escape, but would pay forever to the church until they died. He believed that desperate men would do whatever they needed to do to survive.

And Sam was entertaining. He got along with everyone, except Marian, of course. In a crowd, he mixed well; never without conversation.

"He said his Dad was sick," said Hank, "so he was going to stick around awhile, that's all. We went to East Peking for lunch yesterday. He's real handy with the chopsticks. Said he was in a prison in China for six months and learned how to use them real well."

"What'd he do, scam someone?" asked Marian, disgusted.

"He said something about being a foreigner. Said it was a trumped up charge."

"Oh, come on! Someone finally got him on one of his scams. Probably got some poor Chinese girl pregnant. God knows he doesn't give a damn about anybody but himself."

Hank remembered a pregnant girl. It happened just so.

When Sam and Joe were in the eleventh grade at Collinwood High School, Sam got a girl pregnant. Sam had no money, didn't want the kid, and pressed Hank for help financially. Hank was upset. Abortion was taboo in the Church, and Hank was not in favor of it. Hank was presented with two irreconcilable issues: he had a friend pressed against the wall versus his religious tenets. He was torn apart and couldn't make a decision. Sam couldn't just take the girl to the hospital for an abortion. Abortions were not the sort of thing that anyone was permitted to perform and the stigma attached to it was great. The places where abortions were performed were secret; how Sam located a place was unknown to Hank, but Hank loaned Sam seven hundred dollars, and Sam talked the girl into the abortion. He was a smooth talker.

Hank had refused to accept the return of any money for his contribution to the abortion; he was too repulsed at his participation. His friend had needed the money; and, even though he didn't embrace the activity, he did support his friendship. Sam had begged for the money and tried to convince Hank of the correctness of the decision, but he finally got the money from Hank only out of friendship. Hank concentrated hard to obliterate the reason for Sam's use of the money. It was the only way that Hank could force himself to give the money.

When Sam did finally obtain sufficient money, he only once ever offered to pay Hank back. Now, it was a drop in the bucket of available funds to Sam, but he just didn't want to pay it back. Anyway, Hank had refused to take it back, once.

Sam never had a child thereafter. He had four wives, but no children. The doctors said his sperm count was high, but for some unknown reason, they failed to attach to any eggs, even when artificially inseminated. The eggs shed his sperm repeatedly, some chemical repellant. That didn't stop him from trying. Sam regretted his decision to abort the child only when he discovered he couldn't produce a child. It gave him a tweak as one of the ironies of his life. He should have let the little bastard live; then he would have had a child.

Hank, on the other hand, had three children; Peter, Paul and Beth. They had now completed college and were living with their own families. They were good kids, gave Hank many hours of satisfaction, and provided him many fond memories. He saw them two or three times a year; all three lived out of state. They were independent and Hank accepted that. His grandchildren were the best when he was able to see them. He smiled at the thought of them.

"What's so funny?" asked Marian.

"Oh, nothing, just thinking of the grandkids."

Hank sipped coffee. "Sam's got religion."

"Don't believe it," said Marian, who continued reading and turning pages.

"Well, not exactly as in following a specific religion. But he has studied many religions. Says he knows religion. Says he likes the Hindus best. Lets him worship any God he wants."

"Knowing Sam, he would worship Lucifer."

"Marian," said Hank becoming exasperated. "You really don't know Sam that well. I realize you don't like him. But do you have to make a nasty comment every time I tell you something about him?"

Surprised at the tone of his voice, Marian looked up. "Yeah, you're probably right. I know he is a shit, but I don't have to say it all the time."

"Anyway," continued Hank, "Sam does know his religions. He rattled off all kinds of stuff about Hinduism, Buddism, Confucianism, and, he even quoted from the Koran. He was impressive."

"No one ever said he was dumb," said Marian, then added, "sorry."

"He says no one has faith anymore. Says we're all puppets of the churches, of the priests and ministers. Says he could pick anyone out of this world and show that he has no faith."

"Big deal. Who cares? Like you, you've got your religion, the diocese's legal business. What more is there? Sam doesn't care about religion, he never did. If he cares about anything, it's getting over on somebody. I can't believe you still can't see through that guy. You're like his puppy dog. Been so, ever since you were best buddies in high school." Marian added a sneering emphasis to "best buddies" as if it were some bird gutted by a cat.

Hank wanted to tell Marian about the bet, but he felt she wouldn't understand. She had a bias against Sam, which she wouldn't explain to him, that went back to the first years of their marriage. Sam was aware of it and hadn't been invited to the home ever since. Hank always wondered if maybe Sam had tried to put the moves on Marian. Marian denied it, but the thought persisted.

"Well, we were best buddies, still are, too. You just don't throw those things away. Friendship is a lasting thing."

"Oh, come on. Don't get preachy. You're best buddies with him, I am not so sure the same is in reverse. You haven't seen it for forty years, you're not going to see it now. Go play your silly games. Go pay him the money you owe him for all the two dollar bets you lost to him. Just don't bring him around here. He gives me the creeps."

"Why?" inquired Hank.

"I don't know, he just does. The way he looks at me, or at our kids, or at our things. It's so intense. As if he is trying to get into your mind to make you do things. I just know I don't like it. Never have."

"I know you never have. He hasn't been here since our second year of marriage. I'd sure like to know what it is between you two."

"Nothing! Of that you can be sure," Marian looked back at her paper abruptly dismissing the conversation. Hank knew the conversation was over. He sipped the last of his coffee, turned to the sink, rinsed his cup and put it on the towel upside down to dry. He went to shower.

CHAPTER TEN

▼

SAINT MARY'S

The Joe B family sat in church as a family except for Joe B. Jr., who was one of the altar boys for the nine-thirty Mass at St. Mary's Church. Joe always wore a suit to Sunday Mass. The Catholic Church over time had relaxed the dress standards, but Joe felt that to stand before God, he should at least accord him the absolute respect of wearing his best clothes. Marsha followed his example in a conservative fashion. She thought her best dresses were more for evening soirees than for church, so she dressed in a skirt and blouse with matching jacket of forest green and complimentary malachite earrings.

They sat so that the children would not be able to pick on one another during Mass. The order was Edward, Joe, Bobby, Marsha, Jenny and Samantha. Jenny tried to get past Marsha to tangle with Bobby, but Marsha held her back, kindly, gently, and with a smiling look of reproof. Life was good with the Joe B. family.

They watched with pride as Joe B. Jr., walked up the aisle with the other two acolytes and the priest. The lector was announcing the opening hymn. The church was filled with the sound of the organ and guitar accompanied by the lone voice of the choir director, then joined by the multitude, uplifting their spirits.

Marsha again pointed her finger at Jenny to move over and leave Bobby alone. Joe swelled with the presence of God. His son, Joe Jr., serving so close to God. What magnificent training for a child. He would be a right and proper son. He would do well in this life. God had rewarded Joe well in this life. He was thankful. He honored Jesus. Joe tried to do his best for the church. He offered his services. He helped on committees. He set up tables when needed. No job was too lowly for Joe; ask and he would help.

Father Bill, standing at the vestibule, greeted parishioners exiting after Mass. Joe Jr. went to the sacristy to remove his cassock, he'd meet them at the car. Joe took his time leaving the church to give Joe Jr. time to change clothes. They moved with the crowd slowly out the church.

Joe and Father Bill were close friends. In addition to golfing several times a summer, they jogged in several ten kilometer races. Joe always finished before Father Bill—a little bit more competitive, and in better shape. They practiced together and became close friends. Neither hesitated to lean on the other when a favor was necessary and neither ever refused to help. Father Bill often picked up the kids after school and took them to baseball practice when Joe was tied up in a trial. Joe delivered Communion to the sick whenever the Eucharistic Ministers were ill and needed a substitute. They didn't need to speak of their friendship, it was just there, ever present and comforting.

"Good morning Joe, Marsha," said Father Bill extending his hand to shake, smiling and nodding.

"Good morning, Father," answered Marsha, taking his hand and shaking it.

"Morning, Father," said Joe. "A little run later, maybe about six miles. Looks like you might need it." Joe smiled and poked Father Bill in the stomach with his index finger.

"I do. I do," admitted Father Bill, rubbing his hand over his stomach. He reached to shake hands with each of the children.

"About four-thirty sounds good. Meet you at the school. We'll do the school route?" said Joe.

"Sounds good."

Joe met Father Bill at the high school track, took two turns around it and went on the six mile route they had mapped out several years ago when they were in training for a ten kilometer run. They traversed this six-mile route about every three weeks.

They slowly covered distance, huffing and puffing, and occasionally talking.

Father Bill said: "I have been saying a prayer for you each day so that you get to be made a partner. I think it's time my prayers paid off, don't you?"

"I think, after that win last week, that it won't be long now. I am kind of like a protege to Hank Smith and he was keenly interested in this last case. I do a lot of work for him and he seems to like it. I'd sure like to make partner. Lord knows, I work hard enough for it and I'll continue to work hard for it."

"I can feel it in my bones. There are great things for you ahead. When I was praying this morning, I felt something pass through me when I was thinking about you. I know it sounds strange, don't look at me so funny. I tell you," Father Bill panted, "that I felt a wave pass through me from the top of my skull, down the back of my neck, slowly through my spine and down my legs. I actually felt it leave my toes."

Joe turned his head momentarily. Father Bill was serious. "Why?" he asked.

"I don't know. I was saying the morning prayer I always do when..."

They turned a corner, Joe was on the inside and turned quicker than Father Bill. Joe slowed for Father Bill to catch up. They were both sweating profusely. Joe adjusted his baseball cap to catch the sweat dripping on his forehead.

"I was just saying my prayers, and I was focused on you at the moment it happened. It was like I was communicating with Jesus. Direct contact. It's never happened before. Maybe, it was a physical reaction to my prayers. Like a response. I can't explain why, I just know it happened. I could feel that it had to do with you. Great things for you. Like your faith was to be rewarded. I don't know. It was eerie. I don't expect you to know what it was. I don't know what it was. I just wanted to tell you about it. I'm puzzled."

"Yeah, me too," puffed Joe.

CHAPTER ELEVEN

▼

THE PARTNERS MEET

Six senior partners at Smith, Post and Trivisonno were seated at the far end of a very long conference table. Hank was at the head, Mr. John Post on his left, Mr. Anthony Trivisonno on his right. The room was forty feet long. Huge pieces of contemporary artwork, some of it 3-D, hung on the walls. One wall was made entirely of glass with thin partition lines. Anyone could see into the room and anyone in the room could see out into the hallway, but no one could hear anything spoken on either side. When the senior partners were in the conference room, no one except their personal secretaries were allowed in the room with them. Coffee, tea and mineral water was available on a table next to the wall. Each of the men were tall, good looking, not thin, but more ascetic than fat, in good physical shape, and dressed in the perfect legal suit of grey with ties of reddish tint. The only visual difference between the men was that some had button down collars and some did not, and the color and quantity of their hair.

They discussed various donations. The American Cancer Society, The American Heart Association, The Catholic Charities, and on and on.

National organizations were particularly effective in requesting funds from large law firms. However, because Smith, Post and Trivisonno dealt largely with the Catholic Diocese, they were in a unique position to say no to many of the charities. They only had to say yes to Catholic Charities, and they did so with large amounts of money. They contributed monies to the missions in San Salvador and Guatemala, to Catholic Charities earmarked for counseling or adoptions, and to each local parish in which any partner and junior partner was a member, whether either to the St. Vincent de Paul Society or to the church's benefit functions or general fund raisers. Giving money was only one way they could repay the benefits they received from The Catholic Church. And they did so conservatively and steadily.

"St. Noel's is having a carnival at the Feast of St. Mary. I suggest we send Father Iammarino one thousand dollars," said John Post.

Hank glanced at Anthony Tivisonno, Bud Beck, Paul Davis, and Tom Stillwell. They all gave a thumbs up at the same time. The partners had developed a sign language when going through these requests for money; thumbs up or thumbs down. If the vote was not unanimous, then the minority voters could express their point of view and another vote would be taken; it would be determinative. They didn't waste time, time was money. Hank put an entry on the legal pad in front of him.

"Any others?" Hank asked. No one said anything. "Okay," said Hank, "let's move along. Next on the agenda is the question of promoting one of our junior partners to senior status. Not to our level, but to the level just below us."

Smith, Post and Tivisonno had five levels of membership to the firm. The first was associate. This was the admitting level for first year lawyers green out of law school. The general rule was that if you were not promoted from associate to junior partner within six years, then you were either going to stay in the associate position forever, or you would move to another position in another firm voluntarily.

The junior partner position was a promotion with a modest increase in salary. All the attorneys were on salary so they were exempt from the federal labor laws and made to work as many hours as necessary to get the job done. Most of the work was accomplished by the associates and the junior partners. But, to be a junior partner was an acknowledgment by the senior partners that you were on the partnership track.

The next step was senior status. You were considered a senior partner, but you had no equity interest in the law firm. Ten percent of your salary, which usually represented your raise when you were made senior status, was put back into the firm. This then was your contribution to the firm which was a method used to purchase an interest in the firm when you were made senior partner. Senior status made as much as two hundred thousand dollars per year. Much of the salary of a senior status member depended on his work output or his ability to bring in business.

The next step was senior partner, which were the six men clustered at the end of the conference table. They shared in the profits of Smith, Post and Trivisonno equally. In a good year, they shared well. In a bad year, and there were never any bad years yet, they would all share poorly. The senior partners were good men, upright, moral, and good businessmen. And, as morality and business might appear to be a contradiction, as it usually was, they worked hard at it so that they tried to do right in the eyes of their church. Because all of the members of the firm were Catholic, the church was an important part of their firm. They acknowledged it, accepted it, and honored it.

The last step was senior retired. No one had occupied that status yet, but the slot was on the flow chart as a space available for filling. When a Senior Partner retired, he would continue to get a reduced salary, have an office to which he could come and watch the world wind down. It was a gentle way to ease him from the business and to keep his income stream flowing.

"I think," said Hank, "that Joe B is ripe to become a member of senior status. He has been here for nine years, five as an associate, four as a junior partner. I realize it is a short time for him, but I think he is doing an out-standing job. His performance in trial last week was superb. Judge Gaines told me he was one of the best trial attorneys he has ever seen. I don't think we risk the chance of losing Joe, but I want to secure him to us. He is a valuable asset and he can do well for us."

"How many senior status do we have now?" asked Anthony Trivisonno.

"Three," responded Hank

"I watched about half an hour of his cross examination of the defense doctor in that case last week. He did do a good job," interjected Tom Stillwell. "I say we let him in. He is good and it will give the rest of the associates and junior partners the impression that we reward good work. That it is just not a time on the job promotion, but a great effort promotion."

Paul Davis gave a thumbs up. Bud Beck looked around and did the same.

"Why not?" said John Post and gave the thumbs up.

"Ok," said Hank. "I will put him on the six-week list. I will tell him confidentially that in six weeks he will be made senior status and we will throw a reception for him." Hank lifted his legal pad, turned slightly as to leave, then said: "Anything else, gentlemen?"

They shook their heads negatively. Hank stood, they all stood to leave.

CHAPTER TWELVE

▼

SAM PREPARES FOR TROUBLE

Sam phoned Hank at the office the following Wednesday. He was put on hold for two minutes before he got through; Hank had to be paged, Sam waited.

"Hank Smith speaking."

"Hank, Sam here. How are you? No, don't tell me, you know that I really don't care how you are because I know you're okay. I need the name of Joe B's broker. Do you know that?"

Hank, caught off gaurd, answered quickly, "Uh...oh yes. It's Holderman-Plank. Why? But wait a minute, Sam, what are you up to?" Hank's voice rose an octave with his concern. He knew the intention of Sam, or thought he knew it. Sam was going to play around with Joe B's investments somehow. "Are you really going through with this?" Hank frowned. "Do you think someone's life should be played with like that, Sam? Don't do anything, just forget it. I think maybe we should call off the bet." An image of Marian at the kitchen counter came to mind. She was so dead set against Sam. So negative against him, maybe this is what she meant. "It just doesn't seem right for some reason. Let's call it off. It doesn't mean anything anyway. What do you say, Sam?"

"Hey Hank, a bet is a bet. This is two bucks. Don't welch on me now. We just got this thing going. We will see what faith is not. It won't take long at all. And don't worry, he'll get it back, I'll see to that. But it will be a true test of faith. Will he damn his god? You bet he will. Just leave everything to me. Gotta go." Sam hung up before Hank could reply.

Sam made an appointment with Edward Vacik, financial broker for Joe B at Holderman-Plank Investments. Sam, shown into the office, introduces himself. He sits across from the broker observing the immaculate desk with only a pen holder and a pad of paper on it. On the walls are a dozen certificates of accomplishments which customers never have time to read or care about. The broker, Mr. Edward T. Vacik, takes some general information from Sam, then gets to the point.

"So, Mr. Hawkins, what can I do for you?"

"Please call me Sam," Sam says in an obsequious tone. "I have a problem. I have a very good friend about whom I am very worried. You see I don't have much faith in the stock market. I know the ups and downs and the vagaries of investments. I don't want to see my friend get hurt financially. I'm looking for a way to protect him from what I believe will be a huge loss in the stock market. I was hoping that you could help me."

"If it is one of our accounts, Sam," Vacik said with delicacy, "I couldn't give you any information. We maintain strict confidence. We would do the same for your account."

"No, no, no," Sam protested putting up his hands as if to fend off a fatal thrust of a blow from a battle axe. "I am not attempting to compromise your ethics or confidentiality in any manner. I already know your client, I already know you are his investment broker. I am just looking for a way to protect him from what I perceive will be a big loss of his investments in the near future. Let me ask you this. In the abstract, don't think about any client at this time, but in general, if a person was afraid of a dip in the stock market because of an incident such as Black Monday when the stock market plummeted hundreds of points and everyone lost tremendous amounts of money, what advice would you give to someone to temporarily protect them from such a loss."

"Sam," Mr. Vacik said in an oily fashion, "you realize that I will have to charge you for any advice I give you."

"Oh yes, yes, I fully intend to pay. In fact, I intend to act on your advice in this matter also, because I also want to be protected from what I perceive to be a dangerous time quickly approaching in the stock market." Sam hesitated as if he was thinking deeply, then said. "I was thinking of making an initial investment of two hundred seventy-five thousand dollars with more to follow. But you see, I want to make sure that it is protected during the time that I believe the stock market will crash."

"I see," said Mr. Vacik. He put the tips of his fingers together and patted them repeatedly together with his index fingers almost touching his lips. He was thinking of the substantial investment, which was only a starter. It would enhance his portfolio, yes, that was good, and it would give him more money to work with. But what was this irrational fear this man was talking about with the collapse of the stock market?

"I see," said Mr. Vacik, once again. "Let me understand you. You want to make an investment, but you are afraid of the collapse of the stock market?"

"Yes, that's it. I want to protect it for—say, two months, and I want my friend's money protected too. Absolute and certain," said Sam with delight.

"When you say to protect it, you want it in some form that will insulate it from the ups and downs that the investment might suffer in the stock market, it that right?"

"Yes, you have it. Can you do it?"

"And how protected do you want it?"

"I want it to be absolute. I don't really care, at least for the next two months whether it makes a whole lot of interest, but I want to be sure that after two months I still have the same principal to invest and to be able to make interest later on. I still want to make some interest on it, but I want it to be safe. Not like cash, I was thinking…" Sam hesitated just a little to make sure Mr. Vacik knew he was a novice at investments. "…maybe bonds, or Certificates of Deposit, or I don't know. You tell me."

"Well, bonds could do it." Mr. Vacik said, seizing on an idea. "I could put the money into bearer bonds which will still be accruing the interest, and depending on which bonds I choose, a very good interest rate. Then after the two-month period, I could negotiate the bonds and invest the money. Bearer bonds are just that, it pays money to the bearer. Anyone in possession of the bonds can cash them in. You have to keep a tight rein on them."

"That sounds good. Do you then put the bonds into the bank for safe-keeping or something?"

"Oh no," said Mr. Vacik, once again tapping the tips of his fingers together, "We put them in our safe, right here. They are safer here than in a bank. No one knows we have a safe. Everyone knows banks have safes. If you want, I will show it to you."

"Yes, later I would like to see it." Sam shifted in his chair. "Now, I would like to invest the two hundred seventy-five thousand dollars. So I just make a check to you or the firm?"

Sam took out his checkbook ready to write a check.

Before Mr. Vacik could answer, Sam added: "And I would like to discuss the possibility of protecting my friend in the same manner. Is there a way he could be protected in the same manner?"

Sam looked at Mr. Vacik wistfully, his eyebrows slightly raised inquiringly.

"I know that you can't discuss his file with me. And I am not asking you to. What I am asking, and it is only between you and me, is for you to protect him. I ask myself what would happen if my friend, Joe B, loses all his investments all at once?"

Mr. Vacik smiled at the mention of the name of Joe B.

"I know that you can't just take his investments and put them into bearer bonds without his consent, but I am, I mean we are talking here so that I can protect my friend. I am not asking you to take a risk for my friend, I am asking that you protect him from risk for just sixty days. If I thought it would jeopardize his investments in any manner, I wouldn't do it. But to save the investments from this strange feeling I have, I just have to do it."

Sam poised to write the check. "To you, Edward?" he asked.

"Holderman-Plank is fine." Said Mr. Vacik who continued to tap his fingertips together. Then he sat up straight, put his hands on the desk while Sam wrote the check. Sam handed him the check. Mr. Vacik opened the top side drawer of the desk, pulled out a form, filled out the top of it, slid it over to Sam. Sam at the same time reached into his jacket pocket and took out an envelope and slid it over to Mr. Vacik.

"Just the agreement to let us invest your funds, some disclosure requirements, a power of attorney, and other details about the riskiness of certain funds we might invest in at some time, with your permission…Sam." Said Mr. Vacik. His eye caught the movement of an envelope sliding across the desk, impelled slowly by Sam's hand.

"What is this?" he asked cautiously.

"This," said Sam, "is my further investment in you." "This!" sliding the envelope further toward Mr. Vacik, "is for you alone. I want my friend protected in the same manner as I am protected. This is fifty thousand dollars in cash. This is a non-recorded transaction. I want you to protect my two hundred seventy-five thousand dollars in bearer bonds for sixty days. And," he hesitated for effect. "And, I want you to also protect my friend's account. I don't want you to risk it, I don't want you to do anything with it other than protect it in the same manner as you protect mine. I don't want you to compromise your ethics at all. If you were risking Joe B's funds, I would consider it unethical. But to assure the safety of his money for a mere sixty days, that's all I ask. I have a strong feeling about the market. I really do. And Joe B is my friend. He sent me to you for my investments."

Mr. Vacik touched the end of the envelope. He had thoughts of pushing it back. It was a lot of money. Fifty thousand dollars. Cash. Why was
Mr. Hawkins giving him a bribe? To protect Joe B's money? How can that
be a bribe? Joe B's money was only about sixty or seventy thousand dollars.
Why would fifty thousand dollars in cash be given free to protect, in
bearer bonds, seventy thousand dollars? He couldn't figure it out. His wife
would surely appreciate the money. It would come in quite handy just
now at this time of his life. Cash. He could filter the money into his own
accounts so the IRS would not see it. The roof needed repair. Just think
what he could do for Christmas presents for the kids this year. He needed
the money. He always needed money. That old junker his wife was driving, he could replace it, she would like that. And, after all, he would not
be risking Joe B's money, he would only be securing it. What was unethical about recieving a gift when it involved nothing but protecting a clients
assets, which was what his job was all about anyways? Any doubts that Mr.
Vacik had evaporated instantaneously. Oh, what the hell, why not? It was
the right amount at the right time of his fiscal career. It was too easy for
him. He should protest, at least protest some, shouldn't he? He needed the
money. Fifty thousand dollars! It would help a lot.

"No, Edward." Said Sam pushing the chair away, standing. "Don't even
think of refusing. The transaction is complete. I thank you." Sam smiled
conspiratorially.

"Could you now show me where you will be protecting my bearer
bonds so well?" asked Sam.

"Sure, oh sure," answered Mr. Vacik sliding the envelope into the top
drawer, inwardly congratulating himself for the new client and great deal
he just made. He got up and led Sam through the door.

▼

CHAPTER THIRTEEN

PARTNERSHIP DISCLOSED

Later that same day, Hank entered Joe's office. Joe was speaking on the phone to a client with a real estate problem. Hank shut the door, sat down in one of the dark green leather chairs and waited for Joe to complete his conversation. Joe knew intuitively that Hank was here to talk about his partnership. He felt it, the look on Hank's face, the hidden smile, the self-satisfied look, the comfortable way he sat in the chair. Joe hurried his conversation.

"Mr. Selleck, I agree with you that the trespass was a trespass and that you are entitled to be compensated for it, but to what extent is what you and I need to sit down in person to discuss and go over," said Joe. He looked at the calendar on the corner of his desk, flipped a page, then another and said: "How about next Wednesday, the fifteenth, at three o'clock, here at my office?"

"That's ok," said Joe, responding to the voice on the phone. "And bring with you a copy of your title…"he was interrupted by Mr. Selleck, then responded: "Yes, the title, or a copy of it will do, we have to show ownership of the property, and the estimates of any damages to your property…" he was interrupted again, then said, "I hope by next week you have some estimates, but bring in whatever you have, Mr. Selleck. I'll see you next Wednesday at three. Ok, til then, bye."

Joe hung up the phone, looked expectantly at Hank, gave a small smile and said, "Oh, oh, it must be something serious."

"It is and it isn't," answered Hank. "It is if you are considering your future in this firm." A small pang of fear leaped through Joe's body from the base of his spine to his scalp, a streak of a shudder, unnoticeable to anyone but him.

"Or," continued Hank, "it isn't, if you think of it as the natural progression of rewarding work performed." Joe knew he was right about the partnership track. The shudder of fear had disappeared to be replaced by a warmth that reddened his ears. A glow of satisfaction. A knowledge interpreted physically by his body with a flush. Joe beamed.

"Joe, in six weeks, Smith, Post and Trivisonno will have a new senior status partner." He looked directly at Joe with a small smile on his face. "Yes, Joe, that is you."

Joe grinned, stood, extended his hand. His face reddened. And, he was extremely happy. "Thank you," He said as he shook Hank's hand. Joe sat.

"The usual procedure in these matters is that we keep it quiet for the next three weeks. Then we, the firm, make an announcement of a reception to be held about three weeks after that in your honor. You will want your wife, Marsha, to be here. Of course, she is invited. But for the next three weeks, aside from Marsha, keep it to yourself. This allows the partners to change their minds. They never have. However, we have accepted this three-week delay as tradition on the off chance that it can happen. Not that you have anything to worry about. Of that I'm sure."

"Hank, this is fantastic." Said Joe. "I have worked hard for this. All I can say is thanks. I am so delighted."

"You have worked hard. And I can say, safely, that we are all delighted. But keep it under your hat for a couple of weeks until the memo comes out, ok?"

"Sure, no problem."

Hank got up, looked at Joe, gave a thumbs up and exited.

Joe sat there beaming. He put his feet up on the corner of his desk making sure there was a piece of paper under his shoes so as not to mark the desk or get it dirty, put his hands behind his head, intertwined his fingers, smiled and glowed at the thought. He was at the brink of committing a sin of vanity and he revelled in it. A promotion. Marsha will be so happy. The raise, the prestige, the new house they had been planning. They could build next spring. Look around for a lot this fall, get the permits, get a builder, the same guy who built Hanks' home..., oh, it was wonderful. The thirty or forty thousand dollar raise that usually went with the jump from junior to senior status, plus the money saved and made with Ed Vacik. Yes, he would have a modest mortgage, still sufficient to live on, and a huge house so each of the kids could have their own bedroom. Kirtland, Chardon, Munson. Get out into the country. What a great life. Marsha would want to know. Joe reached for the phone.

▼

CHAPTER FOURTEEN

JOE INVESTS IN SECURE BONDS

Joe was sitting at his desk still reeling in fantasies when the call came through from Edward T. Vacik of Holderman-Plank, his investment brokers. Aside from his home, all of Joe's money was tied up in investments at Holderman-Plank. He had started to invest with them on the advice of Hank and they had done very well for him over the last seven years. What had started out as five thousand dollars has increased to more than eighty thousand dollars with the additional deposits made by Joe. With this savings, the equity in their home and, hopefully, the promotion for which he had been working so hard, Joe would have enough to build a new home in Kirtland or Chardon, maybe a small farmette for the kids. They all liked animals, especially Bobby.

Ed's advice had always been good advice. He was conservative in his investments. He never went out on a limb with clients' money and he always sought the client's permission whenever he made a major investment change. Joe wondered which investment Ed was calling about today.

"Hello," answered Joe.

"Good morning Joe, this is Edward Vacik."

"How are you doing, Ed?"

"Great, just great." He paused for several seconds, then continued, "Joe, I have been watching the market, like I always do, and there are some things going on that I am a little unsure of. For example, these Litton-Gates stock that you own, I see them going up steadily, but I also see a great fluctuation in the computer industry hi-tech market for several other computer companies. I think Litton-Gates might be next. What I would like to do is to take your money out of circulation for maybe sixty days. Just take it out of the stock market to see if I am right about this. If I am, you will save your money. I am afraid that if I leave it in, it might take a big hit. I see too many indicators for trouble. Do you know what I mean?"

"Not really, Ed. What do you mean take it out of circulation?" asked Joe.

"I thought maybe put it into bearer bonds for, say, up to sixty days. Then, if the stock market has balanced, put it back into something that is growing, but secure."

"Bearer bonds?" queried Joe. "Do they make money at the same time?"

"Oh yes, they continue to make money, but they are at a fixed rate of interest. The ones we are talking about, I have looked into them, are paying six point five percent. That is lower than what your other investments are paying now, but higher than the CD rates everywhere else. It is time to be conservative. Just for a little while. You'll be back on track in no time. But," and he paused, meaningfully, "just to make sure you can still be back on track, I advise you to take this protective step."

"Well, I guess so, Ed. What about taxes? What kind of exposure do I have?"

"There will be a gain on the transfer, but given the low activity that we have maintained on your account, we have spread it out over the last several years. I think I can minimize them somewhat, but yes, there will be a gain. You know we can't avoid Uncle Sam, no matter what we do. Some of the stocks are in your deferred income plan; there are limitations on removing them into bearer bonds. However, I think that I can work them into the program so they are still deferred. We can take them out for sixty days at the maximum, but we will have to get them back into the program at that point. So, what do you say?"

"If that's what you think. Are these something I have to put in a safe deposit box or what?"

"No, no, Joe. We put them in our safe here at the office. It is an actual bond. Anyone can cash them, any bearer. That's why we keep them in the safe. We don't want those getting out. But it is a cautionary measure. You won't lose any big money this way. Whereas, I really do feel uncertain about some of the stocks we are in now, and the whole stock market for that matter. If we just lay low for sixty days, I can get over this feeling of uncertainty. Sometimes there are no objective standards. You just get a gut feeling. And I have that feeling. So I got your ok, Joe?"

"Sure Ed, whatever you think is best."

CHAPTER FIFTEEN

▼

JOE BREAKS THE NEWS

Joe pulled into the driveway looking for darting kids. Jenny stood at the window watching, waiting for him. When she saw his car pull into the driveway, she rushed to the front door, ran and screamed in her shrieking voice at the top of her lungs: "Daddy, Daddy, Daddy…" The daily ritual of running to meet her Daddy, the subsequent hugs, picking her up, walking around, was an unparalleled pleasure.

"What's up today, Pumpkin?" Joe asked giving Jenny a big hug while he picked her up. "Did anyone get into trouble today?"

"No, Daddy. No one is in trouble. We're going to have steak for dinner. Isn't that good, Daddy?" She reached around and gave him a kiss on the neck, just happy to see her Daddy.

"Steak, oh boy, a special occasion. We like steak, don't we?"

"We sure do, Daddy. I want mine cooked medium, just like yours, Daddy."

Joe carried Jenny up the four front steps, through the front hall to the kitchen where Marsha was preparing dinner.

"So," said Joe coming into the kitchen with Jenny still in his arms. "We are having steak today. A special occasion?" asked Joe. He leaned over, gave her a slight kiss, smiled at her.

"Aren't you excited?" Marsha asked.

"Yes, I am, very."

"Oh Joe, I am so happy for you, for us. I knew it. I just knew it." She moved over to him and hugged him with Jenny still clinging to him. "I had a good feeling today and when you called, I just knew you would get it."

"It still won't be official for three more weeks until they announce it to the firm, so we can't tell anyone until then."

"Oh, that's a silly rule. For what reason would they ever turn you down now that they have told you. It's going to happen, Joe. I know it."

"Still," said Joe putting Jenny down, "Let's keep it under wraps. Hank said you could know, but no one else. We can keep it quiet for a couple of weeks." Jenny left the kitchen to go outside.

"We can get the new house. Can I start looking?"

"We can start looking. What with the Holderman investments and the raise, we can get a small farm out in Chardon or some place out in the country. Steak, I'm looking forward to it. Not often we get steak."

"I got the feeling Joe, I knew you would get it today. You've got to have faith, Joe."

Father Bill was waiting for Joe at the school track. They jogged around the track at the school. Father Bill wore black shorts and a white tee shirt that had a logo of the paschal lamb on it. His shoes were the flashiest article of clothing he wore, they were Air Nikes with a luminescent orange wing and stripe down the side and heel. Father Bill felt showy in the bright shoes, but they were the softest running shoes he had ever worn. They were designed for the heavier runner with either a little more air injected into the sole or a little more sole to run on. He liked to think he had more soul on which to run, one of his little parochial puns.

The temperature was in the seventies. Joe wore a bright orange tank top absent writing, green faded cotton shorts, and black Reeboks with short white running socks.

"Well, Father Bill, your prayers worked for me," panted Joe.

Father Bill took in the statement and didn't respond for almost thirty seconds. "Yes, I believe that is the reason that I pray." He knew exactly what Joe was talking about, Partnership.

"But for the next three weeks you mustn't say anything about it to anyone. They will make the announcement then. But I know that you can keep it confidential. After all this is a confession, and there is the confessional privilege." Joe chuckled as he said it.

"Joe, remember when I told you that I had that strange feeling when I mentioned you in my prayers the last time." Father Bill broke into a serious tone and Joe looked at him sharply.

"Yes," answered Joe, inquiringly.

"Well, I had that feeling again yesterday when I was praying for you. I had cleared my mind of everything but my prayers to God relating to you. It was very strange and unusual. This is the second time that it has happened. It was a wave of something, it started at the top of my head and went through my body and to my hands and feet. Not an electrical charge, but like a wave of warmth and a whiff of sulfur. It was stronger than the last time. It scared me, Joe. The first time I thought it was pleasant. This time, I thought it was not pleasant. And the sulfur smell. There was no sulfur around, but I got the impression, strongly, of the smell. I don't know what to make of it Joe. Either I have some medical malady or God is warning me or you of something. Watch yourself, maybe."

Joe looked at Father Bill curiously. "I don't know what to make of it either."

"It's curious, I can't interpret it at all. I don't know whether it is good or bad. But the first time being so pleasant, I knew it was good. But this time," he hesitated a moment, "I just don't know." Father Bill had hit his breathing stride so deeply, he could talk and run at the same time. "I wonder if I am getting hot flashes in my old age. I have never experienced anything like this before. The coincidence is that the two times it has occurred was when you were in my prayers, Joe."

"But anyway, congratulations on your soon to be partnership. You can't have picked a better firm to work for. There can be no way but up for you, Joe. I'm really proud of you."

Joe looked at Father Bill, gave him a frown as if to say don't get mushy on me Father Bill.

Father Bill laughed. "No, I mean it Joe. I am proud of you. I've followed your career ever since you joined the parish. I know it sounds corny for someone the same age as you to say such a thing, but it's true."

Joe waved his right hand in dismissal.

"No way," said Father Bill, "just accept it. Ok. Ok. We'll drop it. Congratulations, anyway."

CHAPTER SIXTEEN

▼

SAM INVESTS IN BEARER BONDS

The exact time was one-thirty in the morning. Sam was dressed in black pants, black nylon long sleeve shirt, black socks, black shoes—actually, dressed like a thief in the night. The only item of clothing with color was his cream sports jacket. He carried a black leather briefcase that contained sophisticated criminal tools that allowed him to enter doors where he was not legally permitted, to enter safes he was not permitted under any circumstances, and to gain entry to almost any passageway he was not legally permitted. He had attached a grayish brown beard and a large handlebar mustache. He knew that everyone who saw him focused on the large mustache and beard and forgot everything else about him. Sam walked to the security guard sitting before the elevators.

"Got to sign in? I forgot to leave some items in the office."

"Which office are you going to?" asked the guard mesmerized by the mustache and beard.

"To the seventh floor, Grand Title Agency. I should be back down in less than half an hour."

"Sign here, and put the time down." The guard looked at his watch. "It's one thirty five a.m." Sam signed "Henry Fabeetz." "Not too many people coming in to do work on such a nice night?"

"You're it. A really slow night."

Sam walked toward the elevators, pushed the up button, the door opened, he entered. He pressed the seventh floor, home of Grand Title and Holderman-Plank.

The elevator stopped at floor seven. Sam walked directly to Holderman-Plank. He put his briefcase on the floor, opened it, put on a thin pair of latex gloves, took out three little picks, inserted them into the dead bolt lock, turned them and heard the lock click open. It took all of thirty seconds to enter the offices of Holderman-Plank. The offices were lit with night lights. He walked directly to the office of the secretaries where the safe was hidden behind a false wall. He pressed the latch behind a file cabinet to release the wall which slid the wall from in front of the safe. Thank you Mr. Ed Vacik for the tour. He then placed four suction cups around the combination plate of the safe. The four suction cups were attached to a small electrical unit which he turned on, a small red light blinked, and a small meter dial glowed with the hushed light of a small reflective bulb. From this unit a wire extended to a pair of headphones. He put on the headphones, adjusted the volume control on the electrical unit. He turned the dial five times to the right then focused on the meter and slightly closed his eyes while he slowly turned the dial.

He thought he heard a small noise, opened his eyes, looked at the meter, nothing. He closed his eyes again, this time, when he opened them, the meter showed a decibel reading. He reset the meter by pushing a black button on the meter and the arrow went back to zero. He turned the dial in the reverse direction, once, twice, three times before he heard a small piece of metal dropping into a slot. He opened his eyes. Again, the meter read a decibel reading. Once again he reset the meter, and turned the dial.

Five numbers, he pushed the handle of the safe down, it opened. He was in. There were no alarms.

There were no alarms because Holderman-Plank did not normally keep cash money, or in this case, bearer bonds in their safe. They kept stocks, which could be reissued in case of theft or loss, certificates of deposit, and a multitude of other transactions. But not cash. However, in this case, they were keeping a number of bearer bonds for two special clients of the firm. Joe B. had the sum of seventy-seven thousand dollars in bearer bonds, Sam Hawkins, the newest client of the firm, had two hundred fifty thousand dollars in bearer bonds. This was a special occasion, a special accommodation for a new client. Whereas alarms were considered when the safe was installed, they were discounted because cash money was never supposed to be placed in the safe. However, new employees did not get the specific information that the safe was without alarms. Edward Vacik had thought the safe would protect the bearer bonds from any thief, but, in this case, he was wrong.

Sam turned on the safe light. The safe was large enough for him to enter. It was lined with drawers on one side and file cabinets on the other side. He opened several drawers, rifled through the files, getting a sense of the filing system. He then went to the G-H file drawer, opened it, located the Hawkins, Samuel file, found the bearer bonds in his file worth two hundred seventy-five thousand dollars. He lifted them and lightly placed them in his briefcase.

Sam next looked under the A-C file, found the B, Joe file, took out all the bearer bonds located within that file and placed them in his briefcase. He then rifled through several other file drawers looking for additional bearer bonds, but he couldn't locate any. So he took, at random, four additional files which included certificates of deposit and some stocks and bonds. He placed everything in his briefcase, threw the empty files on the floor so someone would know that files had been taken. He left the safe door open, turned out the safe light. He left the room, took the elevator down to the ground floor, said "Good morning" to the security guard and left the building.

Sam knew the theft would be discovered; he actually wanted it discovered. He wanted Joe B. to understand the slow taking of all his worldly assets. He wanted to test his faith. Sam could think of no better test than to have a man lose everything. He knew that Joe B, a man who attended church regularly, was a man like every other man. A man who, when presented with the loss of all his assets, would damn his God. Sam had seen men in less despair than the situation in which he was now placing Joe B damn God for the slightest offense. And why not? What would he have to thank God for at that moment? Nothing.

Holderman-Plank discovered the theft the following morning when the early secretaries saw the open safe door. The secretary called the executive secretary, who in turn called John Holderman, the senior principal. John Holderman rushed to the office, face flushed pink, angry, upset—his blood pressure roaring through his arteries and pounding in his ears at a level never before experienced.

The secretaries were told to touch nothing; they left everything as they found it. Four or five files lay on the floor where the thief had thrown them after taking the contents. John Holderman saw that two of the files were those of Edward T. Vacik. One was only two weeks old. The entries on the files told him that they contained bearer bonds. He called Ed Vacik, who immediately rushed to the office. Ed was pale, in contrast to John who was pink flushed. Ed knew immediately that he had been set up. Sam Hawkins. But why would he do this to Joe B? It had to be him, no one else knew he had bearer bonds. He got his own back and Joe B loses. And, Ed couldn't say anything. That extra fifty thousand dollars in cash at home prevented him from saying anything. Ed couldn't believe his eyes, both files gone. He was in shock. How was he going to tell Joe B? How was he going to explain the purchase of bearer bonds in such a good market? Who purchases bearer bonds at a low interest rate when the market was making such great profits for his clients? He could kiss his job goodbye. He had a pulsing headache, throbbing at his temples.

John Holderman, was a man who, obviously by the pink flush of his face, was susceptible to stress and visibly upset. He did not go into his office to talk to Mr. Vacik, but did what managers should never do, he exploded verbally in front of the secretaries.

"Mr. Vacik, didn't you know that liquid assets are never placed in the safe, but put into the bank?"

There was no answer of course. Edward T. Vacik did know, but he didn't follow protocol. He also flushed. Two pink flushed men facing each other.

"Mr. Vacik," said Mr. Holderman, "how could you not know the long standing policy of Holderman-Plank?" He intently stared at Edward, angry, red as a bright rose. "No, it isn't written down anywhere. I know that." Mr. Holderman answered his own question. "No, I don't care whether this is the first time you have ever dealt with bearer bonds for a client. What were you holding assets in bearer bonds for anyway? What kind of investment is that for a client? What in God's name were you thinking?" Raising his voice to an embarrassing level, he almost screamed, "Where do we make money on that kind of investment? Tell me, Mr. Vacik, I want to learn something here. Oh yes, Mr. Client, I can get you a good 3.5% to 5% while everyone else gets at least 9%. Great thinking Mr. Vacik!"

John Holderman, turned away in disgust, "We will deal with you later."

Edward T. Vacik was partially relieved to be out of the presence of this angry man, but he was nauseous. He went to the restroom down the hall, sat on the toilet for five seconds, then immediately stood up, turned around and vomited.

John Holderman had his executive secretary get his insurance man on the telephone. The insurance man listened to the problem and said there might be a small problem on his end, but he wasn't sure, he would have to check it out. The slight problem was that there was an exception to coverage under the policy for theft of cash or its equivalent, which, it would seem, bearer bonds might qualify. But the insurance agent would get a copy of the policy, fax the pertinent pages to John Holderman, and get an opinion from the home office in the next two hours.

In the meantime, John Holderman called the police and the securities exchange security office which required them to be notified whenever anything relating to a theft at a brokerage office occurred. Two men from the local police department arrived. One took a report from John Holderman, then from Edward T. Vacik. The other dusted for fingerprints on the safe, the floor, the file cabinets, and any other spot he thought was important. He pulled many fingerprints off the surfaces. None of them were those of the thief, although the officer did not yet know that.

The fax came over the telephone line; it consisted of three pages. The first was a cover page informing Holderman-Plank that a fax was coming across the line from Great Eastern Stock Insurance Company, specifically, their agent, Bob Warner, directed to John Holderman. The second page was a copy of page sixty-four of the Business-securites liability policy with a hand written arrow pointing to the pertinent secton.

Section 13(d) stated as follows:

Section 13

    The Company shall not be liable for the following:

    (d). The theft of any cash or its equivalent held on behalf of any client on the insured premises.

When John Holderman saw that page, with an arrow drawn toward the offending section, he knew there was no insurance coverage for the theft. He was even angrier than he was before.

The third page was on the letterhead of Great Eastern Stock Insurance Company and was short and succinct. It read as follows:

Dear Mr. Holderman:

In re: Theft of bearer bonds, same date.

Attached hereto is page sixty-four of the policy. We regret to inform you that the occurrence of which you notified this company on this morning of the theft of certain bearer bonds is not a covered loss. Hence, we can be of no service to you in that regard. In the event you are unable to replace the stocks that were stolen, please advise. Thank you for letting us be of service to you.

Very truly yours,
/s/ James Ballen
James Ballen,
Executive Claims Supervisor

John Holderman went to the cupboard in his office, took two aspirins, poured water from his small sink, which was usually used only for an evening libation, and swallowed the painkillers. He sat at his desk, turned his chair toward the window and stared out the window, seeing nothing, but feeling the great increase in his blood pressure. He touched the carotid artery on the side of his neck, felt it pulsing and just sat there.

Joe received the news of the loss with great calm. Marsha, on the other hand, was frantic with questions. She couldn't believe it. Why was the money in bearer bonds? Why was it in their safe at work? Why are they even telling us about it? Why don't they just replace the money? They do have to, don't they?

Joe assured her that they would have insurance coverage for it. In fact he remembered that Edward Vacik had told him that all the investments were insured. Once they had the investigation by the securities police or the local police, they would let us know. So there should be no problem. That quieted Marsha temporarily. But what a bad stroke of luck. Right on top of the good stroke of luck about the partnership. He remembered Father Bill; the feelings that he said he was getting when he prayed for Joe. Maybe this is what he felt; a foreboding. But, things balance out in the end. Joe reassured Marsha that they would get their investment back, that it was just a minor setback in the progress of their lives. It was only money and money was replaceble, wasn't it. That they should pray a little more for God's favor. And pray they did. They extended their prayers before dinner, their nightly prayers, and Joe even attended Mass for the next three days before work. He prayed hard to the Lord. He concentrated on praising the Lord and not on asking for favors for himself. He communed with God.

As a family at Sunday Mass, they prayed together, they thanked the Lord for what they did have.

The police called Joe the following week for a meeting. Joe's initial inquiries at Holderman-Plank were met with requests for patience. They couldn't tell him anything until after the investigation. The police would be in touch. The officer came to Joe's home. He was not in uniform; he was a detective from the Cleveland Police Department. He inquired into how it happened that the investments of Joe and Marsha were put into bearer bonds at all. Joe explained the investment fear of Edward T. Vacik and the request to put the investments into a secure holding for sixty to ninety days, his acquiescence to the plan, and his general faith in the abilities of Edward T. Vacik, broker.

It was then that the detective casually said, "You seem quite relaxed for a man who just lost seventy-seven thousand dollars." The detective looked at Joe, eyebrows raised, questioning, then at Marsha.

Marsha's eyes opened wide, she jerked her head toward the officer and said, "What do you mean? There is insurance coverage for it, isn't there?"

"Oh!" whispered the detective, his mouth holding the oh for several seconds. "No one told you about the insurance?"

"What do you mean?" Marsha's voice became strident and high.

"There is insurance for the loss of all stocks, but there is no insurance for the loss of any cash or its equivalent. Bearer bonds are considered to be the equivalent to cash. So, it's my understanding that there is no insurance. I'm a little surprised Holderman-Plank hasn't informed you of this. I am sure Mr. B knows more about that kind of thing than I do, being a lawyer and all, but it had something to do with an intentional act and the insurance company has indicated that they will not cover the bearer bonds."

Marsha had a look of horror on her face. She grabbed Joe's hand. She exclaimed: "Oh my God. Oh my God." She started to cry, got up from the couch and left the room.

"I am sorry to be the bearer of bad news," said the detective. "I thought you already knew."

"No, we didn't. No one told us about that." Joe looked shaken. "So you mean we've lost that money?"

"Yes, it appears so."

"Well," Joe said slowly, thinking. "We should still get reimbursed from Holderman-Plank. At least on a bailment theory. They had the custody of our money. They should be liable to pay us the money back."

"I don't know the law like you do, but as my investigation has led, it appears that might not be the case. Apparently there is a state statute that grants immunity to brokers for this type of theft. I got the statute from the Ohio Securities Exchange Office. So long as they took the standard precautions to protect your money, and in this instance locked it up in a safe, they are immune from suit."

Joe closed his eyes for five seconds, trying to compose his look of distress.

The detective continued: "I can get you the statute." He hesitated, then said, "But you can get it just as easily, I suppose. It is section 1317 or 1319 something. The commercial code somewhere. I'm afraid that the loss on this is yours alone." The detective looked at Joe's misery. Joe just sat there, his mind racing, asking the question why, why, why?

The detective, not receiving any answer from Joe, continued, "I suppose the only consolation, if there is any, is that you're not the big loser. There was another customer who lost $275,000.00."

Joe looked at him sharply. "Another person lost money, too?"

"Yes." The detective was relieved that Joe was still paying attention and finally responded to something. "The other person lost $275,000.00. Not a small chunk of change."

"Whoa!" Said Joe. "So there were only two who lost bearer bonds though?"

"Yes. There were four others who lost stocks and certificates of deposit, but those were insurable. Although I don't think insurance even comes into play, because the brokers can get them replaced as lost or stolen documents.

But only two who lost bearer bonds. Apparently Mr. Vacik really thought there was going to be a dip in the market."

"Oh Jesus, pray for us," intoned Joe.

CHAPTER SEVENTEEN

▼

THE CASK

Hank heard about the theft of the bonds the day following the incident. He finished pouring his coffee and was walking to his office when his secretary, Debbie, motioned him over to her cubicle.

"Mr. Smith," said Debbie, "I don't know if you heard yet. Joe B had some money stolen from the brokerage firm of Holderman-Plank. Some kind of investments are gone. I know that you invest with them, so I thought you ought to know."

A sinking feeling enveloped Hank. It was bound to come, he thought.

"Thanks for telling me, Debbie," said Hank; and, as an afterthought, "Please hold my calls."

"Yes sir."

Hank walked to his office, closed the door, pressed his head against the closed door, clamped his jaw shut tight, and almost crushed the coffee cup. After a moment he set the coffee cup down on a sandstone coaster on his desk. He looked at traffic on Route 2, didn't pay attention to it, merely looked at it for something to do with his eyes.

Sam, thought Hank. Sam stole the money. Nothing stands in his way. The two dollar bet must be won. Sam, friend and evil person. Marian wanted to be rid of Sam right after they were first married. But he couldn't. He owed his life to Sam and you don't dispose of friends when you owe your life to them.

It occurred when they were in the twelfth grade. On several occasions they went to the University Circle area bars with their fake ID's, where they would get into an argument and then, sometimes, a fight. At a bar called "The Cask," both had gotten in with their fake id's. Getting in was quite an accomplishment by itself. The inside was for college kids only; 3.2 beer was the beverage of choice for anyone not yet twenty-one years old. Aside from the small incandescent bulb behind the bar to assist the bartender in fixing drinks, an ultraviolet light was the only other light. The ultraviolet made their white shirts glow and contrast with their levis. They looked cool. Hank was dancing with a freshman coed, who thought he was also a freshman, when a young man attempted to cut in on the dance. Hank objected. The bouncer, ever alert, scooted them both out the door before they could get into a fistfight in the bar. Once outside, in the cooler weather and with more room to roam and tussle, they were less inclined to get into fisticuffs. Several of the college buddies of the interloper surrounded the pair in a half circle, watching them bluff, bluster, and threaten. They were still talking tough to one another when one of the watchers pushed Hank from the back into the antagonist thereby setting off the fight. Hank and the black haired thin man with white shirt and levis started punching each other. Hank, having had the benefit of wrestling for Collinwood High School for several years, was able to get behind the man, throw him down, and put him in a cross body stretch hold which caused the man to scream to his buddies. One of the buddies then kicked Hank in the ribs with a force that cracked one rib, caused Hank to let go of the man, and knocked the breath out of him. Hank lay on the ground holding his rib, gasping for breath. His opponent got up and was moving into position for a kick at Hank.

Sam came out looking for Hank, saw Hank kicked in the ribs and immediately jumped into the fray. But before he jumped in, he picked up a three-foot length of two-by-four laying by the building. The two-by-four had a rusty nail sticking out which extended 1 7\8 inches through the end of the board on a bent angle. No one saw him approach; they were all standing around watching the fight. Sam swung the board with all his might at the man who kicked Hank. He swung so that it hit the man at the back of the skull causing the man to fall instantly to his hands and knees, then onto his face. The point of the nail entered the skull of the man at the base of the spine—the medulla. The man twitched, his body convulsing. Sam yelled at the men surrounding them that he would hit them the same way. He held the board in the air and swung at them. Hank got up, Sam and Hank backed away toward the parking lot. The college boys yelled that they wouldn't forget them and to look out if they ever came back again. Hank and Sam left quickly. Hank threw up by the car, still holding his rib.

They didn't know when they left The Cask that the college boy had died. They were quite excited, wound up from all the adrenalin surging through them.

"Taught that cocksucker a lesson, didn't we?" Sam said while making a fist.

They found out the next day through the rumor mill that someone had been killed in a bar fight at The Cask the night before. Once again it was Sam who initiated the bond of silence.

"Not a word to anyone. We didn't know anyone there, so no one knows who we are. We used fake Id's, so if the bouncer remembered any names, it won't be ours."

Hank merely said five words: "We are friends, and mum."

No one knew them, they didn't go back to "The Cask" for the next two years. They didn't brag about this fight to anyone after they discovered that the boy had died. Somehow they had learned that there was no statute of limitation on murder and that they could be charged with the crime anytime during the rest of their lives, so they said nothing to anyone and very little to each other about the incident. But this incident was one more weave in the basket of life that bound them inextricably together. They were strong friends. When one was in trouble, the other helped. They joked, they argued, they poked fun at each other, but through it all, these three incidents involving the death of a human being kept them mum and kept them bound to each other.

Again, Hank felt remorse; Sam on the other hand, did not. He felt fully justified at swinging with his full might at that boy's skull. After all, that boy had kicked his buddy. The fact that he had blind-sided the boy didn't make much of an impression on him then or thereafter. His buddy was down when they kicked him. As time progressed, he cared less and less about the boy, feeling more justified in his actions. He had a saying that he always used when he was thinking about it: Friendships are forever and mum's the word. Whenever Hank and Sam would discuss the incident, the saying was sure to be quoted.

No, Marian, Hank thought, you don't just dispose of a friend who has saved your life, even if your wife doesn't like him.

From day one of their marriage Marian resented Sam. Always the snide comment, never a nice word. Hank wondered if maybe she was really attracted to Sam, but put on a nasty bravado to cover her feelings. However, after so many years of ill will towards Sam, he got the clear impression that Marian just didn't like him and definitely didn't like Sam taking up any of Hank's time. Even when they hadn't seen each other in years, Marian didn't let the lapse of time blunt her ill will toward Sam.

Sam and Hank separated after high school. Hank went to college and then on to law school. A draft deferment from the Army kept him away from the military. Sam went directly into the army. He was in a special unit that allowed him to go into several South American countries and also to do secret things in West Germany. He went to Vietnam when that became a political hot potato, but it was after his stint in the army that he was there as some secret civilian. He never fully clarified to Hank just what he was doing, but his knowledge of world affairs was great.

When Sam had leave, the friendship renewed. They parted for several years, then got back together as if no time had passed. Their partings increased in length over time. Hank had gone to Case Western Reserve University, then to John Marshall Law School, which later became Cleveland State Law School. He attended night school while working in a stockbroker firm. He was not afraid of hard work, and had worked hard all his life regardless of the status of his financial position. "Work and ye shall be free" was the underlying motto that formed the basis of his work ethic. He was astounded when he viewed photos

of the Holocaust and saw that same phrase written over the entrance to Auschwitz. The contradiction in application of the concept kept him thinking about it for days, but he still adhered to the phrase as his motto for life. And so he worked hard. He graduated from law school, got a job in a medium sized firm, received training for several years, then because of his connections, he was able to start his own firm with four other partners. The cases floated in. They were successful. They began to represent the Cleveland Diocese. Whenever there was an errant priest, they came to the rescue. They drafted contracts, leases, helped set policy for the church's employees fringe benefits' packages. They did all the things a successful law firm does.

And the firm grew, rapidly, soundly, and honestly. Once again, at least as honestly as a law firm can grow given the nature of the business. There are always some narrow ethical decisions that are made the wrong way, but they were approached in an honest fashion, the decisions were considered correct because of the moral approach. It was as if God was on the side of Smith, Post and Trivisonno. Their success was that great. They were now one of the largest growing law firms in Cleveland and doing fine.

Hank, as the senior partner at Smith, Post and Trivisonno, was in a social group of lawyers who worked hard and performed well. At this prime time of their lives, they exuded financial and social success. They were arrogant, but not overly so. They dressed well, tailor-made suits from Brooks Brothers with embroidered initials on the cuffs of their dress shirts. They wore real diamonds on their tie tacs. They dressed for success, they were successful, and they thrived on success.

Hank and Sam had met at least once a year for a game of golf before Sam had gone away for ten years. They used to play more rigorous sports in their earlier years, but time and age had taken their toll, and they had turned to more sedate sports. Sam traveled the world. He was on an endless quest with no distinct destination. He wandered. He worked for different travel outfits, sometimes for travel clothing, sometimes as a guide. He spoke seven languages including English. He spent much time in Turkey and India. He was in jail in Mongolia for six months for a minor offense on his part but a major offense to the tribal leader. He studied the peoples in the countries he lived in. He studied their religions and their adherence to the precepts of their religions. He liked religion, but he adhered to no religion. He believed in nothing. He had seen much human suffering and pain. It affected him in that he was aware that such pain could be visited on people with no connection to their living good lives or prayers to their gods. But it did not affect him religiously. He could not bring himself to believe in Jesus, Yahweh, Allah, Mohammed, Shiva, Buddha, or anything. He relied on himself. His time on this earth was the only time for him. There was no before, there was no hereafter. Eating a little unleavened bread would not bring him closer to some ethereal being. Fasting for days would not give him grace. Even the chemical imbalance brought on by fasting and drugs—the Ramadan, while it affected him greatly, did not bring him any closer to God, but only to himself, to the realization that he was here on this earth and that was the end to it. Amen.

When Sam inherited his grandfather's money, he became independently wealthy, but it wasn't apparent. Sam didn't spend it outright or outlandishly. He invested, used it when necessary for his travels, and did not share it. His four wives never saw the use of it for themselves except in the courting stage. Once that was over, the appearance of wealth and generosity ceased.

Hank, in contrast, was religious. He married in the Catholic Church, reared his children as Catholics, prayed, volunteered for the church unselfishly, and represented the church in its legal business. The three experiences with death in which he had directly participated caused him to become more attentive to religion. He adhered to the tenets of the ten commandments. He read the Catechism of the Catholic Church. Not many people read that document, but Hank did, and he understood and believed it.

Hank had even confessed his involvement in the three matters that included the death of a human being. He did it separately, and never to the same priest. When he was out of town on a deposition in Boston, he confessed the involvement with the abortion. In Akron, he confessed his involvement with the Nine Mile Creek debacle. And in Phoenix, he confessed his involvement with the Cask fight. Each time the priest asked several questions and sympathized with the great guilt he carried; he was lightly admonished for the length of time it took him to bring it to the attention of a priest. He received little penance. All three priests told him he was forgiven, to move on with his life and Hank did.

Some people in his church might have said he was overly devout, but they didn't know his full background. Some might say he showed off, but then they didn't know what he could have done with all of his money to really show off if he wanted to. Hank was oblivious to any resentment of his intense Catholicism.

The two friends saw less of each other as time passed. Sam was out of touch. The ten year gap before Sam presented himself at Hank's office dressed as a world traveler was the longest parting.

And now, here was Sam, back with another two dollar bet, with another fiasco. What facts did Hank really know, Hank asked himself.

First, he knew of the bet, for a man to have his faith tested by the loss of his money.

Second, he knew Sam had called him inquiring the name of the brokerage firm at which Hank invested.

Third, he knew the capabilities of Sam. He could pull it off without
blinking. He was that cagey, that sophisticated in nocturnal movements,
and, Hank felt, he really was a thief.

Hank's face was hot, his hands cold. He touched his hands to his
cheeks, the coldness felt good.

Oh Sam, he thought, why are you doing this? In the same moment,
counterpoised in the air, was the thought, what will Joe B do? Balanced
with the disgust at Sam's actions was the interest in the outcome. Would
Joe lose his faith over the loss of money. Damn his God? No way. Not Joe
B. The man was a rock.

Hank wondered how long Sam would hold the money, how he was
going to determine when the test was accomplished. Would Joe lose his
faith over money? No. Would Hank lose his faith if he lost all his money.
Now there was a thought, thought Hank. A scary thought at that. If he
lost all his money, Hank pondered, all of it, and was a pauper, just what
would he do? I just might break, thought Hank. Would Joe? Would the
loss of money alone break Joe B? Hank didn't think so. It was surely
insured, anyway.

CHAPTER EIGHTEEN

▼

AN AUTOMOBILE COLLISION

The following week, on a Friday, all of the kids were going to a movie with the babysitter, Jamie. Joe and Marsha were going to spend an evening at home, talking and praying. Their life had turned into a shambles. Even the two-year-old was going to the movie. It was *Jungle Boy*, a Disney production. The children were all familiar with the story. Jenny had a *Jungle Boy* book; she loved to press the buttons that made all the strange noises for each of the animals in the book. It delighted two year olds. The buttons got pressed incessantly until Marsha distracted her to play with some other toy.

The movie started at five. Jamie picked up the kids at four-fifteen. Joe and Marsha had several arguments over the loss of the bearer bonds. Marsha blamed Joe and Edward Vacik. Joe didn't know who to blame or whether it would do any good. They had not paid any bills in the meantime, just piled the letters, invoices, and bills on the table in the family room. Joe would then take the pile to work and put them in the top right drawer in his desk to pay at work, which, in his present circumstances, he could not bring himself to address. They had sufficient money to pay the bills out of their regular income, but the situation had caused them to develop a malaise about things. He ended up looking out the window at nothing. Things seemed not to matter. Nine years of savings down the drain. Not even a thought would pass through his mind. It was vacant. On several occasions, one or the other of the senior partners would come in and give him a task to do. They noticed his lack of enthusiasm, his creeping malaise. They were aware of the circumstances and they were waiting to see what fallout would occur, how Joe would deal with this financial blow.

Joe and Marsha were hoping to spend the evening talking about and analyzing their situation. It had been a great jolt to them to find themselves back to square one financially. All their savings gone in an instant. No one to sue to recover the money. Joe had done the legal research; there was no legal cause of action. They were either going to start over with vigor, similar to what they had when they started their married life, or they were going to collapse.

Joe and Marsha went into the bedroom, lay on the bed in their clothes and just held each other and prayed their individual prayers to God.

The man waited at the drugstore until he saw the babysitter's car go by. He got into his tan car, caught up to the babysitter's car with the five children in it, and began to follow it. The circumstances the man was looking for occurred at the next stoplight. The babysitter's car was first at the stop light. The tan car was several car lengths behind her; a 1973 Chrysler, big, strong, and powerful. The babysitter was driving a Ford Taurus, her father's compact car. Samantha was in a baby seat in the back seat on the left so the babysitter could unstrap her easily when getting out of the car.

The crossroad was a two-lane road with heavy industrial traffic. Many semi-trucks roared past at forty to fifty miles per hour. The kids were asking the babysitter questions nonstop. Who was her boyfriend, how old was he, did she kiss him? She answered some of the questions, but not all. The curiosity of the kids made her smile. She stopped at the stoplight. It was red. Keep talking to the kids. She glanced in the rearview mirror. The tan car behind her kept a good distance, at least two car lengths behind her. That was good, she hated tailgaters, even at lights, but this guy was quite far back, more than usual. Oh well, she thought, better farther than nearer. It was only a brief thought about the traffic and she was once again barraged by the kids questions.

A truck roared by and shook the Ford Taurus with the force of the wind turbulence. Jenny shrieked with delight. The babysitter turned to Jenny to admonish her. Her foot was lightly on the brake, when she felt the impact to the rear of the car. The impression across her mind was that the car behind her had collided with her. He had been stopped. Her foot came off the brake with the initial jolt, the car moved forward. She looked back, the tan car had hit her. She caught a glimpse of the driver, momentarily, the eyes, like ice, focused and hard. She turned to the front, grabbed the steering wheel in both hands, but missed the brake with her foot. She was in the right lane of oncoming traffic. Joe Jr., Edward and Bobby were screaming something, pointing at a huge shadow bearing down on her from her left, she couldn't think, she couldn't act. A truck horn was blowing loudly somewhere. The screech and tearing of metal were the last thing she heard.

The impact of the truck on the Ford Taurus had occurred while the Chrysler was still in contact with it. The Chrysler vehicle turned in a complete circle, but was relatively undamaged. Cars on the opposite side of the crossroad began to stop. People got out of their cars and ran over. The Chrysler, which had stopped running, restarted and drove away in the opposite direction. No one got the license number, no one saw the face of the driver, no one remembered the color of the vehicle, other than the truck driver, who said it was big and light colored. The truck driver couldn't deal with what happened. He sat on the ground and wept and wept. It took several hours for the police to be able to question him in any manner and it had to be in the presence of a psychologist at the hospital because of his condition.

Joe and Marsha lay side by side holding one another. Slowly they began to talk. Joe caressed Marsha's face with his fingertips, stroking lightly along her cheek to her neck and down her back.

"Why Joe? Why? We try to do everything right and this happens. I don't understand it. Is God punishing us? For what? I just don't understand it at all."

Joe, tenderly and softly responded, "Marsha, I don't know what there is to understand. We have told the kids repeatedly that God works in mysterious ways. If he wants us to start over, then we have to. We must believe in Him and continue on. He will look out for us."

"Oh Joe, I don't know. I feel that this is just the beginning. I just feel it. I pray, but it doesn't seem to do any good. I actually think I am losing my faith. There is no reason for this Joe, no reason at all. Our God is supposed to be a loving God. Joe...all our money. What are we going to do? Five kids and we get to start over. It's not fair, it's not right."

Marsha looked at Joe and kissed him lightly on the lips, then added, "Something else is doing it."

"Marsha, I don't know. It's only money. I don't have any answers, but I do know that God will help us if we keep praying to him."

Slowly Marsha relaxed. Slowly the couple began to make love.

The phone rang, once, twice, thrice, and on the fourth ring the answering machine blurted Joe Jr.'s message in his childlike voice to please leave a message because we can't come to the phone.

Joe and Marsha could hear Father Bill as they lay there.

"Joe, Father Bill. I just had another of those strange experiences. Like the feeling I had been telling you about. I'm worried. Give me a call. You know the number, 555-5223, thanks."

Marsha tensed, looked at Joe, and said, "What feeling is he talking about?"

Joe felt uncomfortable all of a sudden. "He told me while we were jogging the other day that he had a wave or something pass through him while he was praying for us. At first he thought it was a pleasant experience, but then he said it became very unpleasant. He thinks it's an omen or something."

Marsha looked at him hard in the dim light. Her body tensed, her grip on Joe tightened.

It took the police three hours before Joe and Marsha were notified. The babysitter's parents were not home when the police tried to reach them and the police did not know who the children were. Marsha peered around the corner in her nightrobe as Joe answered the door. The appearance of a policeman at the door set Marsha off at once. Joe could hear her as he opened the door for the policeman.

"Mr. B," asked the policeman.

"Yes," said Joe.

The officer looked directly at Joe without a smile, without any facial expression. "I'm afraid I have some bad news, Mr. B. There has been an accident."

Marsha erupted from the hallway, rushing forward. "What? What is it? Oh, God, what is it?"

A second officer who had been standing on the porch entered the hallway; assessing the situation immediately, he knew he would be needed.

Joe was numb. He stared at the officers. He couldn't think. An accident? He put his hand to his throat, unconsciously massaging his neck muscles.

Marsha was in front of Joe, her eyes imploring, frantic, scared.

"Was your babysitter named Jaime Keyes?"

"Yes," blurted Marsha, "tell us, what is it?" she added with loud urgency.

"And were the five children in the car, your children?"

"Yes, yes," Marsha said.

"I don't really know how to say this," the officer looked down at the ground, paused, then looked Marsha straight in the face, got control of himself, and said as evenly as he could manage, "Your son, Joe Jr. is his name, I believe, is in Lake Hospital in serious condition. We would like you to come to the hospital with us, if you can."

"Tell me," hissed Marsha. "Tell me, what about the other kids? Are they ok? What happened to them? What's wrong with Joey? Tell me!" She had grabbed the officer's arm and was tugging on it.

"I'm sorry, Mrs. B, they didn't make it."

Joe listened and was numb. He couldn't react, he couldn't do anything. He stood there listening. It was too unreal.

Marsha's eyes opened wide, a sharp intake of breath was the only sound to be heard. She grabbed her chest, stared wildly at the officer, shook her head from side to side signifying the word "No". But it wasn't changing the facts. She couldn't breathe. She reached up and pulled her hair with both hands. She screamed. Not a short piercing scream, but a long, mournful, wail filled with anguish and agony; a wail of anger and helplessness.

The officer winced from the sound. The second officer had tears streaming down his face, but he did not wipe them off. He was as stolid as required of an officer of the law in a stressful situation, but he cried.

"Mr. B," said the officer, "we will drive you to the hospital if you want."

Joe, awakened from his shock by Marsha's scream, put his arm around her and directed her to the bedroom. He told the officer, "We'll get dressed, it'll take a couple of minutes." Marsha sobbed and kept pulling her hair. Strands that she had pulled out caught in her fingers and the hall light illuminated the loose strands for a fraction of a second as they walked to the bedroom.

Joe began to pray, inwardly at first, then outwardly. He repeated The Lord's Prayer over and over. He prayed out loud as he helped Marsha undress and dress. Marsha was helpless. As Joe sat her on the bed and wiggled her shoes on, she finally heard him. She heard him praying out loud.

"Joe," Marsha said between her sobs, "Please just shut the hell up." Joe looked at her for a second, then prayed inwardly, continually. The repetitive droning of the prayer salved his grief, or, at least, put it off temporarily.

Joe and Marsha sat in the waiting room for almost three hours before a blue robed doctor came over to them. The policeman called Father Bill and notified him. Father Bill rushed to the hospital and tried his best at comfort. But there was no comfort available at this time. Marsha's mother was overseas on an African Safari and Joe did not want his family notified just yet. He did not want them bustling about the hospital. It would be too much, he thought.

The doctor, over 6'4", was huge. The blue two piece outfit barely stretched around his extended middle. He took off his blue cap as he approached Joe, Marsha and Father Bill.

"I'm Doctor Flowers," he said, shaking Joe's hand. Marsha nervously clutched Joe's arm, still whimpering slightly. She looked at the doctor's face, she knew Joey hadn't made it. Everything about the doctor's expression told he he hadn't.

The doctor continued, "Your son passed away on the operating table.

Marsha gasped. Her grip loosened on Joe's arm. Joe went to put his arm around her, but she wasn't there. Marsha was falling. Joe grabbed at her, he missed. Marsha slumped to the floor, unconscious.

The doctor yelled for a nurse. Joe and the doctor lifted Marsha and placed her on the couch like seats until the nurse arrived. The doctor took her pulse with his finger on her carotid artery. Checked her breathing.

Doctor Flowers directed a nurse for help. Joe's only thought was he had lost all of his children. His prayers to God had gone unanswered, or if answered, they were denied. And now, Marsha—he might even lose his wife. What was going on?

A gurney was produced, Marsha was placed on the gurney by two male nurses, Joe followed it down the hall. The doctor's last words were: "I'm sorry."

Sorry, thought Joe. Sorry. What a small word meant to express the misery and anguish he now felt. Eddy's and Bobby's baseball games, Jenny running out to the car to meet him every day. His kids, gone. Oh why? There was no answer. Oh, God, answer me.

Father Bill hellped Joe make the arrangements for the children's burial. Family, friends and neighbors brought food to the house, gave condolences, offered help, but there was nothing to do. Marsha's mother was contacted overseas through the travel company and had caught the first flight home. She arrived the day before the funeral and then spent all her time with Marsha. Marsha had been watched overnight at the hospital and released. Joe had spent the night with her. He slept not at all. He couldn't think, he couldn't pray, he merely sat there holding Marsha's hand, sometimes crying, sometimes with his head on the edge of the bed, just holding Marsha's hand.

The cemetery allowed Joe to finance the five contiguous plots. He had no immediately available cash. It was through Father Bill's intercession that the cemetery allowed the financing to proceed; he cosigned on the papers, but Joe was not aware of it. The funeral director was somber throughout the transaction. Inwardly, he shouted with glee at the thought of selling five plots at one time, but outwardly, he was full of remorse and facially serious. He had never had a priest co-sign for burial expenses before.

Marsha continued to cry; Joe could not even talk to her. She paid no attention to anything. Joe wondered if she would be able to attend the funeral. She stayed in bed for two days.

When her mother arrived, Joe was thankful. Someone was there full time to be at Marsha's side. Someone in whom she had one hundred percent trust.

At the funeral home Marsha sat in a corner and cried. Her mother sat next to her, trying to comfort her. Her seat had a view of the five small caskets, each a different size to fit the height of the child within. The caskets were lined up, closed caskets, with a photo of each child on top of the casket above a gold plated nameplate with the child's name, birthdate, and date of death.

Joe stood several feet away in a receiving line formation. Joe was stoic, but depending on who approached him, shook his hand or hugged him, he often shed a tear, had a gasp in his throat, or just said "Thank you for coming."

Marsha couldn't talk to anyone. People approached her to give condolences, but Marsha wouldn't even acknowledge their presence. Marsha had begun to rock forward and back. Only slightly at first, but it seemed to Joe to be increasing the longer the wake continued. She emitted a noise, unintelligible, occassionally. Joe looked at Diane, Marsha's mother, she sligltly angled her head and lifted her eyebrows and turned one palm up. She had no explanation other than the obvious.

Joe himself had a difficult time standing in the receiving line at the funeral home. His friends, his family, his business associates, many people came through the line. The line was endless, Joe stood there for hours, but he couldn't recollect any specific conversation he had with anyone.

Father Bill, thankfully, was the organizer. He moved about making sure that everything was going as smoothly as the situation allowed. But, the situation was…

For the five days between the childrens' death and the funeral, Father Bill took over. He arranged for Joe to take several weeks off from work. He

visited Joe and Marsha each day, brought in the mail, piled it on the dining room table. He noticed the grass had not been cut, so he got a young
man from the parish to cut the grass. Father Bill recognized the second
notice due bills on some of the correspondence Joe received. Joe wasn't
attending to any business, and it appeared to Father Bill, that maybe he
hadn't been attending to business since the loss of his money through the
brokerage deal. That was in fact the case. No bills had been paid. Joe, who
usually paid all of the bills, had not attended to them for almost sixty days.
They would wait. His mind had not been able to focus on paying bills
after he lost his total savings. He would catch up in time.

Father Bill made sure not to intercede where it wasn't wanted. Joe was
at the lowest point in his life. He needed the hand of a friend. The firm,
voluntarily, on its own, but more at the insistence of Hank Smith, sent Joe
a $10,000.00 advance on his salary. They offered help, but there was noth-
ing they could do. Joe's mind was a vacuum. There was nothing in it. He
couldn't focus. He kept asking himself why. He tried to pray, but it was
difficult. As time progressed, and it did ever so slowly, Joe prayed. He
prayed the standard memorized prayers, and he prayed his own prayers.
He conversed with God on a one way conversation, talking, asking, prob-
ing, pleading, supplicating, and abdicating.

The funeral was the most difficult service that Father Bill had ever performed. He browsed the Bible looking for applicable phrases to read to the
people who attended the funeral. He put down the New Testament and
picked up the Old Testament. He thought that a God of Love would not
do this to a man, so maybe it was the Old Testament God that had dealt
with Joe. It was the same God, but the focus on vengeance had passed
with the coming of Jesus Christ, to a God of love. Love thy neighbor, Do
unto others as you would have them do unto you.

His fingers stopped at the Chapter of Job. He read the first chapter and could read no further. The last paragraph said it all:

>...Naked came I out of my mother's womb,
>and naked shall I return thither: the
>Lord gave, and the Lord hath taken away;
>blessed be the name of the Lord.

He looked at the paragraph, over and over. Job, the man who endured pain and suffering and the loss of all he had for a game of Satan's. Satan was given free play to ruin Job. Job had his faith tested, and remained faithful. Is that what is happening to Joe B? Is his faith being tested? Can these things really happen in this world? The more Father Bill thought of it, the more confused he became. He wondered if he would have embraced Jesus Christ when he was on earth or would he have been a doubting Thomas? Joe B has lost his money and his family. All he had left was his wife, who could not function, and a house with a mortgage on it. Can Joe B keep his faith?

The church was filled to capacity for the funeral. The five small caskets, each on its own gurney, draped in purple cloth were moved by the pall-bearers to the front of the church before the altar. The pallbearers had been arranged by Father Bill, they were all classmates of Joe Jr. lending to the scene the tragedy of youth. Nine and ten year old pallbearers caused the assemblage to move to tears quickly.

Joe and Marsha sat in the front row. Diane sat on the other side of Marsha to support her. Diane had purchased a dress for Marsha and made sure she was presentable. Marsha had few moments of time when she was not crying. Joe's parents and brothers and sisters were in the next several rows. Friends, school classmates of the children, teachers, members of Marsha's social groups, Joe's coworkers and colleagues from the Bar

Association, judges, bailiffs, everyone who could came to support and console Joe and Marsha. But Joe and Marsha were oblivious.

Joe stared at the altar and slowly, but quietly prayed. Marsha sat leaning on him, sobbing. It wasn't a sense of physical pain, but an absence, a total loss, a void in their lives. A part of them had been removed from the world, violently. They could do nothing to protect them. It was beyond their control. They would never see their smiling faces. They would never admonish their eating habits. They had nothing without their children, but themselves, a home partially paid for, and…no children.

Father Bill came from the sacristy, commenced the Mass. His purple robes were resplendent. Father Bill had requested the Deacon to assist him because he felt he might falter. The Deacon's robes complemented Father Bill's, flowing white and purple. The three altar boys with their black robes and white surplices walked extra slow in obtaining the cruets of wine and water.

When it came time for Father Bill to give the sermon, he thought maybe the Deacon should do it. He wasn't sure he was up to it. Emotion choked him repeatedly throughout the Mass. He had unconsciously slipped into Latin on two occassions and the assemblage had responded in Latin, at least those reared in the church. Instead of "May the spirit be with you," Father Bill had said "Dominus Vobiscum." The assemblage, without thought, had answered "Et cum spritutu O."

When he realized what he had done, he blushed bright pink. No one, except the Deacon, noticed it and the Mass continued. The Deacon inwardly remarked to himself that Father Bill was under a lot of strain. He hadn't heard the Latin used in Mass in a long time. He liked it. The Deacon glanced at Joe and Marsha, they were statute still.

Father Bill allowed the Deacon to handle the responsorials, then he slowly and formally stood up from his chair behind the altar, walked to the pulpit, adjusted the microphone, peered at the crowd, including those standing at the back of the church and along the side aisles, reached into his robes and took out his notes for his sermon. He usually did not need written notes, but he felt he might not be able to remember. He wasn't going to let his friend down at a time like this.

His peroration began, "Ladies and Gentlemen, Friends, Co-workers, Family members, and Joe and Marsha,

The funeral was a sad affair; they always are when children die for no apparent reason. The turnout of neighbors, members of Joe's firm, friends, and family was huge. Joe supported Marsha, who cried dry salt tears during the entire ceremony, during the drive to the cemetery, and during the burial.

CHAPTER NINETEEN

▼

A BURNT OFFERING

Sam did not go to the funeral. Instead, during the funeral, he went to the home of Joe and Marsha. No one had thought to have security at their home, after all, what more could possibly happen to them? And while it was well known that there were people on this earth who would prey on such unfortunate circumstances and who would break and enter the homes of people attending funerals, there was no thought of such a thing happening in this instance. Most of the neighbors were attending the funeral. Some of the friends had gone to the church hall to set up for the post-funeral gathering. They had collected food and soft drinks.

No one saw Sam drive to Joe and Marsha's home in a small tan vehicle, park in the driveway, go directly to the front door as if he knew what he was doing, as if he had a direct purpose in mind, as if he owned the home. No one saw the two-gallon blue container of kerosene by his side. Sam punched through the window with his gloved hand after opening the screen door, reached through, unlocked the door, entered, walked to the center of the house, looked around, went to the basement, picked up several pieces of clothing from the floor in front of the washing machine, poured kerosene on the clothing, stuck the cloth in the rafters, emptied the container of kerosene on the floor, lit the kerosene soaked cloth, watched it catch fire, and left the premises in a hurry. He got into his car and drove away. No one saw Sam, it was a clean job.

Sam was still in time to attend the burial at the cemetery, which he did. He made sure that several people saw him, such as Hank, so that he could confirm an alibi if he ever needed one, but he wouldn't. His presence at the funeral affected nothing. He saw Joe and Marsha, Marsha still weeping, a silent sobbing, her makeup smeared, eyeliner streaked her face, a red rubbed raw nose. No matter how much people tried to get her fixed up to look good, her tears and agony destroyed the look.

Sam merely observed.

Father Bill had arranged a gathering at the church hall for guests from out of town and those wishing to pay respects and condolences to Joe and Marsha. The friends and volunteers had done a wonderful job of providing refreshments. Marsha didn't want to attend, so Joe was going to drop her off at the house first. Marsha's mother was to meet them at the home. Joe didn't want to leave Marsha alone.

The limousine drove toward their home. Marsha was leaning against the door of the limousine. Joe could not offer her enough comfort. There was no comfort for her. She just sobbed. Joe noticed the fire trucks and traffic immediately. "Oh God, no!" he said.

Marsha jerked up. "What?...what did you say?" She looked out the window, saw the fire trucks, men in long yellow and black heavy raincoats with helmets spraying water on the charred hulk of their house.

"No," she shrieked. "God Damn it. God Damn it. God Damn you, God. Why?"

Marsha screamed, giving full effect from her lungs. The windows were closed and the air conditioner was on, but the sound penetrated the ears of the driver who slammed on the brakes causing the car to lurch. Marsha rushed out of the car, Joe followed.

She stood in the front yard, no longer screaming, just mumbling: "God damn it, god damn you, God, god damn you, God, god damn you, God."

Joe tried to put his arm around her, but she turned with such violence, she looked at him vehemently, she jerked his arm off violently and stared at the house and the busy firemen trying to put out the last of the flames. She had stopped crying. She had no energy left, she just stared and mumbled. Joe motioned to the limousine driver, told him to stand with his wife, not let her out of his sight, and went to talk to the firemen. Marsha's mom, whose car was only a minute behind, came rushing up to enfold Marsha in her arms.

Joe identified himself to one of the firemen, who directed him to another fireman. He was told that they didn't get the call until the house was almost gone. Seems everyone on the street was gone at the same time. The fire seemed to start right in the middle of the house. They would investigate for arson, even bring in Pyra, the fire dog, a dog especially sensitive to petroleum products, to sniff to determine the cause, but because they got there so late and the heat was so intense, it was unlikely they would be able to find the cause. Once a house falls and burns, it destroys its own evidence. But they will check it out. The fireman took Joe's name and where he could be reached, asked his insurance company's name, told Joe he would notify the insurance company and assist them in making their investigation. Other than that, there was nothing he could do here. The fireman gave him a card with the name and address of social services if he should need emergency lodging, if he didn't know anyone who would be able to put them up for a while.

When the driver took them to the church hall, Joe sent the driver in to get Father Bill. Joe informed Father Bill. Together, with Marsha's mom, they got Marsha out of the car, into the Rectory where Father Bill showed her the bathroom and bedroom. Joe, with the help of Marsha's mom, put her to bed. Father Bill heard her mumbling: "God damn you, God, god damn you, God." He looked at Joe, raised his eyes inquiringly, and said nothing. Marsha's mom stayed with Marsha.

"I will also send one of the ladies from the hall over to help keep an eye on her. Looks like she might need some medical help, Joe. Plan on staying here until we figure out where you are going to stay." Father Bill looked at Joe with great concern.

"Joe, I don't know what is happening to you." Father Bill said. "Somebody has it in for you. It is very strange, all these things happening at once like this. Your money, your family, your house. And, I don't have any advice to help you in a time like this. All I can say is that I am here for you and Marsha for whatever you need."

Joe nodded appreciatively. Father Bill continued, "I don't know anything I could say that would help you, but please pray and keep your faith in God. Lean on him. That is what He is there for. As down as you are, you must still trust in Him, He is Almighty. I like to think that everything He does has a purpose, but I cannot personally think of any purpose for this." Father Bill took hold of both of Joe's hands and held them in his as if he was trying to drain the pain from Joe. He tried to mask his pity mixed with the concern.

"Oh Father Bill." Joe sobbed, "I don't know why this is happening to us. I'm totally confused." Joe sat down, put his elbows on his knees, his head in his hands, sighing deeply.

Father Bill sat next to Joe, put his arm around him. "There are times," said Bill, "that confusion reigns."

Joe continued, a firm resolve in his voice, as if Father Bill had not spoken, "But my faith in God has not been shaken. As you said in your sermon, 'Naked came I out of my mother's womb, and naked shall I return thither.'"

Father Bill winced at his words. All his troubles, thought Father Bill, and he still listened to the sermon.

"I am shaken to the depths of this earth," said Joe, "but my faith in God is not shaken. I don't curse Him when I have good luck, I am not going to curse Him when I have bad luck."

Father Bill sat in rapt attention next to Joe. Maybe Joe didn't know, but his comments were the same comments Job had said to his friends. Uncanny, coincidence?

"I know there is evil in the world," said Joe, "and for some reason it is directed at me. I hope to be able to keep my faith. I intend to persevere. I am a sinner, the Lord knows. I pray he cuts me off, ends this miserable life I am leading." Joe gasped for breath and paused a moment, then continued, "Yes, end this miserable life, then I would be comforted. I am in pure agony, Bill. I don't know what to do."

Father Bill put his hand on Joe's head and began to pray in out loud in Latin.

CHAPTER TWENTY

▼

A SECOND CHINESE DINNER

Hank hadn't had a lenghty conversation with Sam since their prior dinner at the Chinese Restaurant. When Hank became aware of the money stolen at the brokerage house, he had a strong sense that Sam was involved, that this was the culmination of the two dollar bet. He knew that Sam had the audacity to pull off the theft. The clincher was when Sam had left the message at the office: "Two dollars, it's on." However, when the children were killed, he was praying for Sam's noninvolvement. He was greatly apprehensive about it. It was not part of the bet. It was too much even for Sam who had a tremendous mean streak. He wouldn't involve himself in the death of children, would he? It was unthinkable. Then when the house burned down on the day of the funeral, he was certain that Sam could not be involved. He had seen Sam at the grave site. It was too much. Not even Sam could impose such pain and suffering on another human being. And the children, he kept thinking of the children. Joe's kids were such darlings, so cute and friendly. Dead, all dead. Hank prayed to God to make sure his friend Sam was not involved in this tragedy. He added a prayer for Joe and Marsha.

Hank and Sam arranged for lunch at the same Chinese Restaurant. Sam made reservations for eleven thirty—get in early so there would be no problem with getting seated. When Hank arrived, Sam was already seated and engaged in a deep conversation with the hostess in Mandarin. The hostess was laughing at some small joke of Sam's. When she saw Hank approaching, she said: "Mr. Smith, your friend is very funny, very funny indeed. You had better keep him around. He is very funny."

Sam was grinning, ran his hand through his hair. He wore a dark suit with a modern tie; splashes of color with no real design. The pony tail had been trimmed by a barber. He stood at the approach of Hank. They shook hands. Hank was serious.

"Tell me first," said Hank, "that you had nothing to do with Joe B."

"I did the bonds, Hank. Didn't you get my message I left with your secretary?" Sam admitted, becoming immediately serious, looking directly at Hank. "But that was it. You know I did the bonds. It was too easy." Sam took an envelope from his inner pocket, handed it over to Hank. "Here is the money. I negotiated the bonds, after all they were bearer bonds. You can figure out some way to get them back to him. But that's it. I think your God did the rest. It is a terrible thing that happened to the man and his family. The papers are making a big deal out of it. But no, Hank, I wasn't involved with any of that stuff. I am surprised you would have thought I was involved." Sam feigned a hurtful and remorseful look at the same time. "I couldn't do such a thing. Kill kids, give me a break, Hank. Jesus." Sam tossed his head in disgust.

"I just had to hear it from you. The timing was too coincidental. I'm not saying you were involved, it's just that we were talking about it, then all of a sudden everything bad in the world happens to the poor guy. I just wanted to make sure it wasn't all connected. I really don't think I could live with myself if I knew I was the cause of his troubles." Hank's voice cracked, he faltered, looked at Sam, quickly dropped his gaze and looked at the teapot as he spoke. "I can't even believe the money part. It's like you started the ball rolling and everything went downhill for the guy from there. Have you ever seen such a tragedy in your life?"

"No, and I don't choose to again. How's he doing?"

Hank ignored the question. "What the hell am I going to do with this money? How am I going to get it back to him? You stole seventy something thousand dollars? I can't believe it. Wasn't there another couple hundred thousand stolen?"

"It was my own money I took back. I had the broker put my money into bearer bonds also, then I just took them back. They were uninsured by the way. What a way to run a brokerage house." Sam laughed. "I wouldn't invest there if I were you. I even had to talk to the police who were investigating the theft; showed my righteous indignation that I lost so much money. Pretty good act, if I do say so myself."

Sam was lighthearted and mocking in his speech. He had it all tied up, his friend believed him, he returned the money, he was back to square one with his friend.

"Jesus, how did you get in? What do you know about burglaries?"

"Don't ask. You can probably make a loan to the kid, Joe. Loan him fifty grand, tell him he can pay it back when he can, then don't take the payback. I'm sure he could use it."

"The firm gave him an advance of ten grand. He is on partnership track, maybe," Hank rolled his eyes and thought of the figure of Joe sitting at his desk getting nothing accomplished. Hank asked himself: would he be able to think of work if such a thing had happened to him? Probably not. "I wonder if he will ever be able to be an effective lawyer again. He's in shock, I'm sure. God, what a terrible thing to happen to a guy. I don't wish that on anybody."

The waitress came and took their order. Chicken subgum for Hank, a cashew vegetable combo with egg drop soup for Sam. And, don't forget the fortune cookies, he added.

"Sam, why are you involved in this? Why did you even steal the money?" asked Hank, dumbly.

Sam put his two palms up defensively, a feigned look of surprise and said, "Hey, we wanted to test his faith, right? Why am I involved? Two bucks, remember? You bet me the two bucks, buckaroo. Well, his faith is being tested now; he is a real Job now. I'm not saying it is good, but for the purposes of our bet, we will really see if he is going to be loyal to his faith. Now I will admit," Sam said apologetically," this thing kind of snowballed on its own. I did the bearer bonds thing, but those other things, they must have been done by your God, his God, or just bad luck. Maybe your God heard us and got in on the bet. The kid has had terrible luck. I don't wish that on anyone. But, you've got to admit, this will test his faith, if he ever had any."

Hank, distressed, but somewhat relieved his friend affirmed his noninvolvement in anything other than the theft, "Good thing the bet wasn't on his wife, she has God Damned herself into a mental hospital for the last week and a half. She keeps saying God damn you, God." Hank knew and felt his bet with Sam started this thing to Joe. He felt guilt. His friend stole bearer bonds from Joe. Now he has given them to Hank. Conspiracy to commit theft! What if Sam really is involved in the other activities against Joe B? A feeling! What is it? Can Sam be trusted at all? Could he really be trusted when he knew him? Not trust, so much as the ability to depend on him. Sam did what Sam wanted for Sam's benefit. But why would he do such a thing? And Hank was involved. And he didn't like it. He was agitated, angry, upset, guilty, and uncomfortable. His prior ease at seeing Sam again after a lenghty absence had dissolved. Sam sensed it, Hank saw. It must be obvious, his nonverbal language was speaking volumes. He didn't like being with Sam anymore. He didn't know Sam anymore. He had changed. Or, he was always the same and Hank was older or mature enough and experienced enough to see him for what he was. He wasn't sure, but he did know that he wanted no part in the terrible act that had put Joe B in this horrible position. He stole money after he set up the broker, knowing full well what he planned to do. All for a two dollar bet.

Two dollars. They used to bet two dollars on everything. No one ever paid the other back, but they kept a tally. Seems like the last time he could remember, he owed Sam something like four hundred dollars of imaginary two dollar bets. That even made this worse. There was no reason to cause harm to Joe by stealing his money. How could that test his faith? It didn't do much for Marsha, look at her, poor soul, stuck in a mental ward. She lost so much so quickly, who could handle such a thing? For an imaginary two bucks, she went crazy.

The more Hank thought, the more distressed he became. The momentary relief he had felt, dissipated. It was too easy for Sam to steal the money, to start the ball rolling. The house accidently burns down during the funeral? Too coincidental. The children…what a tragedy. If he had anything to do with it, thought Hank, well, he didn't know what to think. He didn't know what he would or could do.

Hank was brought back to the present by Sam. "Are you still with us, Hank? I think you were daydreaming."

"Yeah, I was," admitted Hank, "I can't get the picture of Joe out of my mind. The guy lost everything. And I'm involved in starting it. I can't deal with it. I don't know how to fix it." He leaned back in his chair, frowned.

"Fix what?" Sam gave a quizzical look, cocked his head slightly, ran his fingers through his hair and played for a second with his short pony tail. "What is there to fix? The money, no problem, just give it to him. You can't fix the other stuff. That's life as God gives it. There's no solution to it. You accept it. God is not all good, sweetness and light. Remember what he allowed to happen to six million Jews and six million other poor saps,

Polish, Austrians, Russians, French, and twelve million people all told. He killed them. Did they maintain their faith in their god? Ask them when you get to heaven. And ask Him about the twenty million Russians killed by the great warrior, Stalin. God does what he does, or doesn't do what he doesn't want. There is no fixing it. If he wants to put hell on earth for some people, he does it. Maybe it works for their benefit when they get up there, whatever that is. I say these things and I don't even believe in your God, but I know about him."

"Sam, you stole the money, you gave me the money, I am involved. I can't undo that. I know that. But I don't want to be involved. We bet two bucks, which no one ever paid anyway. Two bucks and you go to all the effort to steal seventy thousand bucks. Why Sam? Why?" Hank said in frustrated earnest. He was pleading. He needed a reason. He needed something to salve his conscience. That there was more than just the money. That by participating in the first event of the two dollar bet, he gave acquiescence to the whole of the tragedy. That he gave the okay for Joe to become a Job. He was afraid of the feeling, of a weakness, of something he could do nothing about. It had always been like that when he dealt with Sam. Sam made the move and Hank had to go along for some reason or other; like he was going along with this one.

"Hank. Religion means a lot to me. I have seen it the world over. It means so much that it means nothing. There is no such a thing. It is all myth. Religion is a fantastic made up story to keep the masses in line, under the thumb of the sacred priests. It has gone on since the beginning of time. It tries to explain what we don't know, what we are afraid of. Where we go after death. No one wants to think that they go nowhere, that their lives are insignificant. So they use religion. They buy their way into whatever heaven there is. It is all a dream.

"You wonder why I took you up on the bet. Because." Sam was speaking directly to Hank, no smiles, no happy face, he was serious. "Just because. There is no reason. There is no religion. I hear the word faith.

There is no such thing. The blind adherence to a religious concept. Assume Joe has faith. Faith in what? That god will do him good. That if he is good on this earth he will go to heaven. Give me a fucking break, Hank. Faith." Sam made a spitting sound with his mouth.

"And so you ruin a young man's life for this?" Hank asked incredulously. "You think there is no religion, so you then think that there can be no faith. So you make a bet, of two dollars mind you, that Joe will have no faith. "Hank spoke hesitantly, he knew he was just as involved, but he pointed the blame on Sam. "Then you proceed to destroy the man's life, you steal his money, you…" Hank paused, Sam didn't let him finish.

"I only dealt with the money, Hank. Your God did the rest. Your God made Joe a Job. Your God is testing his faith. Your God said 'Fuck you' to Joe and his family, not me. Your God said, 'Hey, maybe we can test Joe's faith. Maybe I'll joint the bet.' Don't put this whole thing on me. Don't even try it. It is all so much bullshit, Hank. See it for what it really is.

"Obviously, the wife, what's her name, Marsha, has failed the test of faith, but then we didn't bet on her, did we? Well, screw her, the faithless bitch." Sam gave two short laughing snorts. "But what about Joe. Regardless of the tragedy of his life, we still have a two dollar bet. Two bucks, Hank. Let's see how he maintains his faith in the face of the loss of everything he ever had."

Hank sat dumfounded. Such venom, such hatred. Sam's life was a world of anger. And Hank was part of it.

Sam relaxed his tone, then added, "I don't think you should return that money just yet."

Hank, not really listening anymore, catching bits and pieces amid his thoughts, finally said, "Return it, how do I do that." Hank spoke angrily, but with forced repression. The words came out like a hiss. "Here Joe, here is the money that my lifelong friend stole from your brokerage. He didn't mean anything by it. No, it has no connection with the loss of your children or your house, just the money. Here it is back, Joe. Go build a new house. It doesn't fly, Sam." Hank was quiet for ten seconds, then said: "I will get the money back to him, I just don't know how yet."

"When you talk to him, can you find out if he still has faith?" asked Sam. Hank stared at him with total disbelief.

CHAPTER TWENTY ONE

▼

FATHER BILL CONSOLES JOE

Marsha couldn't stop crying. There were no tears. She had none left. She was dehydrated, however, the compulsive sobbing continued. She would sit for a minute, then her body would wrack itself with a spasm, muscles tightening involuntarily like a cold shiver. Joe had called the family doctor, who had her admitted to the psychiatric floor of the hospital. Father Bill drove them, Joe holding Marsha in the back seat. Marsha crying and mumbling, incoherent. Marsha's mother, Diane, came along. She was quiet, said nothing, but her occassional glances at Joe seemed to want to blame Joe for everything that happened to her daughter. He was the most available person to strike at.

The nurses took Marsha directly to the admitting room, put her on a gurney and gave her a shot to calm her down. They wheeled her to a room, helped her off the gurney, changed her clothes and put her to bed. The medication began to take effect; Marsha was a zombie. She lay on the bed and finally fell asleep.

Joe filled out the documentation required at admission on Marsha's medical and mental history. When he completed the forms, the nurse told him to call his doctor in the morning to find out how she was doing. Joe thanked her and met Father Bill in the waiting room. Marsha's mother was arguing with a nurse at the desk, trying to get permission to stay with Marsha overnight. It was an argument she could not win. Hospital policy prevented it. Diane, furious and frustrated, was without control. She left with Joe and Father Bill.

Joe and Father Bill were quiet for most of the ride home, Father Bill respecting Joe's plight and not wanting to interfere. Diane sat in the corner in the back seat, seething with anger. It took everything she had to say nothing. Finally, Father Bill could take the silence no longer; he thought Joe needed someone to talk to. The silence was too oppressive, too heavy with sadness, almost a feeling of guilt.

"Are you okay, Joe?" asked Father Bill.

"Yeah, I'm okay," sighed Joe, "I just don't know what is happening to me. I can't get a handle on it. If it is not one thing, it is another."

"I see it and I don't believe it," Father Bill responded. He knew he had to say something, but he didn't know what to say. So he just said something to keep Joe in conversation, hoping that conversation would keep Joe from turning into a mental disaster like Marsha. It would be very easy to go absolutely insane given the things that had happened to Joe.

Marsha's mother did not join in the conversation. She glared at Joe when he spoke. She fidgeted with the door handle. She resigned herself to not getting her way and tried to relax.

"Why not me, Father?" Joe asked, turning to Father Bill. "Why has nothing happened to me directly?" he paused for about five seconds. Father Bill desperately thought of something to say, when Joe continued. "Why has nothing happened to me personally? My money, my kids, oh God my kids..." A gasp escaped from Joe. A gasp of desperation, like losing one's grip on a wire hundreds of feet in the air, a letting go, a knowing that there is no further reason or ability to continue to hang on.

Joe continued. "My money, my kids, my house, and now my wife. Why is it everything around me and not me, Father? I don't understand it."

Diane purposely blocked out the conversation.

"Joe." Said Father Bill after an appreciable time of silence, after he thought Joe wasn't going to say anything more.

"There is only prayer at this point. I can only tell you to pray to God, to Jesus, to ask for his help, to ask for his mercy. I know he hasn't shown any to date, but you must pray. There is no other answer. You must have faith in God."

Joe said nothing, Father Bill continued, "If God the Father almighty, the Creator of the ordered and good world, cares for all his creatures, even us, Joe, then the question of >why does evil exist,' surfaces. You are undergoing some terrible evil. Something evil has annexed itself to your life. To this question of why does evil exist, no quick answer will suffice. It's as pressing as it is unavoidable and as painful as it is mysterious. Only Christian faith as a whole can constitute an answer to this question. The goodness of creation, the drama of sin, and the patient love of God who comes to meet man by his covenants." Father Bill halted for several seconds, glanced over at Joe to see if he was paying attention. Joe was staring directly at Father Bill. Father Bill was surprised that he caught Joe's attention. Joe was listening, intently.

Marsha's mother gave no outward sign of hearing the conversation, but, intermittently, she listened closely to every word, then phased out the droning conversation.

"Yes, the patient love of God who comes to meet man by his covenants," Father Bill continued and refocused on the road. "The covenants of the redemptive Incarnation of his Son, his gift of the Spirit, his gathering of the Church, the power of the sacraments and his call to a blessed life to which free creatures are invited to consent in advance, but from which, by a terrible mystery, they can also turn away in advance. You have had many evil things happen to you, Joe. God is putting a test to you. He is testing your faith." Yes, Father Bill thought, He is testing Joe's faith. Joe, the Job. Will he survive the test? A short prayer of hope seeped from Father Bill.

"It is more than evil. Why did God create such a world?" asked Joe. "Why didn't he create a world so perfect that no evil could exist in it? I know it is evil that has happened to me. Why is there evil? I cannot understand it! Why is my God allowing this to happen to me?"

"It is true, Joe, that God with His infinite power could always create something better. But with his infinite wisdom and goodness, God has freely willed to create a world in the process of journeying toward its ultimate perfection. In God's plan, this process of becoming, involves the appearance of certain beings and the disappearance of others, the existence of the more perfect alongside the less perfect, both constructive and destructive forces of nature. With physical good there exists also physical evil as long as creation has not reached perfection." Laying it on pretty thick here, thought Father Bill. I hope Joe can handle this conversation. I hope I can comfort him, somewhat, with maintaining his faith in God.

"Angels and men, as intelligent and free creatures, have to journey toward their ultimate destinies by their free choice and preferential love. They can therefore go astray. Indeed, they have sinned. Thus has moral evil, incommensurably more harmful than physical evil, entered the world. God is in no way, directly or indirectly, the cause of moral evil. He permits it, however, because he respects the freedom of his creatures and, mysteriously, knows how to derive good from it. For almighty God, because he is supremely good, would never allow any evil whatsoever to exist in his works if he were not so all-powerful and good as to cause good to emerge from evil itself."

And God permitted these deaths of five children, thought Father Bill. Oh why, God, why? What good can be derived from the death of these good, truly innocent, children?

"I know what you are saying Father, but do you really think good can come from me losing all my children?" Joe had anguish in his voice, incredulity.

He says what I am thinking, thought Father Bill. Uncanny.

"I am having a hard time believing it at this time," said Joe.

"I don't mean directly, Joe." Father Bill said patiently. "But in time it may be seen, that God in his almighty providence can bring a good from the consequences of an evil, even a moral evil, caused by his creatures. Take for instance, Joseph, of the coat of many colors, who said to his brothers: 'It was not you who sent me here, but God...you meant evil against me; but God meant it for good, to bring it about that many people should be kept alive.' Things are not always what they seem, which is why prayer is so important.

"And, think of the greatest moral evil ever committed—the rejection and murder of God's only son, caused by the sins of all men—God, by his grace that abounded all the more, brought the greatest of goods; the glorification of Christ and our redemption.

"So, Joe, I can only say at this point, keep praying. Communicate with God. Evil has been done, but God has a purpose, keep your faith in God."

They did not speak for the final ten minute ride to the rectory.

Marsha's mother began to snore.

CHAPTER TWENTY-TWO

▼

THE INVESTIGATION

The State Fire Marshall's office had been contacted to conduct the investigation into the suspected arson at Joe B's home. Lt. James Finn was the primary investigator, a tall rangy man with a southern accent. He contacted Joe at Father Bill's Rectory three days after the funeral. Lucy, the woman who cleaned the Rectory, a short squat well kept woman, showed Lt. Finn onto the back patio where Joe, in solitude, sat on a lounge chair in the sun.

Joe, half asleep, heard the door open and close. Lucy, moving silently, touched him on his sleeve, "Mr. B. Mr. B, someone is here to see you."

Joe opened his eyes slowly, taking in the tall man in a uniform with a bus driver's cap, or so it looked. On second glance, he saw it was a fireman, not a policeman. Joe sat up, got out of the chair, stood.

"Mr. B. I am Lt. James Finn of the State Fire Marshall's Arson Investigation Unit out of Cleveland. I would like to ask you some questions if you are up to it."

"Oh, yeah, sure," said Joe, waving his hand to a seat.

Joe adjusted the seat on the lounge chair to sit upright so he could face Lt. Finn. Lucy slipped away.

"Here is my card," said Lt. Finn, handing Joe the card. Joe glanced at the red, white and blue card and put it on the white plastic coffee table. "First, let me give my condolences, Mr. B." Lt. Finn paused for an appreciable moment, then proceeded. "My purpose today is to talk to you about some people you come in contact with to see if there is anyone out there who has it in for you?"

"It was arson, then?" asked Joe.

"By all indications we have, and we haven't released the report yet, but yes, we do believe it is arson. However, we won't know until the report comes back from the lab what the specific igniter was. That will take another week or so to get the analysis back from the lab in Columbus."

Joe didn't need the report to know it was arson. There was no reason known to him for the house to spontaneously combust. He just didn't know who or why. He hadn't really thought about it much; his mind was more focused on the children. The image of Eddie coming to the realization that he spit on a girl at school because she made a mistake kept coming to him. He could visualize it, he would smile, then turn sad.

Lt. Finn saw Joe was deep in thought and said, "Mr. B?"

Joe blinked. His half-opened eyes refocused on Lt. Finn. His mind centered once again, realizing he was in the middle of a conversation, he said, "Yes sir, sorry. I go off on these thoughts. Sometimes I don't hear what people are saying right in front of me." Joe furrowed his brow in concentration, paying attention.

"Mr. B, what I would like to know is whether there is anybody out there that you know of who has it in for you? Or maybe in for your wife? Or maybe in for your employer and taking it out on you?"

Joe thought for several seconds. "No," he said. "I don't know anyone who despises me that much."

"How about anyone who despises you at all?"

"Not really. No. Can't say that I do," Joe reflected. "I just finished a jury trial a couple days before, but the other attorney and I got along fine. And it was an insurance company paying the bill, so the client had no personal animosity that I know of." Joe paused again. "No, can't say that there is anyone."

"You haven't received any threats?"

"No, none."

"Hmm." Lt Finn looked concerned and troubled. He cradled and rubbed his chin with his thumb and finger. He appeared to wish he had a pipe in his hand so he could smoke it, the hand movement on his chin was identical to holding and playing with a pipe.

Lt. Finn sat in thought for several minutes. Joe watched him stroke his chin.

Looking up, Lt. Finn said, "We have been in contact with the police on this also. They think there is some connection between the other incidents that have occurred." Lt. Finn did not want to speak aloud about the death of Joe's children for fear of causing more pain to Joe so he avoided it as best he could.

"Do you think the several incidents are connected?" asked Lt. Finn.

"Really Sir, I don't know. I can't believe what has happened. I haven't been able to think straight at all since it all happened. I just don't know. The whole thing is incomprehensible to me. All I can do is pray. There is nothing else left for me to do. I wouldn't know where to start to figure it out."

Lt. Finn brought the conversation back to the investigation. "Don't know a soul who was angry at you at all, huh?"

Joe thought again, then answered, "No, not a soul. Sorry."

Lt. Finn stood, "Well Mr. B, I will be going now. Thank you for your time, and once again, my sincerest condolences." Joe stood and shook hands with him, mumbled good bye unintelligibly.

"I will let you know if we find anything out, Mr. B." Lt. Finn left. Joe sat down not giving Lt. Finn a thought. He once again thought about Eddie.

CHAPTER TWENTY THREE

▼

HOME INSURANCE COVERAGE

It took several days before Joe was able to compose himself enough to attend to business. He contacted Lake Shores Homeowners Insurance Company, the company that had insured him ever since he owned his home. The same company his parents used. They were loyal to the company. They identified the company as their friend. He talked to the adjuster who referred him to the claims supervisor. The company declined to cover the loss. They said that the policy had expired on the fourteenth, that they had not received the premium, that they then sent out the ten-day cancellation notice, which would have permitted Joe to reinstate the policy, but that the premium was never received. As a consequence, there was no coverage for the loss. They were sorry, but they couldn't just pay people because they wanted coverage. They knew that they had collected premiums for years without any claims at all on this particular policy, but an annual contract is a contract. Yes, Joe was a good client of longstanding. In fact, Joe should know that better than most being a lawyer.

Joe remembered the pile of letters and mail stacked on the table in the dining room. The letters that piled up after the loss of the bearer bonds. Marsha didn't attend to the business of paying bills, and he had taken the bills to the office, piled them on his credenza, and didn't attended to them either. Had that much time gone by? Then the kids and the house. He couldn't tell her about this. She had enough problems of her own.

Joe knew that a contract was a contract. He knew he couldn't force the insurance company to pay the claim if he hadn't paid the premium. This insurance business didn't surprise him, why, he expected it. Why should this string of luck—better to have bad luck then no luck at all—be interrupted, Joe thought ironically? Could he predict the next catastrophe? He couldn't even think straight. Insurance, what a business. No insurance for the loss of the bearer bonds, and now no insurance on the loss of the house. Joe had a vague thought about medical insurance for Marsha's treatment, but tossed it off quickly as a thought that couldn't be dealt with at this time. Something he didn't want to even think about.

CHAPTER TWENTY-FOUR

▼

JOE RETURNS TO THE PRACTICE

After two and a half weeks, Joe returned to work. Marsha was still a patient in the hospital, but Joe felt he needed to be busy and work was the easiest place to be busy that he knew. He remained with Father Bill while the police investigated the suspected arson at his home. Although the police were close mouthed about the investigation, they had leaked to the papers that they found petroleum residue indicative of a fire being set with diesel fuel or kerosene smack dab in the middle of the house. They did not contact him and tell him of the results as Lt. Finn had promised, but that was to be expected. It didn't matter to Joe anyway. Who did it meant nothing to him, the fact that it was done and it seemed connected to the death of his children did mean something to him, but it wasn't something that he could change. It was something that had changed him.

The receptionist was the first person to see Joe. She didn't know what to say to him so she used the standard, "Good morning, Mr. B."

"Good morning, Gayle," he responded with a half smile. "I see there are no phone messages for me. Hasn't anyone called me?"

"Not many, Mr. B," she answered. "The messages that I did take are already on your desk. Mr. Bond has been handling your work and returning your messages." Gayle didn't know if she should say she was sorry. Maybe it would open a wound trying to heal, better to keep quiet, she thought.

"Ok," he sighed. "I'll check with him. Thank you, Gayle."

"No problem, Mr. B."

Joe's office had been used, but it was neater than when he left it. Few files were stacked. The secretaries must have put them in the file cabinets. A short stack of phone messages lay on the corner of his desk.

Joe looked at his calendar on his credenza. He maintained a written calendar and a computerized calendar printed out each day by the secretary. There was nothing on it for the whole day, nor for tomorrow. He saw he had a pretrial on the coming Friday at 10:00am in the Lake County Common Pleas Court. That will be a nice drive, he thought. Get out of the hustle and bustle of Cleveland, for the smaller hustle and bustle of Painesville. But it would be forty minutes in a car both ways while not working on some case.

Joe started to go through the mail on his desk. One stack was magazines and catalogs, it was twelve inches high. Another was junk mail, flyers, invites for credit cards (pre-approved subject to passing the financial inspection—thereby negating the pre-approval), winner of $100,000.00 if he is one of the final choices in a selection of several million people and if he subscribes to numerous magazines at short term and high price, and miscellaneous trash. He picked up the entire pile and dropped it into the waste basket next to his desk.

The next pile was old mail stacked up that the secretary thought he should see and be aware he had recieved, but which required no action from him. Copies of pleadings, crossclaims, letters from attorneys to other attorneys, but copied to him. He browsed through the pile. It took him an hour to go through the pile.

The next pile was current mail. All of it opened. The envelope discarded unless there was something unusual about it or it was a time sensitive case. One secretary tore off all the stamps after she made sure the envelope was not necessary. Before Joe started on the pile of mail, Steve Bond walked in, plopped down on a chair, smiled at Joe. "Welcome back," he said.

"Thank you. It's good to be back, I guess."

"Lotta shit, huh?" Steve waved to the mail piles.

"Unbelievable. When it's stacked up like this, it makes you wonder why the post office allows a reduction for bulk mail. They ought to increase the price of bulk mail. It would get them out of financial problems. Then they could pay their employees and they wouldn't be shooting each other."

"I'm sure those people would find some other reason for their aggression," Steve paused. "I've been going through your stuff every day. Nothing too important. Had to answer a couple of complaints, sent off some interrogatories to several clients, but on the whole, it has been pretty quiet. I think people knew you were out of circulation."

"Yeah, feels like I still am."

"Yes, I suppose you are," said Steve looking up at Joe. Joe was fidgeting with the catalog mail pile. Making two stacks, one of catalogs, one of magazines. Then he subdivided the catalogs into ones he would look at and ones he wouldn't. Steve sensed that Joe wasn't in a conversive mood, so he stood to leave.

"Let me know if you have any questions on the stuff I did for you. It's in that pile over there, the small one," he smiled, "see ya, Joe."

"Okay, Steve." Joe did not even look up.

CHAPTER TWENTY-FIVE

▼

A PARTNERS MEETING

The partners of Smith, Post and Trivisonno met in their well appointed luxurious conference room, seated at one end of the huge table in their designated seats. Seats that would remain the same so long as the firm remained the same.

Hank addressed the partners: "Gentlemen, there is only one item on our agenda today; Joe B. I thought we had better discuss his situation. As several of you know, I had spoken to you previously, we made a ten thousand-dollar advance to Joe. We are here today to talk about his situation, figure out where he sits in the firm, and what to do with him or about him." Hank looked at each of the partners, good hard working men.

"Joe has been back to work now for a week and a half. I haven't had much contact with him since he has been back."

"I don't know anyone who has ever gone through what he is going through. It's as if he has a cloud over his head," said Tom Stillwell. The partners darted looks at him.

"Well, gentlemen?" asked Hank.

No one spoke for almost a full minute. They were in a difficult situation. They had an employee whose life had turned into a shambles.

"Does anyone know how he is doing?" asked Anthony Trivisonno. "How's he dealing with the day to day client problems?"

"From what I gather," said Hank, "and I talked to Steve Bond who handled Joe's matters in his absence and to his secretary this morning, he hasn't had much client contact. He avoids calling them back if he can. It is as if their little problems pale in comparison to his, so he passes them by. He is not ignoring the client, mind you, just not giving them the attention he previously gave them."

"I would imagine," said Anthony, "that he just might have a difficult time emphathizing with a whiny client about some soft tissue injury. Jesus, I would. But then, of course," he uttered a small laugh, "I have a tough time empathizing with them now." Several parners joined in the chuckle.

Hank spoke up, "I don't know if you are aware, but his loss at the brokerage of about seventy thousand dollars was uninsured. It looks like Holderman-Plank is going to stand on the state statute that they don't have to pay it back. They have lost my business as of last week on that decision alone." Hank had stood up as he was speaking. "Then, apparently Joe didn't attend to his bills, so when his house burned down, he was uninsured. The time on his ten day cancellation notice had expired by one day. They won't cover the loss."

Hank took a deep breath. This wasn't as hard as he thought it was going to be. "So he has no money in the bank, no home equity, still has a mortgage to pay, had to finance the funeral, five funerals, actually. And, we have the question of his status as pending Senior Status."

John Post spoke first. "You all know the saying, 'Charity begins at home'."

"Is that what is warranted here?" asked Paul Davis. "Are we here to determine the amount of charity we are to pass over to our employee?" His tone was less than kind. "Should we look at this as a business decision, or are we gathered here to give alms. If it is the latter, then just put Joe on the list with the Red Cross and the Cancer Society and we will get to it when we vote on those. But if it is the former, let's properly analyze it."

Paul Davis was then quiet. The partners exchanged glances, but the meanings were unclear. None knew what the other was thinking. None wanted to be the uncharitable. They were, after all, a catholic firm. They were all Christians in what they considered the largest sense. Charity was merely another aspect of Christianity.

Bud Beck spoke in his low rumbling voice that contrasted with his physique. "It is a little bit of both. Joe needs our charity, let's give it. What we must consider, though, that whatever we throw his way, is gone. It will be pure charity. No loans to pay back. No obligations, no ties. If we are going to do something, let us do it. Let us do it from the point of view that it is charity and he is a proper object of our charity.

"I can tell you, I don't think he will be much of an attorney after this. I can't see him coming back and being a good attorney. At least not with the same vigor he had. I can see him lasting four, six months at the most. He will get frustrated, his wife will be a problem, his life is a problem. I don't know that he can get over it. I don't think I could, myself. But we also can't cut him off. We also cannot be indecisive. He is our employee."

"Yeah," contributed Anthony Trivisonno, "how would we look if we let him go. Boy, would the newspapers get a kick out of that. They are already calling him a Job. Channel Five called me to talk about him, but I refused. It might look like a selfish approach to his problem, or our problem, but from a PR standpoint, we must keep him on. And, who knows, he may possibly get over this. I don't think I could, personally, but he might."

Hank said: "Clarify your point a little more for us, Bud, won't you?"

"Sure. Here we have an employee," he explained, "First I am going to talk the business end. We have here an employee who has ten days vacation. For a personal problem, which we will get into shortly, he has already taken those ten days off. He will need more time off, I can see it. He has now come back to work. Given the nature of his personal problem, his ability to come back to work and to be an effective lawyer is suspect. I don't imagine he will get too excited over a fender bender after what he has gone through. So, from a business point of view, we look at him as a lost asset. He probably will never be the lawyer he was a month ago.

"Next, we try to decide what to do about the business end of it. Do we drop him? Not yet. Do we embrace his personal problem? I am not sure of that either. Do we promote him? No. That is the business end we have to decide. He is soon to be on Senior Status; that is a great promotion. Does he deserve it on his past merit? Yes. But where will it put us when he isn't able to produce at Senior Status. Then we are stuck with an employee with vested rights. It would be too hard to get rid of him at that point.

"I realize that I may sound too harsh here, but we are analyzing this in its true sense. Business.

"The next step is the eleemosynary approach. To what degree does he deserve our charity. We are his employers. His tragedy is the worst in the world. He is worse than a Job, almost a pariah. It is not so much that we are saddled with him, but he is our employee. What, if anything, do we give to him from our hearts, separate from our business. However, whatever is from our hearts, is also from our business pocketbooks. It is a loss all around."

There was silence again.

Paul Davis spoke, "Bud, I think you're being a little heavy on the business end. I don't disagree with you, but I think in this instance, charity is the first approach we should look at. We have a colleague, almost a Senior Status partner, who has suffered the worst fate any man could suffer. I say let us use all the charity we can, and then look to the business end. We may lose in the long run. I can see it in the cards, but I think we have to make a bold step to support one of our own in any manner that we can."

Bud interjected, "We have already advanced him ten thousand dollars, I believe?" He looked at Tom Stilwell. Tom nodded in affirmance.

"Let's see." Said John Post, "We gave him, or advanced him ten grand. He lost all his money, his kids, his house. How long will it take him to arrange with the insurance companies to get reimbursement? With his brokerage money uninsured, even if he is successful in getting the money back from them, it won't be for at least a year. We all know the legal process, how slow it is. And the money from the burning of his house. Well, that's down the drain also. Whenever an insurance company can find a way to wiggle out of a claim, they will. We all know that. Joe won't get any money from them for quite some time, if at all." John hesitated, looked at each partner with a casual, but determined, penetrating glance.

"I say we determine an amount of money to give to Joe B outright. We can't count on getting it back, but we have to do it. The degree to which this man has suffered and will suffer; well, I have never seen the equal. Let us dig into our hearts and our pocketbooks and do something for which we will get nothing in return. And who knows, maybe we will get something in return. Maybe he will turn out to be the best employee we ever had. He certainly needs the favor of God at this time."

They all knew he was right. They felt it deeply. Even Bud Beck, the skinflint of the partners, felt it.

"I am not saying let him go," interjected Bud, "but there is no reason to continue to promote him to senior status until we see how he continues to perform. We always wait several weeks after our decision to see how the employee handles the idea. In this case, we have no idea." Bud spoke to Hank. "You did tell him about the Senior Status, didn't you, Hank?"

"Yes."

"Then he is aware of it. But we don't get to watch him under that pressure. I say we hold off on the Senior Status until he can get back on track."

"Great," said John Post. "We can be one more trouble in this man's life. Lose his money, his children, his wife, his home, and now his job. That is really a piece of shit, Bud. Really! A piece of shit."

Bud eyed John, leaned back on his chair, narrowed his eyes to slits. He took umbrage at the comment, but didn't show his anger. He said: "You misunderstood me, John. I'm not saying kick him out. I'm saying put things on hold with respect to Senior Status. What does Senior Status put out of our pocket? About forty grand a year? Do you think he will do

Senior Status work? No way. Why waste the forty grand? You talk about charity. I would rather give him the forty grand as charity. Here, Joe, take it from our hearts. But for the business decision on a business basis, let's keep the Senior Status on hold. I don't think we should promote someone who is not going to be able to do the work. He won't be able to do the work. You want to give him some money, fine, do it. I'm against that also, but that is a different issue. I just don't think we should hide it under the carpet and promote him, then he gets the extra money even though he is not doing the work. It's not fair to the other attorneys."

"Forty grand," said Anthony. "I would go along with that. Give him forty grand, now, for no reason. I like that." He looked slowly at each of the partners. "And..." He drawled, "And, if we are going to give a big chunk of money as charity, which probably exceeds our annual charity budget by ten thousand dollars, it gives us good reason to diminish our other charitable gifts for the year."

The corners of Bud Beck's mouth turned up slightly.

The room was silent for a moment. Hank finally spoke up.

"Bud's right, and so is Tony. But I would like to do a little more. I, also, don't think Joe will be effective as an attorney for at least six months, maybe more. But he is a good attorney. He works hard. We have quite an investment in him and I have a feeling that investment will turn out in the long run. Will we take a hit? Yes, we will, to some degree. But in the long run we can get it back. I say let us give him the forty grand, forgive the ten grand we already gave him, and loan him another thirty thousand dollars."

The partners all raised their eyes at the figure.

"We already gave him ten," said Bud.

"How about ten each, take away the ten, fifty more," said Hank. They all looked at him. Hank continued: "Ten each, gentlemen. It's not too much. He was going on Senior Status, that is at least an extra forty grand per year. We would have contributed that anyway. So I say, let us dig in, give from the partnership fifty thousand dollars with no expectation of repayment. Let Joe get back on the track for his life, if he can. He will know whether he can or can't. I personally will kick in some more on top of that. He is my protege. I want to do it." Hank thought, in this way he could funnel Joe's money back to him, just add it to the partnership money, Joe will think it is partnership money, he will get it back, no one will be the wiser. Holderman-Plank may still get hit legally, but they deserve it if they are going to be so loosey-goosey with other people's money.

"What say you?" asked Hank, looking at the partners and pointing with his index finger at Tom.

"Fifty thousand dollars and the loan on top?" queried Anthony.

"He will be required to pay the thirty thousand back with interest over time starting one year after it is loaned to him. The figure ties in with what was stolen from him at the brokerage. This at least puts him back in the same position as before the theft." Hank hesitated a second. "The same financial position, at least. And, I think Bud is right. Put Senior Status on hold. We can hardly hold a cocktail party for someone who just lost all his children—under the present circumstances. Let us just not make the announcement. See how he produces. If he produces, we can just make the announcement. If he doesn't, well, I don't know what will happen then. That is something we can argue over at a later time. But here you have a guy who is at the bottom of the rung on the ladder of life, not even on a rung, he is sitting on the ground after a big fall off the ladder, stunned. He must be going through hell. I cannot imagine the pain he is suffering. Fifty thousand is a lot of money. It's a write off for us, and will help Joe, I hope." Hank looked at the members.

"Gentlemen?" he asked.

John Post gave a thumbs up. Anthony did the same. Bud Beck gave a thumbs down. Paul Davis and Tom Stilwell gave a thumbs up.

"Well, that is that. I thank you, gentlemen." Said Hank. "Now we will see if he will accept it."

Hank had more than seventy thousand dollars in his desk drawer; money that was Joe B's. Money which Hank did not know how to deliver to Joe B. He could not just go up to Joe B and say: here's the seventy thousand my friend stole, he gave it to me to give back to you. Sam's involvement with the theft of the money troubled Hank. His own friend had started the ball of misery rolling for Joe B; and, also, for Hank. Now he questioned the "friend" aspect. Joe B didn't deserve this treatment. He didn't deserve to have his children killed. He didn't deserve to have his house burned. The fire marshall had determined it to be arson; they were looking for someone to indict.

Hank thought of the various ways to get the money to Joe. He could mail it. He could give it personally to Joe—that might be awkward. How was he going to explain his possession of it? He could act like it was a loan or a gift to Joe. Maybe he needed an intermediary. He would give Father Bill a call and discuss the problem with him. He could talk to the Bishop and have the Bishop give it to Joe. That might be a little difficult. The Bishop may want him to do some penance that would involve disclosing Sam's involvement. He might want Hank to disclose to the police Sam's involvement. That would not do. He couldn't expose himself to an investigation about Joe's predicament. It would not do any good for him, for Joe, or for anyone. But then, he did not have to tell anyone of his involvement, only that charity was to be bestowed on Joe B and would the Bishop help effect that.

His mind reeled at the thought that for a two dollar bet his friend Sam had stolen money from the brokerage house. What did it prove? Joe maintained his faith. The loss of some money wasn't going to affect Joe, even if it was his life's savings. Why, really, did Sam do it? He had always pushed the two dollar bets to the limit. Like the time he bet he could lay between the railroad track while the train went over him. A silly two dollar bet. Hank was physically sick as the train rolled over Sam hugging the gravel between the tracks. Sam won the bet. He pushed it to the extreme. And he'd done it here again.

But the loss of Joe's kids was something else. Children are what we live for. They make the world go around. They are the reason for being here on this earth. They are the only real pleasure in this world. What would the loss of children do to Joe? Would it affect his faith? But that wasn't part of the bet. The bet was only on the money aspect.

A feeling, a doubt, what was it about the kids that such a thought kept coming back to Hank—a thought of Sam. Hank thought it would certainly affect his own faith. How could you believe in anything after such a terrible thing? How could you maintain your belief in a loving God in the face of the loss of money, property, family? The power of the story of Job overwhelmed him. The story of a man who lost everything but failed to curse his God, a man who maintained his faith through it all.

But the angst under which Hank suffered was his own involvement. He did, in fact, participate in a bet for two dollars. A bet that started this evil in progress.

CHAPTER TWENTY SIX

▼

LUNCH WITH FATHER BILL

Hank phoned Father Bill to meet for lunch. Father Bill expressed a desire for Chinese food, but Hank's stomach felt nauseated immediately; he was not interested in going to a Chinese restaurant. Instead, he suggested a diner that served American style foods. Father Bill agreed to meet at noon.

Hank arrived moments before Father Bill. They waited making small talk for several minutes before they were seated. The table tops were a grey colored formica with chrome trim on the edges, Fifties style. Paper napkins, salt, pepper, mustard and ketchup were crowded together at the center of the table. The hostess handed to each a laminated menu of sandwiches printed on both sides.

Hank and Father Bill exchanged pleasantries, studied the menus, decided what to order, until the waitress took their order. Hank ordered a Reuben Sandwich, Father Bill, a Provolone Hoagie. The waitress left.

"So how is Joe doing?" asked Hank.

"As well as can be expected. He is a strong man. He just had another setback. The insurance company for his house won't cover the fire loss.

They say the premium wasn't paid. Apparently, after the money was stolen at the brokerage, neither Marsha nor Joe attended to the bills. It just so happened, coincidentally, that the insurance premium was due then. They sent a cancellation notice and Marsha never even opened it. So they have no insurance coverage. They have nothing."

Hank expressed no surprise. "I heard. They had no insurance coverage for the loss at the brokerage also. You wonder what good insurance is if it never covers anything?"

"You don't have it when you need it, and you have it when you don't need it," said Father Bill. "It's just like life."

"How about Marsha?" asked Hank.

"She's about the same. She has been sedated since the funeral. More like a vegetable than a human being. They are slowly taking her off the medication. It was quite a blow to her. Who can blame her? Joe, on the other hand, is a very strong individual. He has maintained his demeanor. He accepts his fate. He prays to God. He has been going to church every day, sometimes twice a day, just praying. He jogs long distances every day, just to get rid of the pent up anger.

"He is at a loss as to what to do. He lost everything. I think he had several thousand in the bank, but Marsha's treatment is taking care of that. I hope there is insurance coverage for that?" he looked at Hank inquiringly.

"There better be. We have an awfully good plan at work. There might be some co-pay, but it should cover Marsha's treatment." Hank hesitated, he turned a fork over and over.

"As you know, he is back to work. Somewhat desultory at the job, though. It's a concern to some of my partners," Hank said.

"Why I wanted to meet with you, was that the firm has decided to make a donation for Joe, but we didn't exactly know how to give it to him. I was afraid that if I gave it to him, he would feel obligated to the firm and that might cause some concern down the road. I thought maybe you could act as intermediary and give it to him anonymously. What do you think?"

"I don't know," Father Bill said. He inwardly smiled. It was about time someone at the firm thought about charity for Joe. "I think Joe might feel worse if he had to take charity from someone. He might think he was an object of pity."

"He is," interjected Hank.

"He is, but he isn't. He has maintained his faith in God and that has kept him strong, very strong. If someone, like you or me, who are his friends, gave him money, he might feel very awkward about it." Father Bill thought for a few seconds. "It might be better from a third party, not too closely related to him. How much are you talking about?"

"One hundred thousand dollars and an extra thirty thousand dollar loan from the firm." Hank recalculated, fifty from the firm, fifty of Joe's own money back, and twenty some in reserve for Joe. Too bad the Interfaith Foundation didn't give straight charity to people, it would have been a good conduit for delivery of the money. But they were more concerned with religion as a matter of saving souls rather than the individual souls themselves.

"Holy mackerel!" exclaimed Father Bill. "That is a lot of money."

"Holy mackerel?" queried Hank, raising his eyebrows with a slight smile.

"It is our way of swearing, which is what we don't do. I know, you think it's something Batman and Robin would say, and it is, but it fits for me." He chuckled.

"That is a lot of money, and Joe could sure use it. Your firm is going to just give it to him anonymously?"

"Yes. In fact, we don't want him to know where it came from. We want him to get it, use it, and feel no obligation for it. He will be a better lawyer if he doesn't feel the obligation of a large loan hanging over his head. The thirty thousand dollar loan can be made at a later time so as not to commingle the funds." He paused, "At least that is what I think."

"Holy mackerel." They both laughed.

Hank suggested, "How about the Bishop?"

"He could do it." Father Bill played with the salt shaker. "I think you know him, don't you?"

"I do know him. Do you think the Bishop would meet with Joe?"

"If you and I ask him to, he would. You're the attorney for the diocese, and I'm just supporting you. I think he would do it. He could meet with Joe. It might help Joe in his faith also. He is sorely tested at this time. I am amazed that he has maintained his faith. He just keeps plugging on. Not a bad word to anyone about anyone. The name of God is still reverent on his lips. It is truly amazing."

"The Bishop. I like that idea. I will call him and you call him."

CHAPTER TWENTY SEVEN

▼

DIANE'S VIEW

Joe visited Marsha daily at the Psychiatric Institution. On this particular day when Joe arrived, Marsha's mother was already there. She had been there almost as much as Joe. Her initial hostility toward Joe had abated somewhat, at least on the surface. Joe hugged Diane when he saw her. He then gave Marsha, lying in bed, a hug, but the hug was not returned. Marsha had the heavily drugged vacant look. Her mother combed her hair as best she could, but it looked bedraggled. Joe took her hand and held it. He stood at the bed. Joe suggested Diane sit down.

Diane had always been supportive of Joe and Marsha. She loved her grandchildren. Diane, whose husband had passed away two years previously, found herself reliving her youth. She began to travel with a senior's group. At the time of the children's accident, she was on a photographic safari in Kenya, Africa and was barely able to be contacted. She had rushed home in time for the funeral, only to be met by a family, or what was left of it, in complete misery.

Diane wanted to say something to Joe. She squirmed and fidgeted, had an expectant look as if she was about to say something, but was afraid to say it. She had saved and stored up her anger for the past five weeks.

She blurted, "Who has it in for you?"

"I'm sorry, Diane, I wasn't listening."

"Who has it in for you?"

"What do you mean?" Joe asked, puzzled.

"It's obvious, isn't it. Somebody has it in for you. One of your clients, maybe. Or someone you sued. Someone has it in for you. These things just don't happen." She spoke with tight-lipped sternness. "You mean you haven't even thought of it?" A look of surprise mixed with anger crossed her face. "Isn't it clear to you that someone is intentionally doing this to you?"

"No, it isn't clear," Joe studied Diane for several seconds, "I don't know anyone who would do such a thing. I have thought about it a lot. I don't have any enemies who would do these things. Not that I know of. The police asked me the same thing. I had no answers for them either." Joe looked puzzled at Diane's attitude and tone of voice. This was not like Diane, it was unusual to act this way, attacking.

"Well, it is clear to me. Either someone has it in for you, or you are wicked, and those that sow wickedness, reap the same. You did something to bring this wrath upon you and my daughter. My daughter, whose only fault was to marry you. Here you are walking around, healthy, alive, and here is Marsha, almost dead. I curse the day you were born. I wish she never met you." Diane was twisting her hands and dabbing at her eyes with a handkerchief. Her frustrated anger needed an escape and she knew no one other than Joe at which to hurl it.

Joe, humble and discreet, awed by this vituperative attack on him by his mother-in-law, said: "I agree with you, Diane. I must have done something, but for the life of me, I don't know what it is. I wish that I had never been born. I wish that Marsha did not have to suffer like this. I wish I didn't have children if they had to die like they did. I wish the day was darkness." Joe was crying, all the while holding Marsha's hand. "I wish

God would tell me what I did so I could repent. I wish this evil would go away. I wish that God would not set himself against me in this way." The look of anguish on Joe's face was too much for Diane, she looked away.

"I wish God would grant me death and cut me off rather than suffer this misery. I wish I had strength to meet these perils. I wish I was a stone and not made of flesh."

Joe cried silently, tears streamed down his face. Diane cried, embarrassed, whimpering, then left without a word. Marsha lay comatose, having heard nothing, as if in a deep sleep, but awake, not caring, not knowing, totally unaware of her surroundings. Joe massaged her hand. And they stayed that way for a long long time.

Diane had waited a long time to talk to Joe, but it didn't go the way she had planned. As she walked to the elevator, sniffling, she felt helpless about Joe and Marsha. It seemed as if noone was doing anything to find the people who had done this to her daughter and grandchildren. And Joe, he just sits there like a rock. Doing nothing. Praying. What good was it? What did God do for Diane? What did God do for her grandchildren? Why didn't he do something? Anything other than just pray and be the meek, humble servant—some action.

Finally, he'd gone back to work, but there was no vigor in Joe. No desire, he just sits there when he is with Diane, holding her hand, talking to her softly, praying. Sometimes she would come in to see him stoking her cheek or hair. He wouldn't even be embarrassed. It wasn't right that Marsha and the children should be hurt, but that Joe goes unharmed. Diane wanted to hurt Joe, but he just took it as if he deserved it. There was no fight. There is no fight to Joe, none whatever. A real husband would be looking everywhere for the killer of his children, the arsonist of his house and the thief of his money, but not Joe. No, not Joe.

Diane had tried to be supportive. She assisted Joe at all times with Marsha. Marsha made progress, but it was slow. Diane wasn't patient enough, Joe was. Joe never had a bad word for anyone. When Marsha was uncomfortable, Diane insisted on help from the staff. Not Joe, he did it himself, or politely asked for help when they had time. It drove Diane to madness. Why wouldn't he react to this madness itself. Do something, Joe, just-please-do something.

CHAPTER TWENTY EIGHT

▼

HANK CONFERS WITH HIS EXCELLENCY

Hank arranged to meet the Bishop at ten o'clock. He was edgy and nervous, because he was going to have to tell several untruths to the Bishop, God's representative on earth. Hank contemplated a long time on his approach to the Bishop. He wanted to get the money to Joe B without his direct involvement, without compromising his status, leaving him untainted. But he was tainted and it was his lifelong fried, Sam, who had commenced this fiasco. Why had he stolen the money? The thought that Sam was further involved than he let on kept springing into Hank's mind. Hank knew Sam could be terribly mean and he could be terribly nasty, but was he so mean and nasty to cause children to die? Evil? Hank repeatedly dismissed the thought when it arose. It was too horrible of a thought.

Hank figured he could pass the money to the Bishop to give to Joe. It could be done anonymously. The firm would have contributed their share and Hank would have returned the money to Joe that Sam had stolen. It would appear as if Hank was making a contribution on his own to aid Joe, but Hank would just have to deal with that. Better that Hank looked charitable than involved in causing harm to Joe. He couldn't let his involvement be known. How long would his firm continue to do the legal business of the diocese if the Bishop knew of his involvement for a two dollar bet? The Bishop might be understanding and might even forgive him. But in the long run, they would lose the diocesan business. Not even the Bishop could continue to put the church's legal affairs in the hands of someone who contributed so recklessly to another human being's tragic suffering. No, thought Hank, he couldn't disclose his involvement. He couldn't jeopardize the entire firm and their connections to the Catholic Diocese.

Hank's conscience dictated he should tell the Bishop all. But he couldn't. Hank was weak, but if he could just make things right by just getting the money back to Joe so Joe could start to rebuild his life. Then, maybe some relief to his mental agony. How did one rebuild one's life when all of one's children are killed? Hank was wretched thinking of the whole situation, of his personal problem attempting to absolve his blame. He couldn't tell anyone, not even his wife. She would only say, "I told you so." Where was he?

He could pray to God, directly, but that, in his mind, was all he could do. And he had been doing it, but he felt as if it didn't do him any good. The guilt was still there, sitting over his every thought. Every act he performed during the day had a tinge of guilt. The thought of his involvement never left him. He thought of going to an adjoining parish for confession, or to an adjoining city, to some priest with whom he had no connection, but Hank knew, the penance to be given would or should involve disclosure of his involvement. And disclosure would destroy the law firm, would destroy his life as he knew it. There were too many people affected by any decision he made. Hank knew enough priests to know that something this significant may eventually get to the bishop regardless of the privilege accorded to the confessional. The priests were professionals, but information leaked. He didn't trust any priest that much.

If the firm lost the business of the Diocese, what then? Even Joe would not have a job then. And, it did center around Joe. Oh, Joe, all for a two dollar bet.

Opulent was the word to describe the Bishop's office. Leather chairs of a deep rich green, high backed, facing the highly polished black walnut desk of huge proportions. Few items lay on the desk allowing His Excellency to devote his full attention to the person sitting across from him. A gilt frame inlayed with exotic colorful veneers containing a picture of the Pope hung on one wall. A huge fictionalized photo of Jesus Christ as a child speaking with the elders of the temple hung behind the desk.

The secretary to His Excellency had shown Hank into the office of the Bishop. Bishop Pietre immediately rose from his seat, came around the desk and shook hands with Hank. His practiced smile was both sincere and engaging.

"Hank, I haven't seen you around in quite some time. How are you? You look good."

"Thank you, your Excellency, I'm fine."

"Sit down, sit down." Hank was directed to the chairs by the outflung arm of the Bishop. Hank sat. The Bishop slipped into his heavy chair, folded his hands and said: "Well Hank, my secretary seemed to think it was something important. No one is claiming one of my priests is derelict again, are they?" The Bishop smiled a smile of hopeful negativity. He didn't want Hank to be here for a lawsuit concerning any of his priests, but having gone through the process once, and an ugly lawsuit it was, he hoped that by making a deprecatingly slight joke of it, that it would not be true.

"No, no, your Excellency. I am not here for anything legal, it is more of a personal nature. More of a charitable nature."

The Bishop slightly inclined his head, signifying to Hank that he was listening.

"You may have heard or read about Joe B, a young lawyer in our firm. Joe was recently put on senior status notification. It entails about a forty thousand dollar a year raise. The next step would be partner. He was on the move, Your Excellency. Shortly thereafter, he lost all of his savings by a theft at Holderman-Plank, which was uninsured. Then, several days later all of his children and their babysitter were killed in a car accident. Then his house burned down during the funeral. His wife is presently in a mental hospital, in very bad shape, so I hear. Joe is staying with Father Bill of St. Mary's, trying to weather the storm." Hank paused, The Bishop intervened.

"Yes, I have read about it in the newspapers. They are calling him a modern day Job. And it sounds like he is, at least by the disasters that have been visited upon him. I have prayed for him, myself. I wonder, is there a question of his faith?" The Bishop made a sign of the cross, closed his eyes and appeared to make a small prayer. Hank waited for the Bishop to finish his private conversation.

"So, what about our modern day Job?"

"Well, Your Excellency, on top of it all, because of the theft at the brokerage, he hadn't paid his homeowners premium, so he didn't have insurance on the house either. He does have hospitalization, but it doesn't cover everything. A big copay. You know insurance companies.

"The firm has gathered some money together that we want to give to him. We have decided that we can't give it to him directly, or at least we don't want to because we think it will make him feel overly obliged to the firm, which we really don't want. We don't know what kind of employee he will make in the future, and we don't want to saddle him with the obligation that he has to continue working for us, forever. But we do recognize his situation, and we want to put some money in his pocket. We just don't want him to know it is from us or who it is from. Maybe if he survives this tragedy and turns out able to become a productive member of our firm, we might tell him some day. But we don't think it is advantageous at this time to put the burden on him."

"So what can I do for you, or for Joe B?"

"I want, or Father Bill and I want...We want that...maybe you can give it to him. Father Bill thinks that it might help Joe get through this thing if he got money from the church itself. And we, Smith, Post and Trivisonno, don't want it to be known it came from us. It seemed like a logical solution."

"You say Father Bill thinks there might be a problem with Joe getting through this?" The Bishop said it quietly, thinking.

"Yes, he seemed to think that. It has got to be tough. I am surprised he hasn't snapped like his wife."

"Yes, I can see that." The Bishop said slowly. "His faith must be sorely tested by now. I am sure he is questioning all the tenets of the Catholic Church. Yes..." The Bishop was speaking to himself, as if Hank was not present.

"The papers seemed to say that the burning of his house was arson?"

"That is what is said, but no one knows who did it, or why!"

"How much money are you thinking of giving to him?"

Hank recalculated in his mind, fifty thousand from the firm, fifty thousand of the seventy thousand that Sam had stolen for a total of one hundred thousand dollars. Keep twenty thousand in reserve for a future donation to Joe. Hank couldn't just add the seventy thousand dollars to the firm contribution; it would look too suspicious, too coincidental.

"One hundred thousand dollars."

The Bishop raised his eyebrows. "That is a lot of money. Your firm is giving him one hundred thousand dollars?"

"The firm already gave ten thousand to Joe. We want to give another fifty thousand from the firm. I am putting in the additional fifty thousand," Hank lied. Hank felt the warm blush start at his spine and move upwards. He knew his entire face was turning red. He lied to the Bishop. There was no other way.

The Bishop studied Hank for seconds, it seemed like minutes. He watched the blush envelope Hank. Unusual for a man of Hank's age to blush. He's not confessing anything. Merely discussing a contribution. Why is he embarrassed? Why is he personally giving fifty thousand dollars? Who has fifty thousand dollars to give to anyone these days? The diocese needs contributions like that, regularly.

"That is quite a contribution. Excuse me for asking, but why are you contributing so much?"

"I feel I have to," lied Hank, again. He said no more, hoping that the answer would suffice. The less he said the better. Can't the Bishop just accept that he would want to do some charity himself?

"I see," mused the Bishop. "Are you perhaps feeling a little guilt with Joe's problems?"

"Call it what you will, your Excellency, Joe was my protégé. I deal with him every day. I have a great personal interest in his mental health. I just feel I have to do this. I have no real reason. Guilt? Why would I feel guilt? I just have to do this." The urgency in Hank's voice again made the Bishop look closely. The Bishop concentrated on Hank. Something there, he thought. What is it? Something is not ringing true. It doesn't sound right. But does it matter? There is something more involved than just charity from Hank and the firm. What is it? Do I really need to know it to help this poor man, this Job? No, I don't. I can take this money, give it to Joe with the church's sanction, and leave Hank to suffer whatever he is suffering by himself. Or I can also try to help Hank.

"Is there something that you would like to tell me, Hank?"

Hank looked taken aback. He knows, he thought, he knows. He sees right through me. What do I do now? Bluff? Too much at stake.

"No, no, there's nothing that I need to tell you. I am just asking for your help in a very difficult situation. Will you help us, your Excellency?"

Hank wasn't going to tell the Bishop. The Bishop knew Hank was hiding something, but that he wasn't going to get it out of Hank right now, maybe later.

"Of course I will, Hank. Was there ever a doubt about it? How do you think it should be handled…"

CHAPTER TWENTY-NINE

▼

ABIDING FAITH

Sam decided to see for himself if Joe had indeed maintained his faith. After all, a two dollar bet was on the line. It was the principle of the bet that counted. Sam knew Joe was staying at the rectory with the priest. Sam also knew that calling to make an appointment with Joe would be met with a negative response. Instead, he would go to the rectory and see if he could meet with Joe directly. Maybe offer him some help. It was only natural that a friend of Hank's would offer help at a time of terrible tragedy.

The rectory stood across the street from the church. It was a frame house, larger than necessary for two priests to live in, but it was available without building a new rectory. The rectory was well maintained. Vinyl sided, a light gray, with black shutters and white trim. The small yard was edged at the walk, and cypress wood chips had been spread evenly between the shrubs and flowers. Sam could smell the wafting pollen fragrance as he walked up the front walk. He pressed the doorbell and heard the chime sound inside. A squat middle-aged woman in pants too tight for her growing rear-end answered and asked if she could help him. He told her he was here to see Joe B, that he was an acquaintance of Hank Smith, at Joe's work, and he needed to meet with Joe. He gave the impression that he was connected to Joe's employer and that the nature of his business was in connection with that work. Sam was led into a small courtyard in the back of the house where Joe sat in a lounge chair with his eyes closed and his hands clasped behind his head. He appeared to be asleep.

Sam approached, sat on a wire chair, put his elbows on a glass topped table. Sam intentionally coughed, Joe opened his eyes, focused on Sam, sat up, looked around to see no one else was there, and asked: "Can I help you?"

Sam responded, "No, the real question is, can I help you? I'm Sam Hawkins. We met at Smith, Post and Trivisonno several weeks ago."

"Yes, I remember you. You're Hank's friend."

"Yes, I am," he said, decidedly, "I thought I'd come to see if I could offer you any assistance. You have my sincerest condolences. If I am intruding, I can leave. Just say the word, and I will go. But I wanted to speak with you. If I grieve you, please tell me."

"No, no, it's okay. I have to start talking to people sometime. Seems people are afraid to talk to me. But I'm having a hard time communicating lately."

"I can well imagine. Well, maybe I can't. I know you are going through a very difficult time. There is not much I can say or do to help you, I am sure." Sam ran his hands through his hair.

"No one can help me. I am beyond help. There is nothing anyone can do that will help. How does one restore five kids?" Joe gasped, it caught in his throat whenever he uttered it, he repressed a sob. "I'm in shock. I still cannot believe it."

"Makes one lose faith in God, doesn't it?" asked Sam, his head lowered, looking at Joe from a severe angle. This was the question Sam wanted answered. This he had to know.

"My soul is weary of my life. I leave my complaints upon myself. I ask God not to condemn me; show me where I am wrong. It is God alone who can oppress me, who can despise his own work, and who can take counsel of the devil." Joe spoke without moving. He spoke in a monotone, without apparent feeling, but the emotion was there, a deep abiding chasm full of feeling. Thoughts raced through him with grief.

Sam stared at him, incredulous.

"God made me, yet he destroys me?

"He made me clay; I wish he would make me into dust again.

"I am like a cup of milk curdled into cheese.

Sam began to bounce his right leg up and down, nervously twitching, involuntarily, his knee bobbing up and down rapidly.

"If I am a sinner, then I am marked; God doesn't want to seem to absolve me.

"If I am a wicked person, then woe unto me. But I think I am righteous, yet I cannot lift up my head. I am full of confusion. I am severely afflicted."

Sam put both hands on his face, rubbed upwards, then downwards as if he was washing it. He pressed his eyes hard with the tips of fingers.

"God is angry with me; he is making war against me and I don't know why.

"It would have been better if I had been stillborn.

"I ask that God cease what he is doing and let me alone, let me take comfort." It was a plea, unanswered. Joe stopped, then said nothing.

Sam had listened raptly. He stared at Joe. His leg bobbing continuously, he couldn't believe this man. Joe said not a bad word against God. He still adhered to his faith? After all he had gone through and he still sticks to his religion. What a stupid man, thought Sam. Or, something else. What is it with this man? Why does he maintain his faith? Even in the depths of his tragedy, he leans on and supports God. Does it help him? Is he the better for it? Does he think he is superior to the rest of us?

"They say that God exacts less of us than our iniquity deserves." Sam said. "But knowing you as I have for such a short time, I cannot understand it. I am impressed that you have maintained you faith in God after all this. Maybe I am naive, but how can this be?" Get right to the heart of the matter. Find out what makes this man tick?

Sam's knee increased in speed, rapidly.

"The Lord made all. How can we dispute that? He is the be all and the end all. He made the earth, the animals, the fishes of the sea. It is his hand that is the soul of every living thing and the breath of all mankind."

Sam wanted to put his finger down his throat and gag. This was too much. Did this guy really believe this shit?

"With him is strength and wisdom; both the deceived and the deceiver are his.

"Should I speak wickedly of God?

"Should I mock him?

"Though he may kill me, yet I put my lfe in his hands."

Sam saw his knee bobbing, stopped it immediately. He put his hands in a praying position, fingertips at the tip of his nose pressed against his lips. Waiting, listening.

"He shall be my salvation; a hypocrite cannot come before him.

"But tell me my sins, I will confess; just tell me.

"If he calls, I will answer him. Yes, I still have faith in my God. He made me and he can unmake me.

"I have faith, but I have no hope."

Here it is, thought Sam. No hope, maybe he will realize no faith also. Now is the time.

"God has broken me. I am as good as a dead man.

"Everyone looks at me and says I did wrong, that is why God has delivered me to the ungodly.

"He has thrown darts at me till I have collapsed.

"I am cried out. My face is foul with weeping. I am ready to see death.

"And it is not for any injustice that I have done, I know my prayer is pure. My witness is in heaven and my record is known to him."

How long can this go on, thought Sam. The man quotes the Bible? Who talks like this? Give it up, man!

"My friends scorn me, but I pour out tears to God. People say they want to help, but they look at me as if I had done something wrong. It was wrong for me to survive and my family be wasted.

"But it is said that the righteous shall hold onto his way and that he that hath clean hands shall be stronger and stronger. "Where is my hope, it is gone. But my faith, it is not gone."

Joe was silent, his eyes closed. Sam said nothing, thankful for the silence, rose from his seat, walked toward the house, looked back, frowning, and left.

Sam drove away. Strange man, that Joe. Frightening. The man must be insane. I have my faith, but I have no hope…what nonsense.

CHAPTER THIRTY

▼

THE HOLY PALATE

Father Bill entered the patio where Joe stared at the sky.

"Good afternoon, Joe."

"Morning, Bill," answered Joe, glancing at his watch.

Bill smiled. It was eleven forty-five, still morning.

"We got an invite here. A command performance. I think it is time you went out for dinner. This is one you can't refuse this time."

"Hmm," mused Joe. Father Bill handed him the invitation. The envelope was embossed with the seal of the Diocese of Cleveland with red, green and black. Joe opened it.

"The Bishop wants both of us for dinner? Why? What's going on?"

"I don't know, but this is one invitation you cannot refuse. You understand that, don't you?"

"Yes, of course, of course. But why? Is this something you cooked up Father Bill?"

"Don't look at me," Father Bill raised his palms apologetically, "I had nothing to do with it. What day is it for?"

"Friday at 6:00."

"Good, we're open that day. I'll RSVP."

When they arrived at the Bishop's residence, a butler answered the door. Very formal. Father Bill wore a black suit that contrasted with the bleached white clerical collar. Joe dressed in a dark blue suit, yellow shirt, and a tie that coordinated the two colors appropriately, not quite a paisley pattern, but a mixed combination of blue and yellow and gray. They were shown into the library. The dark wooden walls contained multiple volumes of books on shelves behind glass doors. The butler asked for their drink order. Not a request if they wanted a drink, but an assumption that a drink was called for and he was obligated to get it. Father Bill ordered a scotch and soda. Joe hesitated. The butler suggested a small glass of an excellent pinot noir that the Bishop had ordered opened. Joe acquiesced.

The drinks were served promptly. Joe and Father Bill wandered around the room looking at the objects d'art. A statute, in miniature, of David; a replica of a Michelangelo at the Vatican. Joe stroked the smoothness of the marble. He studied the intricacies of a wooden carving, painted vibrant colors, of a Knight of the Crusaders. A beautiful red cross painted on his breast plate. A thought, fleeting, passed through Joe's mind of the thousands of crusaders who marched to the Holy Land to kill for God and be killed for God. Joe moved on. He opened the door to one of the bookshelves. It appeared to be a complete set of Charles Dickens novels: Barnaby Rudge, that was one Joe didn't know; Martin Chuzzlewit, didn't know that one either. Actually, Joe thought, he had only read Bleak House, none of the others. He wondered if anyone in this place had read all of them. Right next to Dickens was a set of Agatha Christie novels. Must have been eighty of them. Mystery novels with all of the religious artwork surrounding the room, interesting mixture.

The Bishop entered at that moment, saw Joe looking at his books, smiled, and said: "You're wondering why Agatha Christie, perhaps?"

Joe turned at the sound of his voice. "Yes, that is exactly what I was thinking."

The Bishop extended his hand. "I am Bishop Pietre, you may call me Bob for the evening, if that is okay? How do you do, Joe?"

"As well as can be expected," he faltered, then said, "Bob."

"That's good, that's good. Bob it is. The less formal we are, the better we will get along here." He then looked at the books. "I like Agatha Christie. Her novels so explain the fine details of English life. Miss Marple, her principal protagonist, is a fuddy duddy with amazing powers of reason. I minored in English Literature in college, so I collect sets of English authors. One of my small passions. It keeps me occupied when I am not so busy."

Father Bill came over to listen to the conversation. The Bishop extended his hand to Father Bill. "Bill, it is good to see you. Good of you to come. How is the scotch? I selected the bottle personally in Edinborough. It is more than one hundred years old. Do you like it?"

"Oh yes," said Father Bill. "A hundred years. Maybe we better shift to the more modern brand. You don't want to waste a good scotch on me."

"Nonsense. It is you God told me to get it for. I am sure I heard him say it when I was looking at the bottles," he joked. "Actually, it was a gift from the Bishop of Edinborough. He let me select a bottle from the cellar in the Cathedral. It's very rare, enjoy it. I don't drink scotch, so it's wasted on me. I'm sure it won't be wasted on you."

The Bishop looked around, spotted the butler, the butler nodded, signifying dinner was ready.

"Gentlemen, let us go into dinner." He walked toward the door, Joe and Father Bill followed.

Dinner was a pleasant affair. Blue point oysters on the half shell served as an appetizer. The main meal, a chicken breast with a mushroom sauce mingled with Swiss cheese and a hint of pepper. On the side were peas, squash fried in butter, and applesauce. The salad was shredded lettuce mixed with mandarin orange slices, coconut shavings, raisins, and a creamy Italian dressing. Dessert was a tray of delicately cut cakes with a dish of velvety vanilla ice cream. Not ostentatious, but sumptuous enough to be made aware that the diocese has money.

But the surroundings were classic. The chandelier hanging over the dining room table had five hundred pieces of crystal hanging in different shapes spreading the light from twenty bulbs throughout the room to a pleasant effect. The dark cherry table shined to a glossy immaculate finish, matching the credenzas. Statues of Joseph, Jonah exiting the whale, and Abraham in the process of placing his son on the altar surrounded the room. Exquisite pieces in marble and stone. The walls held paintings of scenes of Christ's life, Simon the Cyrenian helping Jesus with the cross, addressing a nervous Peter at the edge of the water, and a large copy of the El Greco crucifixion hanging in the Cleveland Museum of Art signifying the darkest hour of Christianity as also being its moment of greatest hope.

The Bishop kept the conversation light. There was no talk of Joe's troubles. Joe's troubles, for a very short while, disappeared. Joe listened closely to the Bishop. He spoke of his worldly travels, light anecdotes of humorous things that had happened to him in various areas. When a lapse in conversation appeared to occur, the Bishop was there with the right thing to say. He inquired of Father Bill's running regimen. It appeared he kept up on all of the sports information in almost every field. If there was a question of any statistic about the Cleveland Indians, then the bishop, as an avid fan, had it on the tip of his tongue.

After the last dish was removed from the table, the Bishop insisted that they each have an after dinner drink and move into the library to enjoy it. The drinks were served in the library. Joe received a small glass of Irish

Mist Liqueur, Father Bill, a Drambuie, and the Bishop, a glass of iced
wine from Inskillin, Canada.

"Joe," the Bishop began, "It has come to my attention about all this
trouble you have had in the very recent past." He waved his right hand in
front of his face, two fingers pointed skyward, in a small circular motion.
"I want you to know that all of our hearts and prayers are with you, especially mine. I give you my sincerest condolences. Father Bill has kept me
apprised of your difficulties. The load is overwhelming. I don't have an
answer from God as to why he has done this to you. He works in mysterious ways. He has a purpose for everything he does, sometimes it takes
years to figure out the purpose, sometimes we never figure it out, but he
has his reasons."

Father Bill sipped his drambuie, Joe listened.

"There are some things that only God can console and fix. But there
are some things that we mere mortals here on earth can attempt to fix. I
know that you have lost a lot of money as a result of a burglary at your
investor's office; I know that your home has burned down and that there
was no insurance coverage for it." The Bishop paused for several moments
to asess the impact of what he was saying.

"This diocese has people in it who are filled with good deeds. There are
people who will go out of their way to help people in need. Sometimes the
people in need will not accept this assistance. That is understandable.
Lamentable, but understandable. I have been approached by some people
of great goodness and they have selected you as the person they wish to be
the object of their goodness."

Joe began to raise his open palms off the table.

"No, no, Joe, don't protest, just listen. Please?" The Bishop also had put
the palms of his hands up to counter the hand and facial expressions of Joe
that objected to being a charity case. "These people know the situation
you are in. They know the newspapers are calling you the modern day Job.
But even they don't know the extent to which your sufferings go.
Notwithstanding, Joe, they have come to me to act as an intermediary to

you. Yes, they thought that a third person was necessary as a go between. They do not want you to know who they are. They want it to be only a giving on their part. If you knew who they were, you might feel obligated to them in some manner. But this is an outpouring from their hearts, they want to do good. This makes them feel good, they are doing what Jesus had told them to do. And it also helps you. These people, they are good people, they are interested in you, they want you to survive and live. And, Joe, I approve of what they are doing and I think it is good for you also."

The Bishop halted for several seconds, appraising Joe's response. Joe, except for the one moment of objection, remained quiet. His face reflected no emotion. He was almost past any display of emotion. The Bishop read nothing in his features.

The Bishop continued: "As a result, Joe, I am authorized to give this envelope to you. It contains a check from the Diocese for one hundred thousand dollars." Joe's opened his eyes wide, brows arched—surprise and astonishment. He flushed pink. "It is for you to begin to repair your life, to get a start on a new home, to pay the doctors for attending to your wife. I won't take a rejection. That is not even an option. This is given to you with absolutely no strings attached. You are not obligated to me, or to the donors, who you do not know, in any manner whatsoever. And please, just accept it; say nothing. And we will not have to discuss it again. Okay, Joe?"

Joe's mind was roiling. Who would give him one hundred thousand dollars? That was more money than he had saved up in all his years of working. It would sure help him get started again. It would make up for the no insurance on the home problem. Yes, of course he would take it. He had to take it. He needed it badly. And the donors don't want to be known. Yes, he would take it without any questions. A start.

Joe finally responded after the longest delay. "All I can say is thank you."

CHAPTER THIRTY-ONE

▼

SAM AGAIN VISITS HANK

Sam had called earlier to make sure Hank was available; he knew Hank was a busy man. Sam entered Hank's large office with its grand view of the City of Cleveland. They shook hands, greeted each other. Hank expessed less welcome than on Sam's first visit after ten years.

"Greetings, Sam," Hank said stiffly. "What are you doing with yourself these days?"

"Oh, you know me, I go to and fro in the earth and am walking up and down on it. I go here and there. I have no anchor," Sam grinned. He sat on one of the seats in front of Hank's desk. Hank looked out the window. Hank then went around the desk, closed the door after glancing down the hallway, and sat at his own desk, a strained look on his face.

"This whole thing with Joe bugs me, you know!"

"I take it you are referring to the bonds?" Sam said lightly.

"The bonds, the whole thing. Look what has happened to the poor guy. How could you do it to him?"

"It's only money," Sam spoke flippantly, looking at one of Hank's wall-hangings as if the converstion were a bore. "What is money? Money is a test in this life. Those with it are tested on their largesse. Those without it are tested on their honesty. He got the money back, didn't he?"

"I arranged for him to get the money back, yes. No thanks to you. But there seems to be more here than just the money, Sam. What is it?"

"I'm not sure what you mean. We had a bet. You won the bet. I owe you two dollars. The man still has his faith. I am impressed," he paused. "By the way, did I tell you I went to visit him the other day and talked to him."

"What!" cried Hank, sharply.

"Yes, I went to visit him, to see if he has really maintained his faith. He has no hope, but faith, he has. I really am impressed." He won't give it up, thought Hank. He persists in the two dollar bet. Why?

"Joe B is an impressive man," Hank said and nodded his head in agreement, but resignedly. "He holds his faith. Everything that was done to him, and he still holds his faith. But, I let you do it, Sam. It should never have happened, Sam. I should have stopped the bet."

"Like stopping a freight train maybe," said Sam, "Hank, our part in this is small in comparison to what happened to him. We only dealt with the money part. Not the rest of it. Your God did this to him. We merely had a test, to see if he would keep his faith. You have won," Sam grinned, Abut I don't really believe it. All that a man has, he will give for his life, but if his own life was touched, he would curse God to no end. You notice that he has not been touched. Nothing has happened to him. It is all around him, his wife, his money, his house, his kids, but not to him. Why? Is his God protecting him? Is this the foundation for his faith? So long as he is not touched, he will maintain his faith? Joe is an impressive man, but his God really hasn't put him to the ultimate test of faith, has he?"

"Are you talking about what I think you are talking about?" said Hank. "Are you really?" he paused. "Don't even think about it Sam. I want no part in what you are even thinking."

"Think about it for a second, Hank. Just as a matter of religious academia. The world has fallen apart around the guy, but as long as he is not physically hit, he can maintain his faith. But if he is struck, then no way would he maintain it," the glint in Sam's eyes shone as he spoke.

Hank sat at his desk, breathed deeply, and said, "Sam, you and I have been friends for a long time. We have been through some rough times together. Nine Mile Creek, the abortion, and the Cask come to mind too readily. I want no part in whatever scheme you have for Joe B. It's over. You have started an action that made this guy's life a living hell. No more, you hear me." Hank never raised his voice, his words trailed into a whispered hiss before he was finished.

Hank seethed. Sam laughed.

"Hank, what do you take me for? Of course it is done. It's been done. Your God did it. I am not planning anything, but you have to admit that I am right. A guy can't even discuss something hypothetically around here. Isn't this the bastion of free thought and ideas?" Sam waved his arm at the law office.

"Yeah, sure, admit you're right." Hank shook his head slowly. "Ok. You're right. Does that make you feel better? You ruin a guy's life just so you can hear me say you are right?" Hank hesitated, "I can say you're right, but you are so far wrong it is pathetic. Our initial bet was pathetic. Say what you want, but leave the man alone." Again Hank hesitated, then asked. "Why does this discussion make me think you might be more involved than you profess? Did you have anything at all to do with the death of his kids?" Hank stared at Sam intently.

"Absolutely not, Hank. Scout's Honor," he raised the two finger scout salute. A What do you think I am?"

"I am beginning to wonder, Sam."

Sam laughed loudly and stood to leave.

"Hank, I am getting ready to leave on a trip again. It looks like my old man is going to live for a very long time, so he doesn't need me around. All we do is argue anyway."

"Where to this time?" asked Hank, relieved.

"To Chile. I am curious about the Andes. I want to see them firsthand. There are several indigenous peoples there that I want to investigate. But I will be back. When I come back, we'll settle up with our bet. I think the guy will curse his God before I come back. You just wait and see."

"Drop it, Sam." Hank said.

"There is nothing to drop, Hank. I'm done. But we will at least let time tell us the answer. I will see you in several months, Okay."

"Yeah, sure, have a nice trip."

They shook hands, Sam left whistling down the hallway. Hank went back to his office desk and vacantly stared out the window. Angry, frustrated, and wondering about Sam's involvement and his own involvement in Joe's life, he was unable to concentrate on any legal work.

CHAPTER THIRTY-TWO

▼

JOE AND MARSHA AT THE HOSPITAL

Joe daily visited Marsha at the hospital. The nurses treated him distantly as if they were afraid of him. His plight was something they treated as a contagious disease.

Marsha was moved to a more open environment. She could walk around her twenty room section. No longer so heavily sedated, she recognized people and slowly began to talk again. When Joe arrived this day, she was sitting in a lounge chair watching TV with six other patients. She stood when Joe arrived. "Hello, Marsha," he said, gave her a kiss on the cheek and a light hug which she did not return.

"Hello, Joe," she responded dully. They walked up and down the halls of the section. Marsha's mother had not yet visited today, Marsha's hair was unkempt, her eyes flat and vacant.

Joe made small talk, asked how she was, what they had her doing on the ward. She explained that she had to talk to the psychiatrist once a day for half an hour. That she couldn't get any medication or drugs until after she had talked to her every day. That the psychiatrist was trying to convince her that life must go on, that this is a serious setback, but that life will go on. She tried to get her to focus on anything other than her loss of her children and her home. He had talked about the Holocaust and the loss of families of generations, about the recent killings in Rwanda, the Khmer Rouge killings and that, although her loss is great, it was no greater than the tragedies these others have gone through. But Marsha couldn't accept the rationale. Her loss was personal. Those other things happened elsewhere, to other people, and were not her immediate problem. She was not faced with the other problems of the world. She was faced with the prospect of how to go on living without her children, her beautiful children.

She began to reminisce about Edward, how cute he was, the things he did. Joe let her talk. He knew she saw the psychiatrist daily. He was kept informed on her care from the psychiatrist's point of view. The Psychiatrist told him to let her talk as much as she can. She has to get it out of her system. He prompted her with un-huh's, and she continued to talk. Her progress was slow, but steady. She needed something to focus on, to be interested in. Something to take her mind off her own loss. It would take time.

They walked the corridors for almost two hours. Joe explained the anonymous gift of one hundred thousand dollars, that he had deposited it in their account. Marsha, even in the unthinking state that she was, said: "Joe, it will all have to go for this hospital expense."

"No, no," said Joe. "I gave the hospitalization information to the administrative office at the hospital. They submit our bills directly to the insurance company. I haven't read the policy yet, but I am sure the co-pay on it isn't much. But don't you worry your pretty little head about it. It at least tells me that all things in the world aren't bad, only 95% of them—that we can at least start something again, that we have some working capital."

Joe had avoided telling her about the lack of insurance on the loss of the home. He knew it would not help her state of mind to know that their own actions had caused them to lose the coverage on the home. He didn't need to add to her mental troubles. He avoided the issue. The thought of the co-pay for her institutionalization in this facility sent a shiver of worry through him. It was something he hadn't thought much about. Insurance. He was having a hard time dealing with it, something he tried not to think about and he succeeded.

Two losses already not covered, and now, a co-pay for a tremendous hospital bill, he was sure.

Joe told her about his going back to work. How uninteresting it was. How people seemed to be afraid of him, like he had a disease. How tired he was of sitting around the rectory drowning in self pity, only thinking on his loss, their loss, and that he needed to divert his mind. He would get an apartment for the time being. He couldn't continue to lean on Father Bill. He felt his time was running short. It was time to move on as best they could.

Marsha shook her head in agreement, or what looked like agreement. She was not fully capable of agreeing to anything yet. But, for Marsha, it was the furthest she had come in her treatment to be able to accept the fact that he had to move forward. They were inexorably bound, life dealt them a tragedy so severe they only had each other.

CHAPTER THIRTY-THREE

▼

HANK CONTEMPLATES THE OLD TESTAMENT

Hank was agitated after Sam left. Glancing at the Cleveland Plain Dealer, he read an editorial that discussed Joe B's plight. The editor complained that no one would speak with reporters about Joe B, not his employer, not the priest with whom Joe B was living, not the hospital personnel where his wife was institutionalized, no one. The article lamented the fact that people should know about the terrible things that happen to people and how they deal with them. It compared Joe B to Job in The Book of Job in the Bible. Everything seemed to be similar except for the visiting of boils to Joe B's person.

Hank sat in his office looking at nothing out the window. He took the Bible from his bookshelf. He had never opened it, it had sat on the bookshelf for fifteen years. Someone had given it as a gift. He opened the cover, the inscription showed it was from his parish priest, long gone. He opened to The Book of Job at the following passage:

Chap. 2,

3. And the Lord said unto Satan, Hast thou considered my servant Job, that there is none like him in the
earth, a perfect and an upright man, one that feareth
God, and escheweth evil? and still he holdeth fast his
integrity, although thou movedst me him, to destroy him
without cause.

4. And Satan answered the Lord, and said, Skin for
skin, yea, all that a man hath will he give for his life.

5. But put forth thine hand now, and touch his bone
and his flesh, and he will curse thee to thy face.

6. And the Lord said unto Satan, Behold he is in thine
hand; but save his life.

7. So went Satan forth from the presence of the Lord,
and smote Job with sore boils from the sole of his foot
unto his crown.

He read The Book of Job once, then twice.

"And the Lord said unto Satan, Whence comest thou? Then Satan
answered the Lord, and said, From going to and fro in the earth, and from
walking up and down in it."

Hank focused on the passage. An eerie feeling creeped along his spine.
The language used by Sam was identical! "From going to and fro in the
earth, and from walking up and down in it." It was the very same greeting
Sam used when he first saw him after a ten-year absence, and today, too.
The idea struck Hank instantly. His body reacted, his bladder applied
pressure and he leaked urine momentarily before he caught himself. A
moment of total lack of control. Hank spoke out loud slowly to himself,
"Is Sam Satan?"

Sam had acknowledged that Hank had already won the bet, that he
would pay him when he got back from Chile. Chile, why was he going

to Chile? Why wait until that time? No one ever paid the two dollar bet anyway.

But Hank had called off the bet. It was over. Hank was no longer involved. He told Sam it was over. Was Sam not letting it go? Sam expressly told him he had no involvement with the death of the children. The house burned the day of the funeral. Too coincidental. If Sam was Satan, wouldn't he lie to get whatever he wanted? Sam, Satan!

The issue of Faith. Hank reread The Book of Job. He had a difficult time understanding the arguments of the three friends of Job. He had an even more difficult time understanding the arguments of Job. It was as if the statements made a comparison, but didn't say anything.

> Chap 4.
> 11. The old lion perisheth for lack of prey, and the
> stout lion's whelps are scattered abroad.

What did it mean? Hank scanned the words. He reread Job's plea to God to leave him alone. He read Job's adherence to faith. His God was his God whether he did good or evil to him. He read of his loss of hope, but not his loss of faith. Sam told him, not more than an hour ago, that Joe had lost all hope, but not his faith. Is Sam really Satan? It seemed so. Could it be? But this is the twentieth century! Time makes no difference with evil. It persists. It is persisting in Sam.

What next? The boils. Hank again read the passage on how Satan struck Job with boils. Sam had stated that a man isn't really tested until he personally was afflicted, then he would reject his God. Was Sam planning to strike Joe B with boils, or something worse? What could he, Hank, do? What was there to do? Call the police. He could, but would they even believe it? Would they even entertain the thought? Could he talk to the Bishop, or Father Bill? Isn't he implicating himself then? What really did he have? He reread the Book of Job and his view of the statements of Sam. Great investigative work that is. What would happen to the firm? All these people rely on him for their livelihood. What is the right thing to do? Can he do the right thing? Does he even know what the right thing is?

Hank, agitated, strode around his desk, exhorting himself, thinking, perambulating, lost in his quandary. He did nothing.

CHAPTER THIRTY-FOUR

▼

SAM COLLECTS VEGETATION

The picture of activity of human beings is sometimes like watching an anthill. People go bustling here and there with no obvious purpose to the observer. But to each individual there is a purpose and a direction, a destination. If you focus on one individual and you follow him, you will see that there is a purpose and direction. It is this way that we get a vision of Sam in the Cleveland Metroparks System gathering and searching for various plants. One of the plants can be identified; it is poison ivy. A two-inch thick vine winding up a large oak tree. The vine sprouted richly colored green shiny three cornered leaves grouped in threes. Sam wore latex gloves to prevent contact with the many leaves he picked and placed into a brown paper bag.

He went to a pond, actually, more of a marshy area. He looked for an alga with a reddish tinge. He gathered as much as he could find. It was similar to a lichen, but was an alga.

The beneficial use of these two biological specimens is left to man's imagination; after all, it was a fungus that provided penicillin that has saved an untold number of lives. Sam took his two arcane gatherings back to his father's kitchen. He sliced, diced, used the osterizer, added some olive oil, and created a slurry which he placed in a pot and let sit for two days. He then pressed the slurry through a cheesecloth to eliminate any solid matter. A light greenish oily thick liquid of approximately half a cup remained. This he poured into two vials with rubber stoppers and threw the rest into the sink. He took meticulous care to clean the used pot and dishes. He washed them twice, once with ammonia, and once with fels naptha soap.

Sam held up one of the vials to the light. The greenish tint was a wonderful color. He knew the oil is primarily urushiol, a fierce allergen. A drop spread on the skin would give a serious rash that would take three weeks to clear. Sam had read that an ounce of urushiol can cause rash in twenty eight-million people, that a drop the size of a pinhead can cause a rash in about five hundred people. Sam held the vial to the light, gave a slight chuckle, passed his hand through his hair and placed the two vials in his pocket.

CHAPTER THIRTY-FIVE

▼

SOME EXERCISE AND A FAREWELL

Father Bill waited at the steps to the Rectory for Joe when he came out dressed in his running togs.

""We're doing five miles today," announced Father Bill.

"Suits me," acknowledged Joe.

"We might have to change our route if there are any cameras around."

"Idiots."

They started north, slowly, increasing the pace slightly as they began to sweat and loosen up. After the first mile they were at a good seven and a half-minute per mile pace, clipping along, occasionally talking, running together, two friends. Talking was not necessary. Joe was all talked out. Everyone wanted to talk to him, but most friends were hesitant to talk to him. And, he was not up to talking. Newspapers had tried to get him to talk to them; television stations wanted him on their talk shows. He was a freak. Everyone wanted to expose him, to use him. He was having none of it. Father Bill interceded very nicely for him.

"I am sorry, but this is of such a personal nature, Mr. B will not ever be available to talk to the press about this matter. Thank you."

And he would cut them off. He protected Joe in every way he could. He had refused visitors. One or two had gotten through, but they had caused no damage. One of them, Sam, some friend of Hank Smith's had even gotten Joe to talk more than he had talked in a long time. It was nice to see people who were really concerned, who just wanted to help, but most people just wanted to ogle, to point the finger at Joe, to see a person dealt life's severest blows.

They ran past yards, staying in the street even when there were sidewalks. People recognized Father Bill, waved to him, called to him. He always responded.

Thirty-five minutes after they started, they came within sight of the rectory. There were no video cameras chasing him. They must be off work today, thought Father Bill.

"Last five hundred yards is a burner. You're on. Loser gets the drinks." Before Joe could answer, Father Bill had shot ahead at a fast pace. Joe quickly accelerated just off Father Bill's left shoulder. They didn't speak. They were running too hard. Faster. They were neck and neck as the saying goes. Both even now, feet hardly slapping the pavement as they ran on their toes. This was not a time for heels to hit the pavement. Joe slowly edged ahead, both were panting heavily, pulling in deep lungfuls of air. Joe finished a car length ahead of Father Bill.

They stood at the end of the walkway to the Rectory breathing heavily. Joe bent over, put his hands on his knees, and sucked in as much oxygen as he could. He pulled his cap on and off to wipe at the sweat dripping off his face.

"That will teach you to mess with me." Joe exhaled loudly.

"You were lucky, this time," answered Father Bill. A pang of guilt went through him instantaneously when he said it. He didn't look at Joe. He knew it was the wrong thing to say. Joe, lucky? The two words were oxymoronic. They couldn't exist in the same sentence. He would let it go. Better to not focus on it. Maybe it passed Joe by. But what an insensitive thing to say. Say something else. Father Bill looked toward the Rectory, there was a man sitting on the front steps. He walked toward the steps.

"Hello, may I help you?" Father Bill managed to say.

"Oh, no, I just stopped by to say goodbye to Joe. He is an acquaintance of mine. I'm leaving town and I wanted to give my last condolences." The man was Sam. Joe recognized him.

"Hank's friend," Joe said to Father Bill with a slight question in his voice, extending his hand. "Excuse the sweat."

"No sweat," laughed Sam.

So this is the man, Father Bill thought, who gave Joe a quiet time to talk. Someone who really cared.

Father Bill looked at the Rectory door, Lucy, the housekeeper stood at the screen. "Could you get us some water, Lucy?" Father Bill requsted.

Sam moved into action. "I'll get it. Here, let me get it for you. Gotta do something to earn my keep." He moved up the steps with lightning speed before Lucy could react.

"Which way is the kitchen?" Sam rushed by her. She looked at him strangely, but pointed and said nothing.

Sam found the kitchen, opened several cupboards, located glasses, selected two, ran the water for ten seconds to get it cold, then filled the glasses. Lucy came and stood by the doorway, watching. He opened the refrigerator freezer, found a plastic ice cube tray, twisted it over the sink until half the cubes fell into the sink, put two in each glass, refilled the tray and put it back into the freezer. He picked the glasses up, started to walk back, instead, he glanced at Lucy and asked, "Restroom?"

Lucy pointed down the hallway. Sam put the glasses on the counter and brushed past Lucy in the direction she pointed. Lucy wiped up the mess made of her kitchen.

Sam looked down the hallway, walked towards the end and peeked into a bedroom. It was too lived in, not a guest room. Proceeded down the hall, looked in another room. It was used. This was Joe's room. Looks like a guest room. Went straight to the bathroom, opened the shower, saw the liquid soap with a press dispenser, a washcloth hanging on the edge of the shower, Sam felt it, it was damp.

He removed the two vials from his pocket, poured one onto the washcloth, it soaked in slowly. He made sure not to touch it. He opened the soap dispenser, emptied the contents into the toilet, squeezing the container. He poured the second vial's contents into the soap dispenser, shook it vigorously, and put it back in place. There was enough residue liquid soap and vial contents to mix evenly.

He flushed the toilet, came out of the room and bumped into Lucy. "Oh excuse me," Sam apologized. He smiled and moved toward the kitchen. He retrieved the glasses of water and went out the front door. Lucy watched him walk down the hallway. Wonder why he didn't use the front bathroom? It was closer.

Sam pushed open the door with his foot. "Here you go. I put some ice in the water. Ice is not supposed to be good for you right after a run, but it won't cool the water off quick enough. And you can chew the ice when you finish the water. Don't drink it too fast. You'll get cramps."

"Thank you. I'm Father Bill," he extended his hand.

"Sam Hawkins," answered Sam shaking his sweaty hand.

Joe gulped the water. "This hits the spot."

"Well, Joe," Sam said, "I'm leaving town and I just wanted to stop by to say goodbye and good luck."

There was that word again, thought Father Bill. Luck, something Joe hasn't seen in a long time.

Sam continued. "I know you haven't had any for a while, but I am wishing it for you. I will keep you in my prayers. If there is anything that you think you need, ever, just give Hank Smith a buzz and I will come running. He usually knows where to reach me."

"Uh-thanks," said Joe. "I will." Joe, puzzled, thought, why is this man offering help? What kind of help? Kind of overly friendly, isn't he? I hardly know him except for the two times I met him. He speaks like we are old friends."

Sam extended his hand for a final handshake with Joe. Then he shook Father Bill's hand and said goodbye. Joe finished his water. Sam left.

Lucy spoke through the screen door. "Father," she spoke lightly, "there is a phone call for you, a Mr. Hank Smith."

"Tell him I'll be right there, Lucy, thanks," he turned to Joe. "What a coincidence, a call from Hank right after his friend shows up."

Father Bill and Joe entered the house. Joe went to his room, Father Bill to the phone.

"Hello."

"Father Bill, this is Hank Smith."

"Yes, Hank, I know. What can I do for you?"

"Well, Father, I have a rather unusual request. And I don't know how to ask it, but I will anyway. If a man named Sam Hawkins comes around, don't let him see or talk to Joe at all. Will you do that for me?"

"Would you care to explain why?"

"I can't explain it. It is only a feeling I have. I may tell you someday, but not right now. Just don't let him talk to or have any access to Joe. It really is important." Father Bill felt the urgent emotion in Hank's voice.

"I'm sorry. You're too late."

"What do you mean?"

"He was just here. Just this moment. He just left. Just came to stop by to say goodbye to Joe, shook his hand and left."

"That's all? Just shook his hand and left?"

"Yes, that's all." The thought that Sam had gotten water for them never crossed Father Bill's mind. It was insignificant.

"Okay, Father Bill, but if he comes back, don't let him talk to Joe."

"I don't generally like secrets of this sort, but I will go with it. He won't have access to Joe if I can prevent it. I will tell Lucy, my housekeeper, to refuse him entrance. You can tell me about it later. Someday."

"Thank you, Father." Hank sighed relief.

CHAPTER THIRTY-SIX

▼

MEDICAL BILLS

Joe began to sort and open the mail left on the hall table after he showered. He saw the return address of Great Erie Life and Health Insurance Company. Uncertainty gripped him. It was a bill. He knew it. The typical window envelope where the bill is folded in three so the address shows through. He opened the letter. It consisted of three sheets of paper itemizing the services provided for Marsha and the amounts of money that the company paid pursuant to the policy and the amounts still owed by the owner of the policy.

The bill was enormous. He quickly reviewed the services, the private room, the medications, the two people to constantly monitor for three days, the psychiatrist sessions, the consultations with other professionals, and on and on.

In looking at the numbers, Joe easily calculated that his obligation for Marsha's care was fifty percent of the total bill. The total bill listed at the bottom of the page was $110,604.00, half of which had been paid by the

company. The other half in the column titled "amount you owe" was
$55,302.00.

Joe groaned. There goes more than half the amount of money donated
by the Catholic Church. There goes the good start they had. He knew
Marsha would be in the hospital for at least another month, maybe another
fifty-five thousand worth. The psychiatrist had told him Marsha's progno-
sis to leave was about another month if things continue to go well.

Money, gone in a flash. But, (and Joe actually thought of the but),
Marsha was alive and, after all, it was only money. He had learned that
money didn't mean anything when you didn't have your wife or your children. He would throw all the money in the world away if he could have
his children back. Just to have one of the hectic evenings around the dinner table with the kids babbling and making noise. It was so lovely. They
were so lovely. Oh God, how he missed them.

Bringing his mind back to the present he looked at the bill in his hand.
Maybe they would give him terms, a monthly payment. Of course they
would, if they wanted to get paid. He would call and talk to them tomorrow.

He opened the rest of the mail, threw away the department store advertisements, made a pile of the bills he would attend to the next day and
began to page through a magazine.

CHAPTER THIRTY-SEVEN

▼

THE INVESTIGATION CONTINUES

The secretary buzzed Hank over the telephone intercom.

"Mr. Smith?"

"Yes."

"There is a police officer here to see you."

"A what?"

"A police officer, sir."

"Did he say what he wanted?"

"No sir."

Hank, puzzled, knowing, with an unconscious feeling, that it had something to do with Joe B and Sam, said, "OK, tell him I'll be with him shortly."

Hank stood and went to the window, looked, and saw nothing. He wondered what the police wanted. In connection with what—the theft, the death of the children, the burning of the house? He had the increasing feeling they were all connected. He made the connection that Sam was behind them all despite his protestations otherwise. He had no evidence other than Sam's obsession with the two dollar bet. Only two dollars, right Sam?

A flash of memory brought to mind the Nine Mile Creek incident. Nausea passed through him. Another child who had died because of a connection with Sam and Hank. Is he doomed to be connected to the death of children as long as he is connected to Sam? The words of Sam identical to the words of Satan in the Book of Job. Who would have ever thought he could use the same words, but he did. He used the same words: "From going to and fro in the earth, and from walking up and down in it." Was he just being cute about it? Did he know those were the words in the Bible? Coincidence, or, and once again the thought struck Hank so strongly he had to support himself with his arm on the desk, was Sam the devil? Was he just evil itself?

Hank led the police officer into the office.

"Have a seat, officer."

The officer in plain clothes, wore a dark gray tweed sport jacket, matching gray tie with a white shirt and dark blue pants. He handed Hank a card and introduced himself as Detective Sprague. They shook hands.

Hank closed the door and took a seat. The officer looked around, impressed with the surroundings, their richness, matching colors, just the right luxurious feel.

Looking at the card, Hank said, "What can I do for you, Detective?"

"I am looking for information on a Mr. Sam Hawkins. Do you know where I can find him?"

"Chile."

"Chile, did you say?" exclaimed Detective Sprague.

"Yes, the last time I saw him, several days ago, he said he was going to Chile. Something about some indigenous tribes he had to learn about."

"Do you know if he left?"

Hank wondered at the question. "No. I don't," he answered, tentatively. "What is this all about, Detective?"

The Detective gave a grimace as if he didn't want to tell, but he said: "Well, if you don't know where he is, I guess I can tell you. We are investigating the death of Mr. Joe B's children and the babysitter. We have reason to believe it was not just a casual hit and run accident."

"What!" burst forth from Hank. "How?"

The Detective regarded him studiously, then answered openly: "We had been looking at the accident as a hit and run initially, got the paint scrapes, hit the various auto body shops looking for someone who repaired the car, anything. Then the driver of the truck, who went bananas as a result of the death of the kids—excuse the language..."

Hank nodded, understanding.

"The driver was put into a psychiatric hospital and the shrinks attacked him. They put him under heavy sedation, then they started to play with him, mentally. Then they let him off the drugs long enough to allow him to be hypnotized. They got into a regular schedule so he could fall into a hypnotic trance and he would talk. They finally got around to talking about the accident. He related a very interesting story. He said, although he didn't remember it, he said that the car had been stopped at the red light when he proceeded into the intersection. That area is fairly open, so he could see a good distance up the road to the left and right. It was to the right that he noticed a car stopped about three car lengths behind the car at the light. It had been stopped for several seconds, a dead stop. It wasn't until he approached the intersection that the car accelerated into the car at the light with the kids and pushed it into the path of his truck. It didn't just have an impact and stop, no it continued to push and push the car until it was in front of the truck. It was an intentional act."

The detective paused for several seconds watching the impact of what he was telling to Hank. Hank's face was a look of horror. Hank knew what was coming but he wished it wasn't. He could feel it. It was Sam.

"The truck driver," continued the Detective, "had a view of the car, a 73-74 Chrysler, probably a New Yorker or Fifth Avenue, a big car, tan color. Now it is almost impossible for us to track down a specific color on a car. It is usually listed on the manufacturer's statement of origin, but it never gets put on the titles. But then, most people do not change the color of their cars."

Hank listened with rapt attention.

"So we looked a little closer into this Joe B. He had some bonds stolen from his broker's place. That was a real hush-hush affair, but we found out about it. There were two people who had bonds stolen, one was Joe B, the other was a Mr. Sam Hawkins. So we followed up on Mr. Sam Hawkins. This Mr. Sam Hawkins has a father, who says he knows you, and who has a registered 1973 Chrysler Fifth Avenue. This particular Chrysler had evidence of a recent collision. Red paint marks on its bumper. We tested them with the paint on the Ford Taurus that the babysitter was driving at the time she was killed, and, do you know what, they matched. The father says he hasn't driven the car for six weeks. He has been ill. I guess his son came home to see him before he died, but he doesn't look like he is going to die at all now. He doesn't speak too highly of his son, not highly at all."

The Detective watched Hank. Hank agonized. He tried to keep a straight face, but he couldn't mask the arrow piercing his mind, the arrow that finished a friendship of more than forty years. Sam had actually caused the entire tragedy; he had done the whole debacle. All over a stupid bet, but it wasn't really about a bet, was it? And he did lie. A bald lie. Yes, that was Sam. He cared nothing about anything, but himself and what he wanted. Hank was involved also. Did they know that? Did they know about the bet? Was he an accomplice in the eyes of the law, probably not, but surely he was in the eyes of God? In his own eyes, he let it happen. He probably couldn't have stopped it, he didn't even know it was happening, but after the bearer bonds, he could have turned Sam in. He didn't though, and look what ultimately happened.

The Detective continued, "The only clue that we have to the connection between Joe B and Sam Hawkins is you. From what we have found out, you and Sam have been lifelong friends. Mr. Hawkins recently came back from no one knows where, and he came here. He talked to you. You went to lunch and dinner together. You went to the same high school together. Mr. Hawkins was expelled from China after spending some time in prison for rape of a child."

"Oh Jesus…" moaned Hank.

"And the last connection, which you already know," the Detective paused dramatically, "is that Joe B works in this firm."

The Detective finished. It was Hank's turn to talk, it was expected of him, but he didn't say anything. His mind was in turmoil, churning like the waves of the ocean on the rocky beach in a gale force storm. Beating and beating and getting nowhere.

They hadn't said anything about the money going back to Joe B. Do they know about that too? Do they know that he gave fifty of the seventy thousand back to Joe in the form of a gift from the church? They will surely find out. Would the Bishop talk?

Finally, the Detective, realizing Hank was in a dream world and was not going to start talking, began to ask questions.

"You did know Sam Hawkins."

Hank started. "Uh, oh,… yes, I did."

"For a long time?"

"Uh, yes." Hank realized he'd better have some sound answers to the detective's questions. He was too connected to this thing. "All my life."

"You were friends, I take it."

"We were the best of friends," he stressed the word were'. "I am stunned at what you've told me. I don't know what to say."

"Just let me ask some questions and we will see if we can get through this."

"Uh, yeah, sure."

"Did you have any knowledge that Mr. Sam Hawkins was involved in the theft of the bearer bonds?"

"No," lied Hank.

The Detective looked at him calmly. The man blushed a deep pink, quickly, from the neck to the bright glow on his ears. Whoa, we have a liar here. Why is he lying? What is he covering up? There is something here, for sure. Was he part of this?

"Did you and he ever discuss Mr. Joe B?"

"I introduced them to each other." Hank was thankful the Detective got off the subject of the bearer bonds. His lie must have worked. "The first day Sam came to the office after having been away for about ten years, Joe had just won a jury trial on a case I had given him. I introduced them. I don't think they ever knew each other before. But no, we never talked about Joe B. There was no reason to."

Hank was lying steadily now. He saw no way out. He couldn't confess his involvement. It would be the ruin of everything.

The Detective knew Hank was lying, the pink flush persisted. The nervous movements of the hands. Mr. Smith didn't know what to do with his hands. He didn't know if it was all lies, or if some truth was interspersed. All of Mr. Smith's lawyerly abilities couldn't hide his lying. He figured maybe he had better nose around the fringes a little more before he came back to this guy. He was not a good liar. Time to cut this interview short.

"Is there anything you can tell me, if you know, about Mr. Sam Hawkins, that you think might help me in this investigation?"

Slowly, Hank shook his head, "No, not really. I can't..., I can't figure it out."

"Well then, I won't waste your time anymore, Mr. Smith. I thank you for the information you have given me. If you run across Mr. Hawkins, will you let me know? My number is on my card."

"Yes, I will," Hank said forcefully, standing. "I surely will. I can't believe it. You have my word on it."

The Detective thought, yes, just what I don't want, your word on it. He stood to leave, glanced directly into Hank's eyes. What did he see there, briefly? Fear? Yes, this man is greatly afraid. Yes, I will see you again, Mr. Hank Smith IV. Hank stiffened at the piercing look.

CHAPTER THIRTY-EIGHT

▼

A PLAGUE ON THE BODY

The morning following Sam's generous act of getting water for Joe and Father Bill, Joe appeared for breakfast. Lucy always cooked a healthy breakfast. Joe smelled the bacon sizzling; it permeated the entire rectory. He loved bacon.

Joe started itching in the night, only several hours after his post run shower. He awoke a number of times itching. He scratched his neck, his stomach, his groin area; it seemed to be getting worse. In Father Bill's house, you breakfasted first, then showered, shaved and brushed your teeth. Joe was getting into the schedule comfortably.

When Joe entered the kitchen and was greeted by Father Bill, Father Bill's face told the story.

"What happened to you?"

"What?" Joe scratched his neck.

"What? Look in the mirror. What is it? You are full of bumps, red things. You haven't seen it?"

Joe went down the hallway to the bathroom, looked in the mirror and drew back in horror. His face had great red welts as if a cat with infected claws had scratched it. It looked infected but without a breaking of the skin. His neck had the same type of welts but more of a blotchy nature and they were swelling where he had been scratching them. He didn't know what it was. An allergic reaction to something? He pulled up his pants' leg and looked at his right leg, same thing. He lifted his tee shirt to look at his stomach, same thing. Joe groaned. Inwardly, he knew this was another test by God. This was what happened to Job. Joe had read the Book of Job, the final indignity to Job was to be visited with boils. Were these boils? Oh God, why are you doing this to me?

Father Bill was at the bathroom door.

"What is it?"

"Boils!" groaned Joe.

"What?"

"Boils. Isn't that what God did to Job after he killed his family and took all his belongings? Boils. What else can it be?"

"I don't know what it is. It doesn't look like boils to me. I have never seen anything like it. Don't scratch it." He added urgently as Joe massaged his neck.

"I am taking you to the emergency room now. There is something in your system. Something is wrong. Get dressed, we're going now." Father Bill hurriedly dressed.

Joe's itching got progressively worse. Father Bill put on the air conditioning because Joe's body temperature was increasing. He itched, he sweated, he was hot. The desire to scratch was irresistible. He lightly massaged his stomach through the shirt he had on.

"Don't do it!" admonished Father Bill.

Splotches appeared on his arms and hands. They covered his entire body. He wanted to scratch. He moved slowly against the seat back and cushion to scratch his back and the back of his legs.

"This really itches."

"Don't. I am sure it will just aggravate it. I am going to the emergency exit. We can walk in. Unbelievable! Boils! I don't think it is boils, though. It looks like something else, but I don't know what."

"Boils. That's what God gave to Job. I read it last week. Since the papers had been calling me Job, I thought I better re-familiarize myself with the story. I read it when I was in high school, but I didn't remember the particulars. I now know that the only thing that God hadn't done to me was to visit me with boils. And now he has done that." Joe hesitated, wanting to scratch and moving slowly over the seat.

"But, what I can't figure out is why? In the Book of Job, Satan makes a bet with God. God brags about his servant Job, and Satan mocks him. He says, yeah sure, take away what a guy has and see if he curses you. So God takes it all away, his family, his house, everything but himself. Then, when he doesn't curse God, Satan tells him that was nothing, take away his health and see what happens. God relents and lets Satan do his dirty work. Why? That was Old Testament stuff. We have a God of Love, not of Vengeance. I can't figure it out. It's too similar, too bizarre and now I'm visited with boils."

Father Bill drove, faster.

"What good would it do to damn God. First of all why is he testing me?" Joe's voice was becoming tense, strained; he looked over to Father Bill who was listening, but concentrating on driving.

"Bill?"

"What?"

"Are you listening to me?"

"Yes."

"Well?"

"Well what?"

"Why, why is God testing me? What is going on here? After reading the Book of Job, it's clear to me that it's not something that I've done that brings these terrible things on me, but something else. Why am I being tested, Bill?"

"I don't have an answer for you." Father Bill was very uncomfortable. He didn't have an answer. He had never seen any human being undergo such repeated tragedies. He couldn't square his God with what was happening to Joe. He knew the Book of Job. He had read it over and over since the accident with the kids. Joe's life was paralleling Job's. But why?... he asked himself. Why did God punish, or even hurt Joe and his family? Why kill the children? The actual reenactment of the Book of Job was unexplainable to him. He didn't know how to counsel Joe.

According to the Bible, the three friends of Job's had counseled him. Was Father Bill one of the three friends for Joe? What the three friends of Job had said made sense, but they were admonished by God. The Book of Job was confusing. So many sentences said nothing. It repeated the greatness of God in a multitude of ways. But it didn't follow logically. Is he just letting us know he is there and that he is almighty? This was so confusing; he had a premonition of these happenings, but he couldn't have prevented any of them. But, thought Father Bill, forget your own thoughts, think of Joe, answer him.

"Joe, I just don't have a real answer for you. I think of a God who will do this to you, and I don't know. I know God is almighty. He can do anything. He can find the slightest transgression and punish it as he wants. He can let the severest sins go unpunished on this earth. We pray to God in the hope that he will be favorable to us, that we can enter his kingdom in heaven. We pray to him out of duty, out of love of him, and we confess our sins to him. We confess and he forgives. He forgives and allows us to enter the kingdom of heaven. He keeps us from hell if we are righteous in the ways of the Lord."

Joe slowly moved his back on the seat, the soothing scratching helped and hurt.

"He enlightens us with the light of the living. He gives us free choice, free will to make the choice of righteousness or sinning. And when bad things happen to us, do we then deter from the route of righteousness in retaliation? Can God, who can do anything, not be allowed to cause us pain? Can he do wickedness? I don't know the answer, Joe." Father Bill turned to look at Joe. The boils were getting worse. Joe's face had puffed up, the marks on his face were blurred by the puffiness. He was blowing up like a balloon.

Father Bill quickly looked back to the road.

"Why, Father Bill?" Joe rasped. The thickness in his throat made it hard for him to talk.

"Yes, why? Why?" Father Bill was angry and scared. "Surely God does not do wickedness, nor would God pervert judgment. He is almighty and he can do anything. He can make man disappear altogether." Father Bill figured he better just talk while he drove so Joe wouldn't try to talk in his present state. Joe was in bad shape and quickly getting worse. Father Bill was speeding between the stoplights, he was scared.

"God has brought down kings. He has elevated paupers. He has supported kings and he has punished paupers. He is truly almighty. He knows all. He knows where those of iniquity reside. They cannot hide in the dark. He can see through the dark. Day is night to him, and night is day. He knows the good works of man, he knows the sins. But the fact that he knows is to acknowledge his eternity, that he is almighty.

"And it is here that we must continue to have faith in God. Faith. It is a word that only has meaning within yourself. You know what your faith is. We cannot think we are better than God. He is superior, our faith acknowledges that.

"You must pray directly to God, Joe. You must pray to him. I am praying to him for you. But you must talk to him, directly, yourself."

Father Bill chanced a glance at Joe. His face was so puffy his eyes were slits.

"God is almighty." Father Bill talked, something to take his mind off what was happening to Joe. He drove through a red light, faster. He heard the beginning of a siren. He couldn't stop now. He would continue to the hospital. Take his chances with a ticket. No choice.

"God is going to help me get past this policeman who is going to chase me. God help me." He hit a yellow light just as it was turning red and kept going.

The hospital was just around the corner. He turned the corner, the siren was getting closer, then it shut off altogether. Too close to the hospital? Father Bill pulled into the emergency entrance, no cars there. He pulled up, put the car in park, rushed around as Joe was trying to get out, having difficulty. The police car pulled up behind him. Two cops, the one on the passenger side hopped out quickly, took one look at Joe and stared.

Father Bill was afraid to touch Joe for fear he might hurt him. Joe was waddling. His legs had swollen also. He moved slowly. Father Bill moved into the Emergency entrance, strode up to the counter. "Please, help. This man needs help." The nurse looked where Father Bill pointed, she shouted to another nurse, and they galvanized into action. One got a gurney, pushed it into the hallway, the other rushed to Joe, told him not to move. She shouted to another, "Get epinephrine, some cortisone, quickly. Get Dr. Domadia down here ASAP." They gingerly placed Joe on the gurney on his back and rolled him through the automatic swinging doors.

Father Bill went to move his car. He did not get a ticket.

CHAPTER THIRTY-NINE

▼

SAM EXITS

Sam hooked the airplane's seat belt after the announcement that they were in the approach to landing. Chile wasn't his destination, but rather, Argentina. Time to leave America for a while. The police were snooping around the car; it would be easy to identify as the one involved in the automobile collision. But it didn't matter, he left his old man with the mess. Served him right for all the grief he had caused Sam during his life. He finished his glass of red wine, handed the glass and small bottle to the stewardess, and closed his eyes for the landing.

Two bucks, he thought. He lost two bucks. Hank must owe him thousands in two dollar bets. Didn't seem right that a man would have that much faith in his God. Most men would have crumbled after the theft of the bearer bonds. What's the world coming to when you can pick a man at random and he turns out to be the one in a million who has and can maintain his faith? It's not fair. Sam grinned inwardly. Fair, yes, there's a good one. It's not fair that I lost two bucks. Who cares about fair to Hank or Joe B? Poor Hank, smug in his big law firm, a big man in town, real close to the Bishop he was. Yes, Hank knew all along and didn't do anything about it. However, don't think he could have done anything anyway. That's always been the way with Hank; let things happen. Don't take action yourself, just let them happen. Hank is so weak himself. Wonder if he returned the money for those bearer bonds? Wonder how he did it?

So much for America. I won't be back there for quite a while. There is nothing there for me anyway, too much faith for me. What is it with this Joe B and his faith? Would a good, benevolent God of love and charity kill an entire family? Truly amazing, grace. Well, screw them, they can all go to Hell. They can all join me in Hell.

▼

CHAPTER FORTY

MARSHA'S PLIGHT

Diane heard about Joe's malady from Father Bill. She was momentarily delighted. Something happened to Joe. So Joe wasn't immune to the bad luck after all. In the same instant, she was apalled at her own delight. What happens to Joe also happens to Marsha. So Joe wasn't immune to the bad luck after all.

Father Bill asked her to inform Marsha that Joe wouldn't be able to visit for a number of days. She might want to check with the psychiatrist first to make sure there wouldn't be a relapse or something, or whether the information would upset her even more.

Marsha's progress had been steady. The psychiatrist expected her to be able to leave the hospital within three weeks, but she would have to continue with therapy for at least a year thereafter. She had been deeply wounded.

The psychiatrist gasped when she was told what had occurred. She needed to think it over for an hour, then she would meet Diane with Marsha at 2:00pm. Don't say a word until I am there.

Diane was late. Marsha was surprised to see Dr. Fell come into her room. Marsha was sitting in a chair reading a Silk Clothing Catalog. She put it down and stood up.

"No, sit down, Marsha," said Dr. Fell.

"What brings you here at this time of the day, Dr. Fell?"

Dr. Fell sat in the opposing chair. She watched Marsha. Saw the mix of emotions caused by her own unexpected appearance. She'd better get right to it.

Diane entered. She looked at Marsha, then at Dr. Fell. Dr. Fell looked down. Diane made the assumption that Dr. Fell had already told Marsha. Marsha looked puzzled.

"Oh, I am so sorry, Marsha," said Diane, breaking into tears.

Marsha, alarmed, quickly stood. "What,…What has happened?" she insisted.

Diane, immediately realizing her mistake, said, "Oh my God."

Diane's hands covered her face.

Marsha began to let out a wail, but Dr. Fell grabbed her by the right wrist, "Sit down, Marsha," insistent.

Marsha, wide eyed, open mouthed, quieted, then sat slowly.

Dr. Fell paused. "Marsha, Joe has had some kind of allergic reaction."

Marsha, expectant, listened. Her fears softened, somewhat. He wasn't dead.

"Joe has been admitted to the hospital for observation. He has welts on his body and needs monitoring."

"I have to go see him," Marsha said.

"Marsha," Dr. Fell answered, "I don't know if that is such a good idea at this time."

"I have to see him, Dr. Fell. I have to."

Dr. Fell placed her palms together, fingertips touching, pressed against her lips, breathed deeply, making a rasping sound with her breath. She watched Marsha, glanced at Diane wiping her eyes, smearing her eyeliner.

"Alright. Just for a couple of hours, Okay?"

Marsha, relieved to have overcome this hurdle, answered, "Oh, yes."

Chapter Forty-One

▼

HANK'S ANGUISH

Hank Smith's legal production waned; he had sat at his desk for the last three hours and performed no legal work at all. His thought processes were churning, but they couldn't focus on legal work. He was a snowflake in a storm, tossing, flying, spinning, getting nowhere. He received several phone calls, but he put the clients off, he would get to it next week, he was extremely busy, he said there was an emergency hearing so he hasn't been able to attend to their particular matter. He finally activated the do not disturb button on his phone. A computer chip capable of telling the receptionist and everyone in the office that he was unavailable by phone.

But the time he had devoted to thinking wasn't helping him. He kept coming back to the same issue. He had done wrong. His conscience screamed at him. Hank, you let it happen.

But that was always the way of his relationship with Sam; Sam did something and Hank went with the flow. When Sam made his mind up to do something, he was hell bent to do it. Sam was strong, Hank was weak.

The relationship, the long friendship with Sam was over. It was really over. Kids. Who kills kids? Sam, you are deranged. You must be absolutely crazy. You sweep into town after a ten year absence, you steal money, kill people, you burn houses, and you somehow make a man blow up with huge boils that almost kill him.

Was it to best me again, Hank? Your best friend? You would kill five children to best me! But I didn't care about the bet. You can't just kill people and get away with it. But you did, didn't you? You got away. You came, stirred up the shit that brought a thousand flies, and you left, you got away. Sam, I truly hate you, and yet, in me, there is something, I still love you. You are an evil man. You are my history. But you are the devil, Satan, Beelzebub, Mephistopheles, Lucifer. The fallen angel. Were you ever a good person? No, never.

But what does that make me? And this was the sticking point to all of Hank's arguments. This was the bottom line of what he kept coming back to: I have been your accomplice! I have been your accomplice all of our lives!

That child died as a result of me back at Nine Mile Creek. I never owned up to it. That young man I fought at the Cask, while still in High School, died as a result of contact with me. I never owned up to that either. You aborted a child with my money—another death. And now, five children have died as a result of their father's connection with me. I am guilty. I could have prevented it and I let it happen. I know it.

Hank sat at his desk, head in his hands, elbows on the desk, crying. Guilty and weak. I let things happen. I don't stop them. I let Sam have his way. After the discovery of the bond theft, I should have reported him. I still haven't reported him. Why? I am weak. I don't want to lose the firm, my position with it. And now that Joe has come back to work, how can I look at him without thinking every day that if it wasn't for me, his kids would still be alive. How can I face that? I can't. I can't face Joe. I can't face my partners. I can't face anyone.

And so he decided there and then his course of action. He gathered all the strength he ever had in Sam's absence, focused and made a decision. He must quit.

I must do it in a fashion that only benefits. I will leave and only leave good. As much good as I can. It is the least that I can do after all the hurt I have allowed to happen. I am not needed. I cannot live with myself, let alone live with the presence of Joe in the firm. It is my weakness of morals, my weakness of spirit, my weakness of faith.

CHAPTER FORTY-TWO

▼

MARSHA REVIVES

Marsha's visit to Joe at the hospital was the first positive action she had taken towards her self healing. The Psychiatrist watched her prepare for the visit. She showered, combed her own hair for the first time since the accident, groomed her nails, and made sure the dress she wore was neat and clean. Diane hovered, helping her do this and that. Upon inquiry, Diane didn't know Joe's malady, only what Father Bill had told her on the phone. Diane was happy at Marsha's activity, but puzzled. How could Marsha turnaround so quickly? Dr. Fell smiled, watched a few more minutes and wished Marsha good luck. She gave her a hug before she left.

Joe had been admitted immediately. Because his esophagus had contracted as a result of the enlargement of the tissues, a large tube was inserted to his lungs. Because his lungs had expanded with the enlargement of the tissues, oxygen had to be pumped into them forcefully until the swelling subsided. As a consequence of the increase of the multiple tissues throughout Joe's body, and his increasing itchiness, Joe's hands and legs were secured by bands to the bed. He couldn't move anything except his head. The nurses, because Joe's temperature was so high, put ice on him immediately. They monitored him closely. The doctor in the emergency room diagnosed him initially as having an allergic reaction; therefore, he injected epinephrine to counteract the poison. He injected Benzedrine to dull the itching. They took blood samples to analyze. The laboratory technicians in pathology analyzed with titration, gas chromatography, infrared, and several other new fangled machines that gave a computer printout and graph of the carbon molecules involved with that particular substance. Results were obtained two hours after Joe's admission. Two separate substances were found to exist in Joe's blood that didn't belong there. One of them they identified as urushiol, an extract associated with poison ivy. How it would get into his blood, they had no idea, but there it was. The other needed further research. They tried to break the substances down with conventional antidotes in the lab, but it wasn't working. They hadn't found an antidote even though they worked on it for hours. By five o'clock in the evening, the physician, after consulting with five other physicians decided to replace Joe's entire blood supply.

A transfusion was started. It would take four hours to completely replace his blood with clean blood. Then, it would have to be done several times because the poisons in the tissues, if they did not break down into harmless substances, would leach back into the blood. It would have to be replaced. It was hoped the substances would be broken down by the bodily protections.

Marsha arrived after the blood transfusion had started. Joe was conscious. He awakened to find himself bound hand and foot, still puffed out like the Pillsbury dough boy. He even felt the fat pressure on his face and arms. The amphetamines had dulled the itching, but not stopped it. He itched all over. The amphetamines had also dilated his pupils into great black holes. He was acutely aware of sounds. He could almost sense movement by echolocation like a bat. He heard Marsha come in before he saw her. He tried to smile, but his face was too tight to smile. He couldn't talk with the tube in his mouth and two smaller tubes in his nose.

Marsha's reaction to his condition showed him how badly he looked. She rushed over, was afraid to touch him, lightly kissed him on the forehead, tried to smile to mask the initial horror of the moment and said: "Hi, fat boy. You sure must be eating a lot." She forced a laugh. It was the first laugh she had uttered in two months. She felt awkward.

Joe laughed inwardly, she could see it in his eyes. He was thankful for the humor. He was thankful Marsha was up and about, and more to the point, concerned.

"You must have been having an affair with those bees?" she added. This was lost on Joe. He didn't know the cause of his malady yet.

"I know you can't talk, just squeeze my hand, if you can." Joe squeezed slightly.

"Good." She said and smiled. "Now I will talk and you just listen and give a squeeze once in awhile. OK?"

Joe squeezed. Joe was the happiest he had been for six weeks and at the same time he was in the greatest pain of his life. Marsha was here. Just having her here was a great victory for him—he thought of it as victory. She was not in the psychiatric hospital anymore. But now, he was in the hospital, what a twist. But his was only a physical or chemical problem. Diane was visible in Joe's peripheral vision standing by the door to his room.

If Marsha was out of the hospital, whatever the reason, it could only mean that Marsha was coming back from the pit into which she had fallen after the house had burned. He offered a short prayer that she had finally started getting over, at least temporarily, her despair. Maybe the boils, or whatever they were, had a positive effect on Marsha. Maybe, she didn't want to lose the last piece of her life on earth—Joe. Whatever the reason, he was relieved, thankful. He prayed thanks to God.

Marsha was talking, but Joe could not make out the words. He saw her, but she was fazing in and out. Then, suddenly, her words came through clearly, A...so Dr. Fell agreed to let me come visit you. She even gave me a hug, that was nice, wasn't it?"

He squeezed her hand, she smiled at him, glowing.

His mind wandered, he thought of the Book of Job. Joe knew his time with Satan was over. And Satan it was. Joe's thinking was extremely clear and precise with all the amphetamines in his blood. He didn't know why he was thinking so clearly. Marsha was talking, he squeezed, but he couldn't focus on what she said.

He thought of the past months. What a living hell. He was tested. He had survived so far. Was there more agony down the road? He didn't think so. But he could take it. God, you are my God. I am your servant. I am what you made me. I am yours. Do with me what you will. No thought can be withheld from you.

Joe was in a dreamland. In real life he had closed his eyes while Marsha was still talking. He appeared asleep, but there were too many foreign substances coursing through his body for him to sleep. He was in a netherworld. He was Moses climbing the mountain. He passed goats, sheep. He was floating up the mountain, hardly a step, yet he was moving easily. The sky was cloudy and overcast, the fog parted to allow him through. There was no temperature. His vision was not more than twenty feet in front of him. He passed the burning bush and kept on going. He passed the broken tablets tossed down by Moses. He passed the altar where Abraham was to sacrifice Isaac, his only son. He came to a wall. He walked along the wall to an entrance, a glowing entrance. Over the entrance was the lighted sign "Work and ye shall be free." He passed through Auschwitz. He left through a dark door into fog with light. Everything was light.

He stopped. A rock stood before him. Steps led up the rock to a platform. He was in a white foggy whirlwind. He climbed the steps, stood on the platform. He was on top of the mountain, on a rock in the shape of an altar. He was the sacrifice, and then he felt it, he heard it, its presence was everywhere.

"Who is this that darkens counsel by words without knowledge?"

Joe listened, stunned, in rapt silence.

"Where wast thou when I laid the foundations of the earth?

"Who had laid the measures thereof?

"Who laid the corner stone for the foundation of the earth?

"Who shut up the sea with doors when it broke forth?

"Who made the light and the dark?

"Declare if thou has understanding. Answer me these demands I ask of you."

Joe stood on the rock, amazed. He answered, softly, silently, "You, Lord."

▼

CHAPTER FORTY-THREE

HANK'S DECISION

Hank made up his mind. He called his life insurance agent and asked about changing the beneficiary on his policy. The agent informed him that a form issued by the company had to be filled out, and that was it. He could send a form to Hank in today's mail. Can you fax one over to me, asked Hank? He then inquired whether a fax on the form filled out would suffice. The insurance agent affirmed that it would, but that a hard copy would be preferable. The hard copy could be mailed after the fax. "Ok," Hank said, "will do."

Hank was in an excellent mood. The best mood he had been in since the beginning of the troubles of Joe B.

He then did something uncharacteristic for him, he took the afternoon off. He looked up the address of a motorcycle sales company, got into his car, and drove over to look at motorcycles. He wanted a motorcycle. Life was going to begin again for him. No kids at home, a wife whose ardor had vanished and whose adherence to the marital relationship was merely perfunctory. She was a good woman, but her life was her own anymore.

She went her own way. Companions of convenience had described their relationship these last five years. It was time to start anew. It was time to do something affirmative in his life for goodness, for right.

He looked at motorcycles. Talked cubic inches, horsepower, balance, and test drove several of them. He finally selected a 1999 Honda four cylinder 1000cc machine. Streamlined and powerful, it could reach speeds of up to 160 miles per hour. The machine would be ready to pick up in the morning. Did Hank have an endorsement on his license permitting him to operate a motorcycle? Yes. May we see it? How would Hank like to finance the machine? No finance? Pay in full? A moment of surprise. A check, we will, of course, have to check with the bank to make sure the funds are in there, you understand, they smiled placatingly. Hank understood. He never understood things so well in his life of fifty-six years. Yes, he understood, call the bank, there will be no problem, he could buy the whole store with what he had in the bank. What time tomorrow? Ten o'clock, that's fine. You will have your own helmet, or did you wish to choose one from our selection. I will get one tomorrow.

CHAPTER FORTY-FOUR

▼

DETECTIVE SPRAGUE INTERVIEWS FATHER BILL

Father Bill fretted. He was told that the admission of Joe to the hospital at the precise time Father Bill brought him was a godsend. Another two minutes and the man's life would have been ended by the closure of his esophagus. He was a very lucky man. That term, "lucky", again. They did not have the results of the tests back yet to determine what fully caused the problem, but surely it was an allergic reaction to some substance. Father Bill explained as best he could what Joe had eaten that day and the day previously. He wasted time in the waiting room for hours until the doctor told him that Joe would be at the hospital for an extended period of time. That the swelling was beginning to go down somewhat and that they were forcing air into his lungs. They were monitoring him very closely, but he would be okay.

Father Bill returned to the rectory. He gave Lucy the report on Joe as she handed him a phone message from a Detective Sprague who wanted to meet with him. He dialed the number: the Dective could either come out to visit or Father Bill could come down to the station, whichever was more convenient. It was about Joe B. Father Bill would come to the station, right now, if it was okay.

Father Bill arraived at the station almost immediately. Inquiring of Detective Sprague, he was asked to wait about fifteen minutes until the detective could be found.

Fifteen minutes turned into thirty minutes. Detective Sprague came through the door, introduced himself to Father Bill and took him back to an office shared with two other detectives. They sat down to talk.

"It's my understanding that Mr. Joe B has been staying with you. How's he doing?"

"Not well," said Father Bill.

"Oh?"

"No, not well at all, he was just admitted to the hospital."

Detective Sprague looked concerned. "What is it?"

Father Bill explained to Detective Sprague about Joe. How Joe lost his money, his children, and his house. Detective Sprague knew all of the information, but he let Father Bill tell his story in full. He told how Joe had stayed with Father Bill, how his wife was in a mental institution, and how Sam Hawkins had visited Joe on two separate occasions at the rectory. How they had just finished a five mile run when Sam was on the steps of the rectory. How he got them both a glass of water. The fact that this man, Sam Hawkins, had hurried to get the water when Lucy was at the screen door of the rectory and the keen interest of this Sam Hawkins in the consumption of the water by Joe got him to thinking. How Joe bloated up with boils and looked like he was going to burst. The rush to the hospital, the police siren following him to the hospital, and how Joe's life had narrowly been saved. But that Father Bill, for the life of him, could not think of anything that Joe could have ingested that would have caused him to have the reaction he did. That he ate the same food as Joe did all day. How Lucy had been at the rectory for ten years and served excellent clean food. The water was the only thing that could have been different. Father Bill finished.

Detective Sprague sat there looking at Father Bill for a long time without saying anything. Finally, he asked:

"Do you know a Hank Smith?"

"Yes, he's Joe's boss at the law firm."

"Do you know anything else about him?"

"Not really, He seems to be a good man from what I do know. He helped Joe get money from the Catholic Church to help him out. I think even some of the money was his."

Detective Sprague arched his eyes.

"Oh? What kind of contribution?"

"Well, the Bishop, with the help of Hank, got the sum of $100,000.00 for Joe. I know a lot of it will be going for the hospital expenses, but it sure was a nice gesture."

"From Hank Smith?"

"I'm not sure. I think his law firm gave most of it, but I think he threw in some of his own. I don't really know where it all came from. Hank could tell you. He's treated Joe well over this whole thing. But, I've met him only half a dozen times, I think. Other than this problem, or problems Joe is going through, I don't know him very well."

"And you met this Sam Hawkins only once?"

"Yes, just at the time we were jogging. But he had been to the rectory one other time when I was not there."

Detective Sprague continued to look at Father Bill searchingly. The Detective was uncertain whether to ask the next series of questions. They were so improbable, so out of line with the continuity of life in the city, but he might as well go forward.

"Father, do you know the story of Job?"

Father Bill looked at him fixedly.

"You know, the story in the Bible? Job?"

"Yes, yes I do. Job was afflicted by many things to test his faith in God."
Then he added, "Just like Joe B."

Detective Sprague considered Father Bill. Then he asked: "So you do
see the parallels in Joe's situation?"

"Yes, the newspapers have paralleled it. Joe and I have discussed it, but
I never gave it much credence. But what would that have to do with Sam
Hawkins...? Oh, yes, I see."

"Sam Hawkins, I think, based on the evidence that I have, caused the
death of Joe B's children."

Father Bill's head jerked.

"Sam Hawkins was the only other investor at Holderman-Plank who
lost any money. Sam Hawkins was the person who induced Edward Vacik
to put the bonds in the safe."

Father Bill's eyes widened. He took in deep breaths.

"Sam Hawkins arrives late to the graveyard after the funeral. We found
one witness who saw him arrive. It would have been possible for him to set
the fire at the house. Hence, the arson connection."

Father Bill wiped the sweat from his brow with the sleeve of his shirt.

"Sam Hawkins is the man who comes to visit Joe B at the rectory twice.
Now you tell me he has an allergic reaction—boils, maybe?"

Slowly, Father Bill shook his head no.

"Coincidence? No, sir."

Father Bill, stunned, said, "That man did all this? Joe's boss's friend?"

"Mr. Sam Hawkins has left the country for Argentina. Today. He told
everyone he was going to Chile, but he went to Argentina. Argentina will
not extradite him unless it is for an international act of terrorism. So we
can't get him."

"Holy mackerel!" Father Bill again wiped the sweat from his forhead.
Father Bill closed his eyes, clasped his hands and mumbled a prayer.

"I am curious about Mr. Hank Smith, IV," said the Detective. "I would
like to know more about him. Mr. B is in his firm, Sam Hawkins is Mr.

Smith's lifelong friend. How does it happen that Joe B is the person selected for the Job treatment? Would you have any insight on that?"

"I'm flabergasted. I can't imagine..."

Detective Sprague paused, then said, "I would like to come out to your rectory, kind of go over Joe B's room. See what we can find, if anything. I don't know how Hawkins administered whatever he gave to Joe to make him get boils, or to puff up like that, but I will check with the doctors to try to find out. In the meantime, do not let anyone touch anything in Joe's room, please? Can you do that?"

"Oh, sure. Holy mackerel."

CHAPTER FORTY-FIVE

▼

HANK DESIGNATES
A NEW BENEFICIARY

Hank reviewed his life insurance policy. Such policies have suicide clauses whereby if the insured commits suicide, then the company will not cover the loss. However if the policy is in effect for more than two years without a suicide, then the company will cover such occurrence. And such was Hank's policy. He had had the policy for well over two years, in fact, he had the policy for fifteen years. It was originally designed to be protection for the other partners as a buy-out of the partnership interest in the event of death of one of the partners. But with the growing success of the firm, the partners had decided to dispense with the buy-out provision; they made other arrangements.

Hank filled out the beneficiary form redesignating the beneficiaries on his policy. One half of the million-dollar policy would go to his wife, which he knew would eventually go to his children. She was too independent and satisfied to remarry. She liked living alone; at least that is what it seemed like for the last ten years for him. He owed her that much anyway; she had produced three beautiful children, now grown and on their own.

The other half of the policy, he split between Joe B and his wife, Marsha, either/or, joint and survivorship. This wouldn't compensate them for the damage that he had done to them by his weak character and his association with Sam Hawkins, but it would give them a start.

Hank made his decision. He couldn't tell anyone of his involvement with Sam Hawkins. He couldn't tell anyone it started over a two dollar bet. He couldn't tell the Bishop, the firm would lose the Diocese's business. The Bishop wanted his attorneys to be squeaky clean. That would hurt the entire firm; they depended on him. He couldn't tell the police; they wouldn't believe him. Who would believe such an improbable story? Sure fella, he killed five kids on a two dollar bet. Where are you coming from? And, telling the police is just what would bring down all that he had built up.

It was better, he thought, to make it look like an automobile accident. That way no one would get blamed. He had enough blame in his life.

He couldn't embarrass his wife by telling her. And, the final straw was that he couldn't face it himself. He didn't like himself. He was weak. His morality was weak. He was a follower. He let Sam commit evil, mask it, and he, a best friend, did nothing about it. And today, he is still allowing it, but it is going to stop now. He would, at the very least, leave a legacy to someone he has hurt more than anything in the world. A half a million dollars won't bring Joe's kids back, but it will surely make it easier for Hank to leave this world with a conscience as clear as he could obtain given the circumstances. He should go to confession. But why, he was getting ready to commit a mortal sin—eternal damnation. Hopefully, having money will make it somewhat easier to live with the grief; at least money would not be a problem in addition to everything else.

Hank faxed the beneficiary designation form to the insurance agent and mailed a hard copy through the office mail.

Hank took the bus to pick up his new motorcycle. He hadn't ridden a bus in fifteen years. When he arrived, he was treated like royalty. Not many people write a check for the entire amount of a motorcycle. They seated him in the office, offered coffee or soda pop, which Hank refused. He was in a good mood. A little nervous, but entirely happy with himself for the first time in a very long time. He felt that he was doing someone, primarily himself, a very good deed.

The salesman showed the motorcycle. The store threw in a helmet for free. A clean white helmet with a face guard that surrounded his entire face and head. There was a helmet lock on the back of the cycle so when it was parked no one walked away with the helmet. Hank tried on the helmet, an exact fit.

"It's all tuned up perfectly, Mr. Smith. I greased it myself. A smoother riding bike, you won't find. Yes, sir." The mechanic smiled at Hank, patting the bike as if he was permitting Hank to fondle his own beloved girlfriend. Hank looked at the mechanic and laughed. He saw all these things: the mechanic was jealous of Hank. This man has money and can afford this motorcycle; it just ain't fair. Too bad, thought Hank. Life just ain't fair, and I'm the one who knows it. I am out of here.

Hank put on the helmet, sat astride the motorcycle, revved the engine and waving goodbye, edged out of the parking lot. He cruised down the road. Lots of red lights. After several miles of riding, he pulled over, took off the helmet, attached it to the helmet lock on the back, got on the motorcycle, and started to drive. He drove for hours. He had to stop for gas twice. It was a beautiful machine. Smooth, powerful. The acceleration was astounding. The machine just stood up and lunged. He had to hold tight to the handle grips to stay with the bike. The wind across his face added to the impression of speed and power. He loved it. Sure beats breakfast with Marian.

He cruised for several more hours, looking for a likely spot to crash. What would be the best way for him to commit suicide on this motorcycle? It would have to be a situation where he was assured of a head injury that would be fatal on impact. He finally found a location. At the exit ramp off Route 90 at East 156th Street, there was a building that he could hit squarely and fast. He would have to keep up his speed from the freeway, jump the curb, and collide into the building. His angle of collision would be at about sixty degrees. Maybe even more if he could turn the wheel at that speed.

He tried a dry run. He sailed off the freeway, kept it at sixty miles per hour up to the building and then brought it to a hasty stop at the stop sign. Maybe, he could go even faster than sixty. He got back on the freeway, went to the next exit, got off, doubled back on the freeway for three exits, turned around and decided he was ready and committed. He was nervous. He had to pee. He remembered, he peed when the kid was shot. He he is ready to commit suicide and he's still embarrased about peeing. But he wasn't going to worry about that, he would pee soon enough.

Hank traveled at sixty miles per hour past the 260th St. exit, he increased to seventy miles per hour past the 222nd St. exit. He was at eighty-five miles per hour at the 185th St. exit. When he started off the exit at 156th, St., he was traveling at one hundred miles per hour. The motorcycle handled smoothly, but he was traversing ground so rapidly, he was afraid to turn the motorcycle for fear he would lose control before he got to the building. There was no traffic. He went faster than cruising. The wind was terrific. His eyes were slits, tears streaming and tearing at the edge. He closed his mouth. The wind was pushing his face backwards.

The building rose up ahead, Hank jerked the wheel toward the curb, leaned into the bike to help it turn; it hit the curb, sailed into the air, and he let go of the handles. He was flying above the bike by inches, the distance increased. Gravity pulled the bike and it was on the ground when it collided into the wall. Hank slammed into the wall at a fifty-eight degree angle. As he wished, his head hit first. He died upon impact.

No one exited at East 156th St. for fifteen more minutes. The first two cars that passed Hank, or what was left of him, didn't even notice that there had been a collision. They went right on through. The third driver saw the motorcycle and the man lying next to the building. He stopped his car, ran over, looked, ran back to his car and drove to the nearest gas station to call the police.

CHAPTER FORTY-SIX

▼

JOE RETURNS

Joe awoke from his troubled sleep. The swelling had reduced considerably. Marsha sat next to him, holding his hand. She looked tired: but, she looked alive. She appeared different than in the hospital. Marsha didn't want to lose Joe, too, after she had lost all her children. She had come to the realization, although not the full acceptance yet, that she had lost her children, her home, her money. But she recognized too that she still had her own life and her husband. And now her husband was threatened. Her husband's injury triggered her revival; brought her out of her self-pitying misery. She had a husband who loved her and she loved him. He needed her. He was a good man. He was upright, he feared God, and he eschewed evil. Marsha looked up and saw Joe was awake. He squeezed her hand.

"Good morning," she smiled. She squeezed his hand. "The doctor says he thinks the swelling has gone down enough to take out the tube. What do you think?"

He again squeezed her hand. She got up, told the nurse at the nurse's station that her husband was awake and would like the tube removed. The

paged doctor appeared within two minutes like an archangel, strident, tri-
umphant, and knowing.

"Good morning, Mr. B. You look much better today. I am going to
remove this tube." He gripped the tape attaching the tube, lightly loosed
it, slid the very long tube out, put it on the tray, poured a glass of water
from the carafe of water, handed it to Joe and said, "Drink it slowly. Slosh
it around in your mouth in small amounts first. You have a tendency to
dry out a little when your mouth is open for that length of time." Joe
drank little sips. His throat hurt, but he could feel it. He could breathe.
He could swallow.

"Thank you." Joe said in a scratchy weak voice.

"Good, good," intoned the doctor, "you can still talk. Take your time.
Drink some more water, don't talk too much, and I will be back in about
an hour to check on you. You are a lucky man to be alive. Puffed up you
were. You looked like the Pillsbury Dough Boy. You can thank your friend
for his quick action one of these days." The doctor left.

Marsha sat on the chair by the bed. The restraints were removed
overnight since the swelling had decreased, he did not appear to have that
itching sensation anymore.

"So,how do you feel?" asked Marsha, taking his hand and massaging it.

"I feel alive. I feel great. How do you feel? They let you out?"

"Yes, I insisted. I'm done with that. I don't need it anymore. I need you,
Joe. You're my therapy. I'll have to go back, but I'll deal with it."

Joe chuckled as best he could with the pain in his throat. He smiled at
Marsha. A tear slid down the side of his face.

"Marsha," he said. "You're not going to believe this. But I had this
dream just now, before I woke up. I talked to God. I mean, I actually
talked to God."

Marsha looked at him, quizzically. She slightly cocked her head.

"He told me things will be all right now. That I have fulfilled his expec-
tations. That we will have seven sons and three daughters. That he wants
the name of the first daughter to be named Jemima, the second Kezia, and

the third, a very difficult name, called Kerenhappuch. He said that we would be wealthy, that we wouldn't have to worry about money, ever."

He looked at her. She was crying. Not sobbing, not painful, but a happy crying.

"Don't you believe me?" he asked.

"Yes, I do." She stood up, and turning sideways, patted her belly. "Look, we have already started."

"What?"

"I think I am pregnant."

EPILOGUE

There was a man in the land of Cleveland, whose name was Joe; and that man was perfect and upright. And one that feared God and eschewed evil. He was a good catholic. He atended church regularly, participated in community activities, and tithed generously.

And there were born unto him three sons and two daughters. He was active in their education, their sports, and their religious upbringing. They had all been baptized in the church; the two eldest had received first communion. The girls belonged to the children's choir; they sang like angels.

Joe's substance was wealth in family, wealth in religion, and wealth in health. His income was modest. A hard working lawyer in a modest town. He maintained an honest living. He was an advocate on the side of right. He didn't deceive his opponents, but met them fairly on the battlefield of the court. He won some points and lost others. He held not a grudge, but extended a helping hand to the losers.

His generosity was boundless. Not a beggar passed that he failed to help. Endless hours he contributed to charity. At Thanksgiving he would deliver turkeys for the church to the poor; at Christmas, he delivered hams. He dug into his own pockets.

His pastor was an intimate friend. He helped in his legal profession. He contributed time to the church; he did not bill the church for his services. He confessed regularly, took communion regularly, and believed in God; he had faith. He was a perfect catholic of the twentieth century...

Catechism of the Catholic Church, copyright 1994, Paulist Press, Mahwah, New Jersey 07430.

The Holy Bible, Containing the Old and New Testaaments in the Authorized King James Version, 1977, Consolidated Book Publishers, Chicago.

Oriental Mythology, 1989, The Apple Press, London N7 9BH